D1755466

SHOES *of the* DEAD

By the same author:

Death of a Moneylender
Riverstones

SHOES *of the* DEAD

KOTA NEELIMA

RAINLIGHT
RUPA

First published in 2013
in RAINLIGHT by Rupa Publications India Pvt. Ltd.
7/16, Ansari Road, Daryaganj
New Delhi 110002

Sales centres:
Allahabad Bengaluru Chennai
Hyderabad Jaipur Kathmandu
Kolkata Mumbai

Copyright © Kota Neelima 2013

First impression 2013

This is a work of fiction. Names, characters, places and incidents are either
the product of the author's imagination or are used fictitiously,
and any resemblance to any actual persons, living or dead,
events or locales is entirely coincidental.

All rights reserved.

No part of this publication may be reproduced, transmitted, or stored in a
retrieval system, in any form or by any means, electronic,
mechanical, photocopying, recording or otherwise,
without the prior permission of the publisher.

ISBN: 978-81-291-2396-1

10 9 8 7 6 5 4 3 2

Kota Neelima asserts the moral right to be identified as the
author of this work.

Typeset in 11/14 pt Goudy Old Style by SÜRYA, New Delhi

Printed in India by
Replika Press Pvt. Ltd.

This book is sold subject to the condition that it shall not,
by way of trade or otherwise, be lent, resold, hired out, or otherwise
circulated, without the publisher's prior consent,
in any form of binding or cover other than that
in which it is published.

*To
my father*

Author's Note

The trouble with writing a work of political fiction set in Delhi is that one cannot really name the people who have helped in the research. Instead, I would like to thank those who make Delhi one of the most academically intriguing, strategically dynamic and tactically mischievous cities of the world, as every great political capital should be.

The stories of the Vidarbha region of Maharashtra are the soul of this book. I thank the people of the districts of Yavatmal, Amaravati, Wardha and Chandrapur for the kindness and patience with which they have shared their experiences with me. These include farmers and farmers' widows, taluka and district agriculture officers, officers in-charge of relief and credit, resident and district collectors, managers of cooperative and rural banks, scientists and experts of research institutes, doctors of government hospitals, moneylenders and activists.

I thank my friend Anuj Parti for travelling with me to these districts and for documenting the stories through his photographs.

A principal premise for the book is that the best democracy is one that has the maximum capacity to evolve according to the needs and aspirations of the society. For insight into democratic politics and reforms, I am grateful to Dr Walter Andersen, senior diplomat and director, South Asia, SAIS, Johns Hopkins University, Washington, DC, who shared his knowledge and analyses which have been invaluable for me.

I have come to believe that like individuals, even nations can choose their destinies. For that belief, which is at the heart of this book, I would like to thank Dr Dinesh Singh, scholar, thinker and vice chancellor of Delhi University. The conversations with Dr Singh helped me realize that the search for a better destiny defines a nation, as it does an individual.

As a journalist, I have been fortunate to have worked with the best newspapers in India and with the finest of editors. I am grateful to M. J. Akbar, author and editor-in-chief of *The Sunday Guardian*, for helping me understand and report about the workings of the power templates of Delhi. I also thank him for allowing me time away from work to travel and write.

This book would not be complete without offering my special thanks to Namita Gokhale, scholar and author, for her belief in the concept of the book and for her constant support. Her views have deeply influenced my perspective and assessment of my own work.

This book would not have been possible without the guidance of Kapish Mehra of Rupa Publications. I am grateful for his vision for the book, his professionalism and his passion, and the way he supported the book at every turn. I thank Anurag Basnet for his brilliant and sensitive editing, and for perfect coordination between the two distant ends of the task, Delhi and Washington, DC.

I thank my assistants Shravan Prajapat and Sudhir Kumar

for their efficiency with research, for operating across time zones and, most importantly, for always knowing where the missing papers might be.

This book is the result of the space and time granted by my family to my writing schedules and my travel for research. I thank them for making it possible.

1

Tuesday evening, the Kashinath residence, New Delhi

The November sunlight was like a gentle reminder of an old promise, touching the conscience hesitantly. For those in Delhi inoculated early in life against such evils as a conscience, it was just the month ahead of the winter session of Parliament, and the time to posture aggressively but slip quietly into the limelight.

Such political punctuations in the yearly calendar came in the form of exclusive gatherings of 'personal friends from the media' organized by ambitious politicians. As even some of these carefully chosen journalists could still remain loyal to their profession, the younger politicians had to be often chaperoned and shielded from the 'freer' elements of the press.

One such element, Nazar Prabhakar, parked his car outside the venue of one such exclusive gathering that evening. As he walked along the footpath, he observed the vehicles parked on the road; the labels on the windscreens gave him a fair idea of which of his colleagues he could expect at the meeting.

He walked in through the guarded gates of the government bungalow and was led to the garden behind the house over a narrow brick lane lined with early blooming winter flowers. He was certain that the choice and arrangement of the plants had been made by a government gardener who must have done this every year, irrespective of who lived in the house. Nazar felt that the flowers lost a bit of their charm if their blooming was merely procedural and probably approved by a director of the horticulture department.

But he realized, as he walked into the simmering, slant sunlight and the gentle mist on the grass, that it was not in everyone's fortune to have the sun set in their backyard. The western horizon was one of the various heirlooms inherited by Keyur Kashinath.

Keyur was sitting among a circle of journalists, sharing a joke, the laughter soft and genuine. When he saw Nazar, he walked up to receive him and led him to a chair one place away from his own seat. They had met twice before but were yet to like each other.

Besides Nazar, there were five other journalists gathered in the small circle. From across, Sushila Lal, from an English-language television channel, smiled at him politely. In the chair next to him was Manohar Pandit, from a Hindi television network, and they shook hands. Next to Pandit was Girish Das, a friend who worked for a magazine. The only other newspaperman was Param Singh, a senior journalist and a friend of Keyur's father. As Nazar wished him good evening, Param nodded, the waning sunlight travelled through his silver hair, making it look almost golden.

Nazar had been to this garden before. On the western side, it extended up to the rear garden of the neighbouring bungalow, the official residence of the union minister for chemicals and fertilizers. The minister was a fourth-time member of Parliament and an important ally in the coalition government. On the southern side, the garden touched the flank of the residence of another MP, a lady who held a crucial post in the organization of the Democratic Party, or the DP, the principal party in government. To the north was the home of the minister for heavy industries, who had wanted an even heavier portfolio but had to settle when the party compensated by offering a palatial government residence instead.

In fact, Keyur should not have been in that garden as he was only a first-time MP. But the house belonged to Vaishnav Kashinath, Keyur's father. Vaishnav was one of the two general secretaries of the DP, the right-hand man of the party president, a close confidante of the prime minister, a sixth-term MP and the only man in the party to have ever resigned from a ministership taking moral responsibility for an accident that happened on his watch. It had been a decade since the resignation, and Vaishnav kept away from government positions, reaping the respect bestowed on him due to his selfless act of the past, untarnished by the risks of responsibilities of the present.

The story of how Vaishnav inducted Keyur into national politics was now a legend in Delhi circles. As a member of the panel which selected candidates for national elections, Vaishnav moved a proposal which sought the resignation of panelists whose family members might be aspirants for party tickets. This thwarted the dreams of other panelists, other parents, who were counting on inheritance as the best way to carry forward their political legacy. The proposal fell through but no one had the courage left to push for the candidacy of their sons or daughters through the panel. They cursed Vaishnav's politics and got busy finding an antidote.

Keyur had been stunned; it was impossible for him to receive a ticket, at least not while his father served on the panel. Vaishnav heard, unmoved, Keyur's many attempts to induce guilt, an infallible weapon since childhood to get his way with his father. Unsuccessful and disheartened, Keyur took the advice of a friend to go abroad and stay away from the country till the elections. At the end of two long days, he was reconciled to the future, discarded the khadi clothes, returned to his designer jeans and T-shirts, and tweeted about his plans to work in the US to 'broaden the horizons of experience'. No one was fooled and all wondered why Vaishnav wanted his son to stay out of politics. And when a colleague mentioned about the speculations, Vaishnav did not answer. But he did not deny them either.

Three days after Vaishnav's first proposal was tabled, one of the panelists moved a second one. Those three days were spent by members of the panel with lesser options than Vaishnav, and lesser average lifespan left, in gently but urgently spreading the rumour that Vaishnav feared his son would lose the election if he contested. The new proposal sought that panelists could consider their relatives as contestants, but would have to resign if the relative lost the election. No one could object to candidates who came with such a fail-safe, not even Vaishnav. The proposal was quickly approved by the party and rapidly adopted as a resolution. To mark its acceptability, Keyur was offered the first ticket, which he humbly accepted after publicly seeking his father's permission. Vaishnav's high morals and ethical conduct were appreciated by both friends and rivals within the party.

It had been eight months since Keyur won the election from Mityala, a Parliamentary constituency in south-central India, and he had proved to be a disciplined MP. Vaishnav kept his son away from the party, sometimes treating him with undue harshness. This protected Keyur from criticism from other, more formidable, quarters. Keyur understood this and was grateful for the distance he could maintain from the vicious politics of the DP. But he was also growing restless in the wings and eagerly waited to emerge on to national stage. So, despite knowing his father's strategy, Keyur subtly kept up the pressure on him by playing martyr to his tactics.

❖

Keyur stood up to receive a short, elderly man wearing a white turban, a thick jacket, white cotton dhoti and black shoes. He had the look of someone who had been satisfied with the precautions he had taken against Delhi's winter, until he discovered that the meeting was being held outdoors. With a look of dismay frozen on his face, he settled in the empty chair between Nazar and Keyur, and rubbed his hands together, his rough palms rustling as if about to catch fire.

Two more people walked up, a woman wearing an amber yellow saree with a brown tunic, and a well-dressed, thin man with a thick file under his arm.

All the chairs were now occupied, and Keyur politely let the small talk settle down. The honest anxiety in his eyes for the comfort of his guests was now replaced with a smile. Keyur was thirty-one years old, well-educated, unmarried. Not all the advantages of birth he enjoyed were political. He looked good without effort, and had a face that people trusted easily. He was born with the mask; he did not have to acquire it.

The media loved him because he always returned their phone calls and answered their messages, flattered them by asking for advice and won them over by sharing information trivial to him. And yet, no one really gave him credit for settling down so quickly and with such ease in Parliament and in the party. They believed it was all the result of Vaishnav's careful guidance, who seemed to be meticulously arranging the future of his son.

Like some politicians, Keyur spoke better when addressing a small gathering rather than a large crowd. 'Let me thank you all for being here this evening, especially you, sir, Mr Param Singh and Dr Daya. I am honoured that you accepted my invitation.'

Everyone waited. A peacock perched on the low-hanging branch of a nearby tree, its plume almost touching the ground.

'Dr Daya, as you all know, is director of the Centre for Contemporary Societies. Sitting next to him is the assistant director, Dr Videhi Jaichand. And to my right here is a man who has travelled fifteen hundred kilometres to be with us, Lambodarji, the chief sarpanch of the panchayats of Mityala district. Before we begin, I would like to reiterate what I had mentioned to you all over the phone two days ago. This is an informal meeting and I would request you to keep everything said here "off the record".' He politely repeated, 'No one is to be quoted.'

Letting this message sink in for a moment, Keyur began, 'I know there has been concern about the rising numbers of farmer suicides in my constituency. Twenty-eight farmers have committed suicide due to unpayable debts in Mityala, according to the local administration, in the last forty days.

'I was deeply worried and began investigating the reasons. In this, I was helped immensely by Lambodar maha sarpanch's knowledge and Dr Daya's expertise. I want to place the facts before you as they are and present an authentic perspective of the problem. Each one of you has done a lot of work in the field of agriculture and on issues concerning farmers. I look forward to your views on the subject,' he smiled, 'especially on what is expected of me.

'Dr Daya's Centre is conducting a study for the government on remedial measures needed to address agricultural distress. May I now request him to discuss with us some of his findings?'

Daya thanked Keyur and introduced his Centre as an interdisciplinary research institute set up to facilitate the convergence of thoughts from different fields. Speaking about the study, he said, 'Mityala was one of the twenty districts we studied and Mr Kashinath has been associated with us as the MP representing the constituency in Lok Sabha.

'The causes of distress have been in the making for a long time,' he continued. 'Poverty, indebtedness, land fragmentation, private moneylending, technological stagnation and the lack of follow-up on welfare schemes are just some of them. Other than these, there are also specific reasons for suicides by farmers. What we have done in our study is not merely offered solutions, but identified target groups and worked out implementation.

'The study will be presented to the government in a few months' time and is in the process of being finalized now.'

He paused, then added apologetically, 'I cannot talk about it till the government makes the study public. However, my colleague, Dr Jaichand, will present before you the gist of our findings.'

Daya, Nazar observed, had found a way round the procedural limitation of maintaining secrecy before a report was made public; he would have a proxy speaker in his place. He found her sitting on the other side of the small circle.

'Thank you, Dr Daya,' Videhi began, opening a slim file. 'First, we believe that agricultural extension services should be individual to each farmland. Often, fertilizers, pesticides and sprays are applied disproportionately to increase yields. A separate corps of scientists, experts, even students, can build case studies in villages so that examples are set.

'Secondly, subsidies for fertilizers and power should be withdrawn. The overuse of fertilizers is killing the soil and the overuse of borewells is depleting groundwater. These also add to the expenses borne by the farmers and result in debt escalation. The subsidy withdrawals might have the added advantage of dissuading people from agriculture, thereby reducing pressure on the land so that it becomes sustainable for others.

'Thirdly,' she continued, 'the expenditure of farm income is connected to the increase in exposure to urban lifestyles due to television and cinema. To mitigate this, urban youth should be drafted to rural areas for a period, mainly to interact with rural youth. This would, we feel, help in the exchange of information on adapting to modernization and the realization that life in cities is as much of a struggle as it is in villages.

'Finally, religion is the support system of rural society and spiritual discussions can yield solutions to many problems. This trend is fast fading away in many villages due to its incompatibility with the modern age. As a result, lives have become isolated and prey to unshared tensions. Our suggestion is to begin spiritual counselling centres, mainly by reorienting the local people, especially the elderly.' She glanced up from the file when she was finished and thanked everyone for their attention.

Keyur then invited the chief sarpanch, who was sitting next to him, to speak. Seated on the other side of Lambodar, almost cut off from the group, Nazar heard the maha sarpanch softly ask Keyur if he should mention names. Nazar could not hear Keyur's answer. He looked away, noticing how the blue dusk mixed in layers with the nascent night.

'Namaskar,' Lambodar said finally, clearing his throat and pausing as tea was served in shallow white cups, accompanied by cookies that tasted of coconut and summer. The pens in one hand of the journalists flew across pages, the cups in the other were steady.

'Keyurji, I do not have much to say... I am merely one of the two maha sarpanches...' he began hesitantly in Hindi.

Keyur held Lambodar's hand on the armrest, interrupting him. He turned to the journalists. 'A panchayat, as you all know, is a village assembly and is headed by a sarpanch. In some districts, the honorary position of maha sarpanch has been created for people who have long served as sarpanches in their villages and can now provide valuable guidance to others. A maha sarpanch is a chief sarpanch who is elected by the village sarpanches of an entire district.

So, you see,' Keyur smiled, 'Lambodarji is being modest when he says he is "merely" one of the two maha sarpanches of Mityala.'

Lambodar chuckled with pride, his eyes wary even in happiness, like wild beasts at watering holes. 'Well, if you put it that way...The truth is, dear friends, the recent increase in the suicide figures has little to do with distress. It has everything to do, however, with a decision made by the district collector two months ago in September.'

Though what he said was off the record, everyone made notes, some noted down issues to be researched later, others like Param, made mental notes of people to be researched later. The dusk sounds of winter, scattered and forlorn, filled the space around them.

Lambodar's voice was low and metallic, as if inseparable in spirit from the hookah he had smoked for the better part of the sixty-two years of his life. 'In August, Sudhakar Bhadra, a thirty-two-year-old farmer from my village, Gopur, committed suicide by consuming poison due to alcoholism and depression. But his family claimed it to be a suicide due to debt distress and sought the one lakh rupees that the government offers as compensation in such cases. In our state, these claims are taken up by the district suicide committees set up to examine and validate farmer suicides caused by debt. The Mityala suicide committee decided that Sudhakar's death was not debt-related and refused compensation.'

He cleared his throat a little self-consciously before continuing, 'I pride myself on my memory and as a member of this committee since its inception seven years ago, I remember almost all the cases that have been examined. I remember this case distinctly because I have known Sudhakar and his family for a long time. His father was a good farmer and educated his two sons, sending them to the school in Mityala town. Sudhakar was very good at studies and wanted to continue his education through college and university. But these dreams were curtailed when the family slipped into serious debt due to persistent drought. Sudhakar had to return from the city to Gopur, leaving his studies halfway. It was soon evident that Sudhakar was not good at agriculture; his heart was not in it. It seemed that education had given rise to aspirations in him which agriculture could not fulfil.

'His younger brother, Gangiri, however, continued with his own education, went to college in the state capital and found a good job as a teacher. It was said that he kept requesting his brother to come to the city, and even Sudhakar was keen to move.' Lambodar paused.

'The truth was that Sudhakar was waiting for that one big harvest after which he could have left Gopur and lived his dream in the city. The truth was, Keyurji, he was a not a farmer. He was a dreamer,' Lambodar said, his strong face melancholic. 'And he failed.

'Sudhakar died three months ago in August after delayed rains devastated his crop. Instead of planting the crop again when the rains finally came, like hundreds of other farmers did, he plunged into depression. He became an alcoholic and never recovered. His brother came to Gopur village to perform the final rites. People told me that he held agriculture and the farmland responsible for causing the death of his brother. He was ready to sell off everything and leave Gopur with his sister-in-law and the two children; a four-year-old girl and a five-year-old boy. That would have been the right thing to do for the little children...' Lambodar sighed. 'Instead, soon after the district suicide committee's verdict against Sudhakar, Gangiri resigned from his job in the capital and chose to stay back in Gopur.'

Lambodar glanced away, a spark of anger sharpened the metal of his voice as he said, 'In September, this man managed to get himself appointed by the district collector as a member of the district suicide committee. Since then, there have been three committee meetings. As if avenging the verdict passed by the committee in the matter of his brother's death—which I still believe was not caused due to debt distress—he has managed to put pressure on the committee members and has got them to endorse many farmer deaths as debt-distress suicides.

'Members of the committee, including myself, took up this issue with the collector and demanded that Gangiri's appointment be revoked. But the collector,' Lambodar said helplessly, 'seems to be under some pressure not to overturn his own decision.

'These, dear friends,' Lambodar concluded, 'are the unfortunate reasons why the numbers of distress suicides show an unnatural increase in Mityala district. The toll now stands at twenty-eight in just under two months...two of them from Gopur village itself!'

Lambodar stopped on this emotional note. The performance made Nazar smile.

'You said he was just a school teacher. How could he put pressure on members of the committee?' Girish asked.

Lambodar shrugged. 'Gangiri is a clever man. His full-time occupation these days is to learn about the lives of the committee members and their families. Sooner or later, he comes across something he can use to blackmail them. And he does.'

'So you are saying,' Girish said, 'that these are not really farmer suicides due to debt distress. They are merely suicides by farmers.'

'Yes, and in some cases they are not even suicides,' Lambodar said. 'We have had dozens of cases in which death from medical causes—heart attacks, strokes and other ailments—were passed off as debt suicides. I have even heard of tales about family members pouring poison into the mouths of the dead to claim it was a suicide.'

Sushila was shocked. 'Ghastly!'

Lambodar glanced at her. 'The most notorious case was that of a farmer who was electrocuted when trying to steal power from the main line. His family members placed a bank pass book in the dead man's pocket to show that he was returning from a visit to the bank. They then argued that he killed himself after the bank refused him a loan, given his history as a defaulter.'

Param shook his head. 'Terrible! How unscrupulous!'

Daya interjected, 'It is one of our findings that if the compensation is suspended, there will be no incentive and the suicide figures may actually decline.'

'I think it is still sad that they are killing themselves for any reason,' Manohar said. 'The suicide toll will certainly become an issue in the forthcoming state assembly elections, Keyurji.'

Keyur nodded solemnly. 'You have seen others in my place, you know what ought to be done, what ought not. Please tell me, friends, what should I do?'

'I think you are getting the best advice possible, Keyur,' Param said, smiling.

Keyur smiled at Param, 'My father is one of the two general secretaries of the DP. I am just a first-time MP. I assure you, sir, he has no time for my minor problems.'

Sushila said, 'I think the remedies suggested in the study sound promising. I recommend you try them.'

Manohar said, 'Yes, I agree. We have heard of the methods of increasing credit access, granting loan waivers and introducing modern agricultural practices. But nothing has made an impact. Perhaps the solution should be of socio-economic nature, as Dr Daya suggests.'

Others agreed with Manohar. Only Girish differed, saying that solutions for any sector would have any real success only if they included inputs from people who belonged to that sector; in this case, the farmers themselves.

The empty cups were set down near the chairs, the light porcelain balanced on the long blades of grass and tilted, as if with hidden motives. A chill touched Nazar's leg above his tan boots and he glanced down at the wet grass. It was getting cold, the temperature the previous night had hovered just a few degrees above zero. As he shivered a little, Nazar wondered whether it was due to the winter or the smooth rhetoric he had just heard. He thoughtfully turned to watch the afterglow in the west. A fleet of bats flew over the garden across a cobalt sky, their silhouettes emerging from the silhouettes of trees, before vanishing into the night.

'What do you think is the solution, Mr Prabhakar?'

Nazar heard Keyur ask the question, a genuine curiosity behind the words. He glanced at Keyur and wondered how a man just a few years younger to him could pretend so convincingly to be earnest. Nazar still could not convince his father of his indifference.

Nazar then turned to Lambodar who was sitting next to him. 'What is the name of the brother of the farmer...the new member on the suicide committee?' he asked.

'You mean...Gangiri...Gangiri Bhadra?'

Nazar thanked Lambodar and looked across at Keyur. 'Gangiri Bhadra is the solution, if you are committed to resolving this, Keyurji.'

A brief silence followed his words and the night waited for someone to speak so that it could continue its stealthy advance.

2

Keyur asked, 'You mean, arbitrary distribution of compensation?'

'I mean,' Nazar replied, 'I do not believe Lambodarji, however senior a sarpanch he might be. I think he is being selective with the truth.'

Lambodar was stunned and his bushy white eyebrows rose steeply in surprise.

'Just as you claim that "normal" deaths are being called distress suicides by farmers,' Nazar continued, 'you might have dismissed farmer suicides as "normal" deaths in the past. There is political comfort in keeping suicide figures low. It disproves debt distress, it shows the success of policies. So Lambodarji, who must be no stranger to crisis management, might have done in the past exactly what he claims Gangiri Bhadra is doing now.'

The maha sarpanch glared at Nazar but seemed confused about how to respond.

Girish said, 'I agree. Figures that make governments look bad are usually fudged.'

Keyur looked steadily at Nazar, his dark eyes assessing.

'Yes, this looks bad for you, Keyurji,' Nazar smiled. 'The issue of farmer suicides in Mityala is your first major crisis as an MP. Besides, the crucial assembly elections in the state are due in six months. You are constantly judged against Srinivas Murty, your rival in the Democratic Party, who is also a first-time MP. Both of you aspire to the same institutions of power and the competition is keen. But he has risen through the ranks, and has weathered many storms. You fear he will use this crisis against you. So you want to bury it, "handle" it when you can so that it is under control before the elections. I understand. You do not have to put up this show, Keyurji.' Nazar added, 'We all understand.'

Keyur nodded thoughtfully. 'And I understand your cynicism. You have been to this "show" before. Only the players have changed. But when I ask you, what do you think I should do to help the lot of the farmers, Mr Prabhakar, I do mean it.'

'If you had meant that sincerely,' Nazar replied, 'you would not have Lambodarji here telling us the story of a renegade farmer falsifying the figures of farmer suicides and about the failed attempts to get this farmer out of the district suicide committee. I find it interesting that this farmer has survived all these efforts to oust him and has remained, despite everything, committed to the purpose of the committee. If you had meant what you are saying, Keyurji, you would have had Gangiri Bhadra to meet us here this evening instead of Lambodar maha sarpanch.'

There was once again an absolute silence amidst them, making audible the gentle sounds of birds settling in the trees around.

'You are entitled to your views, however far they may be from the truth,' Keyur said calmly. 'But be fair and consider the solutions we have offered here tonight.'

'Solutions! Well, this city is famous for its eyewashes, Keyurji,' Nazar chuckled. 'I hope that by now we can recognize one when we see it!'

He glanced at the woman in the amber saree, the blue mist in the garden obscuring the details. 'Urbanization is required, I agree. But what is the best that we have done with our cities? Polluted, dirty and cramped, which is our model city? You are right; it might help to have an urban-rural cultural exchange programme, the kind that takes place between two countries. But what if the urban youth who are "drafted" into this programme find that the cities and villages are indeed two different countries in this nation? What if they ask who is responsible and hate us for it?

'Now, we all know,' Nazar continued, 'subsidies have passionate lobbies, both for and against. But there are facts that are neutral and must be considered to find solutions that are in the interest of those who have no lobbies, like the farmers.

'Farmers may be using heavy fertilizers for better yields, as you said. But, without these high doses, the seeds do not deliver profitable crops. Farmers use heavy pesticides, facing personal health hazards, because the genetically modified plants have sidelined traditional pest-control measures. These seeds have succeeded in some parts of the country because of factors like better irrigation facilities. But where they have failed,' Nazar paused, 'the dying crops have taken the lives of the farmers with them.

'Don't you think, ma'am, that you should ask why we give farmers unsuitable and expensive seeds, despite repeated crop failures?' he asked. 'How much did those deals cost the government? How did the payback come? Who gained from the foreign collaborations that made indigenous research redundant?

'Do you have the answers, ma'am? Did you not wonder about these uncomfortable questions when compiling your report? Or are you good with only comfortable clichés that take us for a ride and waste our time...'

Nazar stopped, realizing he had said too much. He had taken the focus off Keyur by targeting a woman. And this one—he once again glanced uneasily across the hazy circle at her—was, perhaps, only following orders.

Only Girish looked like he could forgive his methods.

Keyur's voice was insultingly soothing. 'Thanks, Mr Prabhakar. We would have remained ignorant of all these aspects if you had not enlightened us in such...direct fashion!'

Nazar frowned, but stayed silent.

'And those were not even her recommendations,' Daya added sternly, 'they were mine!'

Keyur glanced at Daya and Videhi. 'As you can see, we are all deeply worried about the dying farmers. Will it be convenient for you to discuss the objections with Mr Prabhakar tomorrow sometime...?'

'No,' Nazar interrupted him hurriedly. 'I am going to be a little busy from tomorrow...so...besides, there is not much to add, actually.'

'But Mr Prabhakar,' Keyur pursued, a little amused, 'we must find a way out for the farmers. If our solutions are eyewash, as you claim, they must be reworked. Will you not help us make government policy more effective?'

'I am available on phone,' Nazar said coldly, hoping his attitude would prevent further attempts.

'Afraid, Mr Prabhakar,' Videhi's voice was icy, 'that you cannot substantiate your criticism?'

Nazar glanced at her, tempted to say yes just to escape. 'I was just staying out of the picture, ma'am,' he said. 'I am merely a journalist.'

'No doubt.'

He could see that everyone was waiting. 'I will be at the Centre whenever you want,' he said in a resigned voice.

She thanked him and he looked away.

Lambodar, who had heard Nazar so far in silence, finally said, 'You seem to resent my presence here this evening.'

'Not at all,' Nazar answered, listlessly. 'It has been a pleasure.'

Lambodar continued to watch with distrust as Nazar turned the pages of his notebook.

To lighten the mood, change the subject, and generally rescue an old friend's son, Param asked Keyur, 'Did you finally go to Nainital?'

'No, sir. The weather reports had forecast rain and everyone backed off. Anyway...we went to Shimla for a bit and stayed at my aunt's place.'

'It's a pity. Nainital can be quite beautiful in the off-season. Of course, in season, it is overflowing with tourists. You can barely walk along the lake!'

Sushila said, 'I don't understand why people go to Nainital when they can easily go to Shimla. The drive is much better and one has a splendid view of the mountains.'

'It has better hotels too,' Girish agreed. 'But I prefer Darjeeling.'

'Nothing can match the beauty of the Nilgiris,' Manohar said.

'I love Manali,' Daya said. 'I have been going there for twenty years.'

'I heard Almora is nice...'

'Have you been to...?'

'I disagree...'

Nazar glanced up from his notebook at the woman across the circle. She was busy with her cell phone and there was not enough light to see her face. The enthusiastic banter improved the climatic conditions within the circle and Nazar wanted to check if it had thawed Videhi's voice.

'Where do you go for your vacations, Dr Jaichand?' he asked, his voice carefully respectful.

Everyone fell silent, surprised.

'I stay in Delhi,' she said. 'I like the city.'

'Really?' He was intrigued. 'For its camouflage?'

'For its snares.'

'So you can see in this darkness?' he asked, amused.

She did not answer.

He never got to see her clearly as they dispersed soon after that. Daya and Videhi stayed back to interview Lambodar at length. Keyur escorted the journalists to the gates, expressed his gratitude and bid them farewell.

Girish walked with Nazar to the cars. 'Thanks for agreeing with me, Girish,' Nazar said.

'What is the use, Nazar?' Girish said, lighting a cigarette. 'The farmer, Gangiri, might have resisted the pressure till now, as you said. But we both know his chances against Keyur Kashinath are slim.'

'I don't know, Girish,' Nazar said, thoughtfully. 'This man seems different, somehow.'

'Then the methods will be different,' Girish observed.

'This is Vaishnav Kashinath's son we are talking about. If he does not want the farmers in his constituency to commit suicide, that is how it will be. The suicides will prove to be heart attacks. You'll see.'

Nazar looked away, curbing his desire to ask for a cigarette. 'I think the increasing number of suicides in Mityala makes for a good story. Perhaps I will file it today.'

'And it will be forgotten tomorrow,' Girish said, smiling. 'Who cares about dead farmers, Nazar? No one even cares about the ones who are alive.'

Nazar looked at him. 'You do.'

'Yes, I do,' Girish said, his smile fading a bit. 'And therefore, I can tell you this. There is no one out there reading your story. There is no one who will take a step because of your story. It is just a numb, self-absorbed world that is slowly consuming itself, from light to darkness, from darkness to darkness.'

Nazar looked away again, hurt by Girish's words. They were silent for a long time, standing on the well-lit sidewalk, alongside the rows of majestic arjuna trees.

'I am sorry, Nazar, forget what I said,' Girish frowned, throwing away his cigarette. 'Must be combat fatigue.'

Nazar did not speak, his gaze far away.

'I look forward to reading your story,' Girish said, smiling once more at Nazar.

Nazar smiled, and nodded.

'Are you going to the symposium on electoral reforms tomorrow? Do you have the details of the venue and time?'

Nazar said he did and they left after some time. As he drove to his office, Nazar thought about what drew him to Girish. Mainly, it was because Girish did not really care for the opinions of people he did not respect, however powerful or influential they may be. They remained good friends, but not because Nazar worked at it. He failed at nurturing friendships, he was bad at follow-throughs and follow-ups.

It was dark by the time Nazar reached his office, a short drive from the Kashinath residence that still took almost an hour through rush-hour traffic. To drive in Delhi was easy, if one kept to 40 kilometres per hour. So, the Ferraris, the BMWs, the Mitsubishis, the fastest cars in the world, humbly stayed in the lower gears. But the pace of traffic always quickened as the night advanced. And even the policemen did not chase the few who took their speed machines out to race on the six-lanes, the cloverleaves and the flyovers.

Nazar drove with patience, parallel parked, and made his way to the seventh floor of the building which housed the editorial offices and newsroom of the newspaper he worked for. He was a thirty-three-year-old, ordinary-looking man who was always dressed well. The tweed he wore that day matched his brown eyes, his white shirt was too white to have been washed at home. The cufflinks and the tan boots might seem like the result of careful thought. But, in fact, he was an instinctive dresser, never comfortable with looking too long in the mirror.

Nazar was meticulous because he was impatient. He wanted to do things only once and do them well. He knew it made him appear reckless and he did not care. He was vain and opinionated. He was harsh with soft people, soft with harsh people and never cared for friends who remembered his birthday. He also never forgave those who forgot.

Nazar suspected himself to be a traditionalist. Only that explained the intense pleasure he derived from breaking every framework he discovered in life, whether it was about his family, his women or his work. He searched for affection that could remain unchanged, love that was unconditional and integrity that could not be compromised. He knew he was defined by his search, and his failures. But being a good man at heart, he contained all the failures and the destruction to just the frameworks which concerned him. As a result, few understood the extent of healing he required. And he chased away those who tried discovering.

Among the few whom he could not chase away was Haridas Tulsi, the seventy-one-year-old editor-in-chief of the newspaper. Just a few months earlier, Nazar had been seriously contemplating resigning from his job because he was fatigued by the predictability of journalism and its results. As if reading his mind, Tulsi called Nazar in for a rare cup of tea. He gave Nazar a brief lecture on the stupidity of reinventing the wheel just because of seniority and argued in favour of beaten paths that led to great destinations. Taken aback by how perceptive Tulsi was, Nazar, for only the second time in his life, spoke about his convictions.

'There aren't many things that really motivate me, sir, and I am not excited by money,' he said. 'I thought journalism would be different, but it is not. I find myself out of place even here if I do not chase money, power and fame. I only wanted to be a small part of opinion-making, I wanted my words to contribute to action that brings about change. In return, all I wanted was to be judged as a chronicler and a commentator. I now get the feeling that such things do not exist.'

'That's an unnerving thought!' Tulsi smiled. 'You will, however, never truly understand people unless you fathom the human desire for money, power and fame. Access to people is of no use if you cannot think like them, Nazar. It is wrong to measure the world according to your priorities. You cannot want what you already have.'

Nazar smiled at the old, knowing eyes which scrutinized him across the wide desk. 'I *did not* want what I already had,' he pointed out.

Tulsi saw the change in his expression and smoothly changed the subject.

Later, Nazar reprimanded himself for still letting his past affect him so much. He never wanted to recall in front of anyone, especially professional acquaintances, the pain that lurked just below the surface. He wished he could detach himself from the past, as simply as he had separated himself from his family.

Some of that crucial training in detachment was provided by Mandip Srivastav who was promoted two months ago. For a while, Mandip was happy thinking his promotion had happened because he was better than everyone else in office. However, that phase did not last long. Mandip was one of those interesting people who disbelieve their personal success so much that they can almost turn it into a failure. He dug so deep looking for the reasons for his promotion that he discovered, instead, that Nazar was being paid a better salary than him. Though Nazar's designation of 'assistant editor' was junior to his, Mandip was sure Nazar had secured himself a better deal by some manipulation of paperwork. That, to him, also explained how Nazar's room even had a window!

Mandip derived his main consolation from the fact that Nazar's wealthy family was periodically in the news for some excess or the other. Just the week before, it was a lavish wedding abroad. The 'leaked' guest list included Nazar's name but he had not attended the event. At one of the daily editorial meetings, Mandip suggested a feature on the 'Weddings of the Remorseless'.

He had instructed, with evident relish, 'Let's find the bills of the bastards'.

Nazar was a man of little vulnerability, except when it came to his family. Eight years earlier, and that was for the first time in his life, he had put into words his long-standing discomfort with pursuit of wealth as the single goal of life. No one was really shocked, his parents were only hurt that he did not respect their endeavours and his siblings conveniently followed their lead; one brother less meant one claimant less for the family fortune. No one stopped him from leaving London when he could still have stopped, and stayed. That was eight years ago. Now, he was convinced he would not have stopped for anyone.

Nazar had worked in two other publications before this newspaper; he had resigned from both because of the stories he had filed. The editors of both the papers told him he nurtured an ego no journalist could afford. He wondered about it sometimes during the weeks of unemployment that followed his resignations, and between jobs.

Nazar also made no bones about why he quit his previous two jobs. He candidly even mentioned the reasons under the category of 'past experience' in his résumé.

The first case was a story about a dam and the complicity of the state government in causing the needless displacement of lakhs of people. It turned out that the contractor who changed the design of the dam, and caused such damage, was a friend of the father-in-law of the newspaper's proprietor.

Nazar got his next job because of the heat generated by that story and his sensational exit. It was said that when the editor asked him to retract the story, Nazar reached for the nearest piece of paper on the editor's desk and wrote down his resignation.

He quit his second job because of a story on a series of murders among the followers of a godman. Under great pressure from the godman and his influential followers, the newspaper published a denial of Nazar's story without consulting him. He e-mailed his resignation a few minutes after he read the retraction in that morning's paper.

Tulsi had asked for Nazar and met him briefly before offering him a job. He asked Nazar the question he usually did to assess a journalist; where he or she would like to report from, given a choice. He had heard many fancy answers: 'Koraput, Kalahandi; Kanker, Dantewada; Srinagar, Kashmir; Adilabad, Telengana...'

'Delhi,' Nazar had said, without blinking. 'Why would I be in Delhi if I wanted to be anywhere else?'

Tulsi saw the honesty in Nazar's questioning eyes, and confidence about honesty, almost pride. Tulsi knew that by hiring Nazar, he was buying trouble. But he wanted to be able to afford it.

❖

The white lights and reflective glass slowed Nazar down as he walked to his room from the elevators. He reminded himself, as he did daily, that he had to wind down his thoughts to writing speed. His corner office shared walls with the photo editor and the news editor, and only the corner rooms had a window.

Nazar found a small blue envelope among the post on his table, his name written in black ink. He opened the rest of his mail, but left the envelope unopened. He knew who it was from and he wanted her to wait. There was nothing about Nazar that should have recommended him to women. At least, that is what the men thought. But the women waited for him.

Nazar logged in to his computer, checked mail, and began replying. Finally, when he was free, he sat still for a moment, comforted by the sounds of the busy newsroom. In his mind he made his way back to the newspoint, salvaging it from the layers of the day.

A few years earlier, villages from about a hundred districts in the country had been declared in desperate need of development. They required everything, from clean drinking water to food to sanitation. They were promised all that and more; schools, roads, electricity.

Following up on the welfare schemes that had been announced by the DP government, Nazar visited some of the villages and discovered that, except for the new signboards announcing the projects, nothing had changed. He wrote about funds that were waiting to be spent, work plans that lay idle, costs that were appreciating for the taxpayer. He wrote about the deficit of political will for welfare which kept these villages backward.

In response to the stories, the DP government promised quick action to prove its commitment, reprimanded a few junior officials and set a vague deadline that was never kept. When Nazar persisted with his stories, some of the junior officials were suspended for inaction. But nothing moved on the ground.

That experience had taught him not to aim at the small fish. The big fish were tough to catch, they were too smart to be drawn into the dark corners of the Great Indian Growth story. But Nazar hoped that in the case of Mityala, the big fish could be dragged into dealing with the distress of the poor farmers because it threatened the prospects of one of their own, Keyur Kashinath, the son of the big fish.

Nazar typed a mail to Mandip, outlining the story he proposed to write. It was not based on the informal, off-the-record briefing he was just at. He suggested a brief analysis of the three worst-affected constituencies represented by MPs of the ruling party, highlighting the increasing number of farmer suicides.

He did not have to wait long. Mandip walked into the room, nodding a greeting.

Mandip was older than Nazar by about four or five years; he was a short man with a chubby face and bright eyes. He was famous for his cool head. It was commonly held that any news crisis could be sorted if Mandip was in charge.

Mandip paused for one thoughtful second and said, 'I wish you had told me about this story in the morning.'

Nazar shrugged helplessly.

Mandip shook his head. 'Page one is packed.'

'Inside will do. A three-hundred-word analysis. Three high-profile constituencies. Half an hour.'

'Do it.'

Mandip smiled as he walked out of the room. Whatever he felt about Nazar, he never let it come in the way of a good story idea.

It took forty-five minutes to write about Ichalgunj, Warni and Mityala. All three districts had 90 per cent of their land under cotton cultivation. All had seen suicide notes left behind by a husband, a father, a brother, a son. Every second house had a widow. Every other child had a question.

'Death Districts of the DP Government', he suggested for the headline. *There are no doors in Ichalgunj*, Nazar began his story. *Once, that was because no one wanted anything more. Now, it is because no one has anything left.*

He finished the story and sent it to Mandip. As he waited for his response, Nazar once again felt like lighting a cigarette. Even though he had quit some months earlier, he still felt the urge whenever he had nothing to do. Worried that he would reach for the 'emergency' pack of cigarettes in the top drawer of his desk, Nazar stood up and walked away from it.

Finally, the phone rang. Mandip was curt. 'It is fine. Late, but fine.'

Nazar refrained from answering that. Instead, he wished Mandip a good night and left office for the day.

3

Tuesday night, Gopur village, Mityala district, South Central India.

The people of Gopur were asking themselves a question that night. Almost everyone wanted to know what had happened to their sense of shame? Where, in the journey of life, had they shed their manners and their sabhyata, their code of civilized conduct? And yet, they could not help smiling and even exchanging jubilant greetings with each other. Except for the very young, and the very arrogant, everyone felt guilt for their overwhelming happiness.

That day, two widows from the village had received compensation for their husbands' deaths due to agricultural distress. Of the total amount, 30 per cent was given to the widows in cash and 70 per cent was deposited in a bank account. The amount could be invested in any of the various schemes the government offered to the distressed families. These and other related issues were explained to both recipients personally by an official of the district administration.

The children of the village stared with worry at the tear-streaked faces of their parents. People followed the official from one house to the other as he went about explaining the disbursal of the compensation. Then they stood watching as the jeep drove away with the official, carrying the widows' signatures on the necessary documents. When the widows smiled, the people smiled with them. This was the first disbursal to have happened in Gopur in seven years.

When farmers committed suicide in Gopur, no local sarpanch had the courage to fight his or her way through the district suicide committee and get compensation for the widows. Every sarpanch aspired to be the next leader of the district and, perhaps, one day, one of the leaders of the state. After a few failed attempts, no one tried pushing their reputation too far with the suicide committee.

Lambodar, a highly respected member of the committee and a native of Gopur, had earned a nickname in Mityala. He was called 'apatra' Lambodar. The name had been coined by a rival candidate during one of the local elections. It was formalized when, at a function to celebrate his re-election, a member of the Legislative Assembly praised Lambodar in a routine he-has-a-finger-on-the-pulse-of-the-people speech and ended with, 'I wish apatra Lambodarji many more victories.'

Lambodar swore to make sure Gopur never voted for that MLA again.

But the name stuck.

The suicide committee decided whether a given case of farmer's suicide was 'patra', or eligible, or 'apatra', or ineligible, for compensation, by ascertaining if the suicide had been caused due to farm debt. Lambodar was notorious for giving the maximum apatra verdicts in the district and, thereby, denying compensation to the widows. To emphasize his stand against compensation, he never supported any death from his own village, Gopur, as a distress suicide.

The tears and smiles of the villagers that day were also

because the grip of the influential Lambodar on their lives, and their deaths, seemed to be slowly slackening. They smiled, saddened that they could still smile, despite the vacant looks in the eyes of the widows, despite the hardening faces of the children.

The sum of one lakh rupees was meagre, and even the officials knew it. It could, perhaps, pay for a five-acre cotton crop and support the farmer's family for a while. But not for too long. And if there were new loans to take, or old debts to repay with the harvest, the money would run out even quicker.

But there was still time for that darkness to arrive, people knew. Today was a day to retell how this miracle happened, to narrate how a village which had forgotten justice, discovered it again.

Two months ago in September, everyone had been stunned by the news that the district collector's office had made changes to the district suicide committee. Such committees had, as members, top people drawn from the village and the administration, and once constituted, were rarely changed. Members were replaced when they were either posted out of the district or died. No one had ever heard of a new member being added to a new category of the committee. The suicide committees of the neighbouring districts had stayed intact for over ten years, whereas the Mityala committee was only seven years old.

Besides Lambodar, the other maha sarpanch of Mityala, Gauri Shanker sarpanch, was also a member of the committee. Gauri was older than Lambodar by a few years, an important seniority in the village system. Their forefathers were zamindars who had owned most of the village lands.

The extent of their holdings was now diminished but not their claim to the prestige. Gauri Shanker was apolitical, but Lambodar routinely helped candidates from the DP win elections in the district by cashing in on old loyalties and debts.

Both were respected for the fact that despite their stature and achievements, they had lost elections to the state assembly a few times and were now reconciled to living in the safety of their past glory. They were also respected for the fact that both had children who, despite their best efforts, stayed away from the district and, when visiting it, refused to step into their fathers' dusty village shoes.

One of Lambodar's principal, though untested, beliefs, which made him deem every suicide apatra or ineligible, was that he thought of debt-distress suicide as an act of deception against the state. Though Lambodar lived in Gopur, he knew almost all the families of the district, some as far back as three generations. Villagers who knew of his memory seldom crossed his path. Memorizing names, faces, and who said what and when was a passion of his and a cause of irritation for others. People tried not to get recorded, indexed, and stored in his memory to be recalled at inconvenient moments in the future. Lambodar mistook their prudence for reverence and lived under the presumption that the distance they kept was out of respect for his conservative, patriarchal ways.

In contrast, everyone in the district loved Maha Sarpanch Gauri Shanker. He was from Chira village, situated about 30 kilometres from Gopur, which was surrounded by hills and water catchments that turned into great lakes during the monsoons. Chira was best known for the big cement plant which had brought roads and jobs to the area. But the water drained quicker than ever before, the soil got rockier and the farmers toiled so hard that there remained no difference between shedding sweat and blood.

Gauri Shanker always validated suicide cases brought up before him to be debt-related and patra or eligible for compensation. The slender old man had always been driven by his passions, nervous but unshakeable in his beliefs. He had founded five schools in the district and was nervous about improving their performance. He was raising funds for a new hospital and was nervous whether he would see it ready before he died. He was nervous about his son's forthcoming foreign trip, and whether he would return and still be his son. He was even nervous about the dying eucalyptus tree in the backyard which loomed ominously over the house.

He never asked for any proof when voting for farmer suicides, and went through the procedures of the committee to prevent questions. He never needed to recall names and faces, but he did so to fool everyone else. At times, the suicides were not just debt-related, but he always voted 'yes' to the compensation. His did so mainly because he believed it was the duty of the state to take care of the families of farmers who had become victims of the state's oversight. But Gauri Shanker did this also because he knew that as the oldest and seniormost member of the committee, he was the only one stopping Lambodar from monopolizing the verdicts. Without him, no farm widow would ever get her due.

The third member of the committee was the enigmatic Durga Das, from the distant village of Nula. Durga Das had worn the same set of clothes for the last two years, clothes he had got tailored for his daughter's wedding. The blue of the shirt had now almost faded to white and the brown of the trouser was turning khaki. His shoes had long given up hope of a good polish and he carried a pouch on which the original leather remained, like a mischievous clue, only in the folds at the sides.

The villagers, however, knew that the deep poverty his state reflected was just a lie. He loved to keep the true extent of his wealth hidden from the world. It was, though, impossible to hide the fact that he was the biggest moneylender in the district, who owned three jewellery shops, one of them in the district headquarters in Mityala town, and had lent money to almost every family in every village of the district at some time or the other. That meant no marriage cost or court expense, fee or bail, purchase or sale, house or vehicle, accident or deliberate, loss or insurance, birth or death happened in the village without his knowledge.

And he knew exactly how much was owed to private moneylenders by the families of the farmers who committed suicide. He was at the head of a delicate but resilient network of informal credit in the villages. He was the one who allowed the crops to be sown, the daughter to be married, the son to be sent to the city, the mother to be taken to the hospital. He was also the one who decided whether a farmer should repay the banks first, or repay the private loan. He allowed the lending of seeds, fertilizers and pesticides to the farmer. In a way, he was the one who could, and often did, decide whether the banks should survive in his backyard. And the banks knew that to survive they must not extend beyond his backyard.

There were only two things about Durga Das which were in sparkling condition and stood out in the cultivated ruin of his appearance. His glasses and his pen. Das wore bifocal lenses set in a frame worth twenty thousand rupees, roughly equal to the crop loan extended by banks for two acres of unirrigated paddy. His pen was gold-plated in the right places with a sheen that was encountering its first winter. These tools, he used to observe and record the lives of his debtors. And because he hated the thought that someone could do the same to him, he maintained his run-down appearance diligently.

His watery brown eyes never missed even the smallest details of the scene on the farms; from the width of the cotton leaf to the height of the farmer's goat; the measure of crop yield and the size of subsidiary income. From the pressure of the water from the borewell to the pressure of the coir cot in the yard; the measure of soil fertility and the leisure of the farmer.

Durga Das never haggled. Before the farmer could answer his questions, Das knew the amount he would settle for. His pen, and its numerous predecessors, never erred in their calculations.

To him the suicide of a farmer too was a calculation and he never went wrong with it, either. On the rare occasions he voted in favour of an eligible suicide verdict, it was with the understanding that debts would be cleared by the widow with the compensation she received. Or, that the money would be routed back as investment into projects he supported, like transportation or animal husbandry.

But mostly, he favoured an apatra verdict so that the farmer's family was denied compensation and eventually lost the land, house or jewellery pledged with him. There was really no way of knowing which equation he was working on when he cast his vote at the suicide committee. There was only suspicion of his foul play. He was too smart to leave any evidence.

The fourth and fifth members of the committee were both from Batoni, the second-largest town in the district after Mityala—the chief of the sub-district hospital, Dr Hemant Rao, and the local head of the national bank, Ramesh Vaish. They were both on the committee to provide opinion on medical and financial issues, respectively, in cases of farmer suicides.

The sixth member was the famously combative and precise Purandar Reddy, the Mityala chief of police. He was on the committee to give his professional opinion that was always heavily laced with local intelligence input which, many suspected, was actually his personal opinion.

Then there was the most important member of the committee, the fashionable and stylish Jivan Patel, the district's agriculture officer (AO) or the man who should know too much. In the past three years, three AOs had been transferred as part of the government's decision to pay more attention to distressed districts. As a result, the AO barely had time to settle in and depended heavily on the local talathis or village officers, who kept records of yield, pests, losses and gains of crops for individual villages.

The AO, like the chief of police, lived in Mityala and went to work every day at 10 a.m. to an office across the road from his residence. He spent more time shaping his goatee than checking acreage changes in the district. An audit of the general administration departments in the district a few years ago had shown that the AO spent as much money on fuel for his official car in a year as an excise officer did in just a month.

As stipulated in the original orders, the committee was required to have a representative of the farmers. This condition was fulfilled by farmer-member Sitabai from the village of Karn, located about 50 kilometres from Gopur. She never vetoed compensation in any case and never let anyone who vetoed it, including Durga Das, get off easily.

Fifty-two-year-old Sitabai was a former sarpanch and was still popular. She resigned from the post after two terms when she was forced to approve harsher tenancy conditions for farmers. Always full of opinion, her usual complaint at the committee meetings was that there were far too many interruptions during the proceedings.

And then, in September, a new category was added by Collector Amarendra Gul for a place on the committee for a member from the families of farmers who had committed suicide. The first candidate in this category was Gangiri Bhadra. As his land fell between Gopur and Allur villages, he represented both on the committee.

Along with the collector who chaired it, the ten-member committee met every fortnight to address the claims for compensation for farmers' suicides in the district.

4

Since Gangiri's induction into the committee, the meetings had become harsh, noisy affairs that were barely under control. No one had physically attacked anyone yet, but Collector Gul no longer thought it impossible.

Gul, who disliked Gangiri for the way he had got himself appointed to the committee, was initially on the lookout for a way to have him expelled. But it soon became evident that Gangiri was not going to say, or do, anything provocative. He had studied the rules of conduct very carefully and always contained his behaviour within the framework. His questions were always factual, his manner unremarkable, his arguments well-researched and even his innuendoes, polite. And yet, Gul issued the maximum censures for misconduct against Gangiri. It was with the hope that one day, if he had to, he could show good reason for sacking Gangiri from the committee.

The other members, unaware of Gul's plans, were disturbed by something deeper. Gangiri's mere presence seemed to change the dynamics of the meetings. Some resented him, some felt guilty, and everyone was unsettled by the fact that when Gangiri's brother Sudhakar had killed himself, the same committee had then refused to validate it as a debt-related suicide, almost insinuating that his sister-in-law Padma had lied in seeking compensation.

Neither their resentment nor acceptance made any difference to Gangiri; he had been both pulled down and patronized enough in life not to be bothered by any of it.

In his twenty-nine years, Gangiri had always wanted what he could not have. And as one of the two children of a poor farmer, the list of things he could not have was long.

He and his elder brother had both studied at the Mityala High School, the first in their family of farmers to do so. They believed they were on their way to college in the state capital, to find paying jobs and earn enough money to send home so their parents could live without worrying about the fate of the crops.

It just took a two-year drought to destroy their plans. Sudhakar was called home to help with the farm and he left school thinking he would return soon. But the drought continued and despite their hard work, they had to sell half their land to clear unpaid dues to moneylenders controlled by Durga Das. It was a blow to everyone, but especially to their father who did not survive it. Sudhakar knew then that there was no turning back for him. He could not run away, chasing selfish dreams.

It now became Sudhakar's goal to help his brother achieve what he himself could not. With letters written full of hope, he made sure Gangiri never gave up, never reconciled to his fate and never stopped wanting the things he could not have. And Gangiri dedicated himself to the single-minded pursuit of his brother's ambition.

But a farmer's son needed to have much more than mere brilliance to succeed. Gangiri fought his way through college with the help of scholarships. He made it to university when people said he had no future to aspire for. He learnt English when they said he had no past to refer to. He taught the sciences to intimidate them and learnt the arts to scandalize them. And now, when he looked back, he was actually grateful for his detractors.

This year was the turning point of his life. A few months earlier, he had received a promotion in the private school where he taught. He wrote to Sudhakar about the new accommodation he had acquired and the increase in his salary. He asked his brother to come along with his family and stay with him in the city for some time. But Sudhakar turned down the invitation, saying conditions were difficult at home. Gangiri had learnt from his brother's letters that the late rains had destroyed the cotton crop, but he had no clue that Sudhakar contemplated suicide.

In August, when his brother died, the road stopped travelling with Gangiri, as if there was no needle in his compass, no signposts in his language. He was lost in Gopur, a village of just 4,500 people.

It felt as if almost every one of the residents of the village came to meet him, and left him overwhelmed by their unconditional affection. But Gangiri wondered why they never spoke a word about Sudhakar. Then his childhood friend, Vadrangi, explained it to Gangiri; he said they feared referring to Sudhakar. He could have been any one of them; every one of them was Sudhakar, a farmer suicide waiting to happen.

Then, slowly, as if answering their own questions, the villagers told Gangiri what killed Sudhakar, what could kill any one of them—debt and organo-phosphate pesticide.

The details of how his brother committed suicide slowly replaced the plans and promises of Gangiri's life. The tall steel glass in which Sudhakar had mixed the deadly pesticide, the empty containers with yellow triangular warnings of poison, the spot in the dust where he had fallen, the shoes that still waited at the doorstep.

People helped Gangiri search for a suicide note, they said it was evidence crucial to prove that Sudhakar had, indeed, committed suicide because he was unable to repay his debts. As an educated man, they felt he would have had no problem with writing a note. They could not understand why there was none.

Gangiri knew why. What was there to say? Sudhakar had surrendered.

Gangiri began to hate the farm that killed his father, his brother, the home in which his mother suffered long for lack of treatment before she died. He was determined to rescue Padma and the children, Sashi and Balu, from it all. Padma reluctantly agreed to leave Gopur and Gangiri set about looking for a bargain for the land and the house. It was a four-acre farm, the house was many decades old, with a concrete roof built in better days but now neglected for years.

His friends in the village suggested that Gangiri wait for the fortnightly meeting of the suicide committee. Gangiri hoped that he could pay off his brother's debts with the compensation money before he left Gopur, so that he would never have to return. That fortnight he spent making trips to the post office, calling people he knew in the state capital, asking for help with finding a second job for himself.

The evening before the suicide committee was to meet at the Mityala collectorate to decide how his brother had died, Gangiri sat on the porch of his home in Gopur, watching the August moon rise behind the tamarind trees in the fields. He could not help wondering why the earth was driving her sons away from her heart. Were they doing something wrong? Were they being punished? Where were they supposed to go? Where were they supposed to return?

His dark eyes sparkled with tears of loss that he could not explain. It was a much bigger loss than the loss of life, and a much deeper loss than the loss of faith. He felt guilt for letting the land go, for not fighting for it. Never, he knew, would he be home again. And never again would he be part of something that contained both his past and his future.

From then on, he would live in the city but never belong to it. A man from nowhere, a man who was just a name on a salary cheque, a face on a photo ID, a voice on the phone. A part of the moving mass of people in a crowded bus, a metro, a local train. A part of the praying mass of people in a temple, a mosque, a church, a hospital. Perhaps he was braver than Sudhakar. He was not merely killing himself, he was killing the farmer in himself.

The news from the meeting of the suicide committee was carried by the village officer, or the talathi, a bald, tall man, who had known Sudhakar well. The committee's verdict was that Sudhakar had not committed suicide due to farm distress, 'as claimed by his widow Padma'. The case had been found to be apatra and, therefore, the compensation was denied. The words sank through Gangiri's heart like lead, hardening every little cell, squeezing out every last emotion.

He asked mechanically, 'Then why did my brother die?'

'The suicide was declared to have occurred due to continued depression and alcoholism,' the talathi explained, 'but not due to the burden of unpaid farm debt.'

Padma argued that Sudhakar was not an alcoholic. If they did not have money to buy food, how could Sudhakar buy liquor, she asked.

The talathi countered, saying that poverty never stopped anyone from drinking.

Her voice was choked as she asked, 'Are you saying we lied?'

The talathi smirked. 'As you said, you have no money. And one lakh rupees is a lot of money.'

Gangiri asked again in a stunned voice, 'Are you saying we *lied*?'

The talathi now squirmed a little. 'I think the committee found reasons other than the ones you mentioned for your brother's suicide.'

'Does the committee know my brother better than me? Or his wife?'

The talathi shifted uneasily in his seat. 'Why do you want to get into all these details? You are right in planning to sell this place. Go back to your job in the capital. You were doing so well, this village was so proud of you.'

Gangiri did not speak.

Then the talathi lowered his voice. 'I heard you turned down Durga Das mahajan's offer to buy the land?'

'He has wanted this land since my father's time, since the time he took away one half of it to settle outstanding debts,' Gangiri said grimly. 'If I can help it, I will never sell him the other half.'

'You misunderstand the man, Gangiri,' the talathi said earnestly. 'He is not like other vaddi-vyaparis or moneylenders. He knew you would need the money, and it is difficult to find buyers at short notice...'

Gangiri suddenly glanced at him, realizing. 'So Durga Das knew the compensation claim would be turned down?'

'You know how these things are, Gangiri. He wants that land.'

Padma stared at them, shocked. After a moment, Gangiri said, 'I have no choice, do I?'

'You don't need a choice,' the talathi insisted. 'I will draw up the papers myself and get your signatures tomorrow. You can pay me later for my assistance.'

'Just one doubt,' Gangiri said. 'If what you are saying is true, then tell me how does Durga Das manage the committee, headed by the collector himself, to vote the way he wants?'

The talathi smiled. 'Durga Das mahajan has the financial records of everyone on the committee—their income, debts, investments. Those he cannot control, he leaves to apatra Lambodar. Together they make sure the majority of the committee votes in their favour. Even the collector cannot question such verdicts.'

Gangiri nodded, his heart filled with anger, but his lips smiling in gratitude. 'You are right, it is kind of him to have spared a thought for me,' he said. 'If you can give me some time, I shall soon speak to you about the land.'

The talathi left after asking Gangiri not to take too long. His motorcycle kicked up a plume of dust as it went up the path that led to the road and vanished round the corner. As he stood at the bamboo gate of the fence, there was a brief debate in Gangiri's mind about the options before him. He could accept the committee's verdict, sell the land to Durga Das and leave Gopur with Padma and the children. A new page could be turned and they could build a new life in the city. Or, he could stay in Gopur and fight.

News of the verdict travelled fast and the villagers came to console the family. Sitting with Gangiri on the porch, Vadrangi recalled the men who had died tilling the land for hope. His own ten-acre cotton field was next to Gangiri's land and fell within the border of the neighbouring village of Allur. The land was so heavily mired in debt that Vadrangi worked like a tenant farmer on his own land. To make ends meet, he took up carpentry jobs in the village but still could not afford to give his family a dignified life. His father had held himself responsible for the debt he had bequeathed his son, and unable to witness his struggle, committed suicide. The district committee had decided it was not a suicide due to debt distress. They said he died of a weak heart. In a way, that was the truth.

There were many such farmers, different names, same fate. As Gangiri heard the stories, he once again found himself wanting something that was denied to him, something he could not have. Justice.

He then made a decision, to make sure no farmer was ever humiliated again, no widow ever called a liar. Suddenly, the small village of Gopur started making sense.

Later that day, Gangiri walked to the post office and called his school principal in the capital. He briefly explained the circumstances and requested to be relieved from work. The principal sympathized with Gangiri and promised to help. The next day, Gangiri sent a formal letter of resignation and a request for his salary arrears to be cleared. Within a week, the school sent him a demand draft for twelve thousand rupees.

By then, Gangiri had a plan.

❧

After a few failed attempts, Gangiri finally met the district collector. Gul met him between meetings, mainly because Gangiri came across as an educated man and spoke English. Gul understood Gangiri's loss but said that he could not reverse the committee's decision on such matters. Gangiri did not argue, but thanked Gul and walked out.

A couple of weeks later, Gul was forced to meet Gangiri again. And this time, he heard Gangiri with attention and realized he was not asking for the decision of the committee to be reversed. He wanted to be included on the committee as a member who represented the families of the farmers who had committed suicide. He supported his claim with a report which explained the communities which were represented by the members on the committee. As compared to the two maha sarpanches and Durga Das, only Sitabai emerged as a member representing the larger majority, the farmers and the women. Gangiri argued that to make the committee truly representative of the district, there should be a member who could represent the families of those farmers who had committed suicide.

Gul pointed out that as the committee had concluded Sudhakar Bhadra's suicide to be ineligible for compensation, Gangiri would not fit the bill. Gangiri countered that if they were to go just by numbers, such suicide verdicts were in a majority in the district and, hence, deserved representation.

Gangiri waited as Gul carefully went through his report. But the question Gul asked at the end was about the phone call Gangiri had made earlier, seeking the appointment.

'How do you know the high court judge?'

'Believe me, Mr Gul, not as a respondent in his court.'

Gul winced, and then waited.

Gangiri leaned forward in the chair. 'Sir, how many times do you get to talk to the special secretary in the prime minister's office? The one designated to monitor districts facing distress suicides?'

'Often,' Gul answered. 'It is of no use, however. It is not in our hands to stop farmers from killing themselves.'

'Not if the district committee, headed by you, represents the very reasons that farmers commit suicide,' Gangiri said. 'Or, so it would seem.'

Gul studied him with calm dislike. Gangiri's dark, smiling eyes promised that he would use the information if he had to. At the same time, it was not difficult for Gul to appreciate the inevitability of the solution Gangiri suggested. The smart, neat man in dusty clothes had done some worrying research.

This was not Gul's first posting as a district collector. And not the first time that he was contemplating an abject, though righteous, capitulation. 'I agree, the composition of the committee is lopsided. But two DCs before me could not touch it. Neither can I.'

'No, you can't,' Gangiri agreed. 'But then, you don't have to.'

Gul knew what he meant. What difference could one more man make? Gul was not sure of the safety of having Gangiri on board, he did not like his tactics. But there were advantages. By including Gangiri, he could silence the activists for a while and Gangiri was right, he had to admit, the PMO might take notice of him.

They met a few more times after that day as Gangiri helped Gul with his antecedents to be included in the proposal. Gul's proposal was immediately accepted; the impressed state government even remarked that more civil servants should think like Gul.

※

The tail end of the rains, whose delay had destroyed Sudhakar's fields, was lashing the state capital when Gangiri arrived. He had come to show the judge of the high court the notification of the committee which announced his appointment as the new member. The judge was the father of one of Gangiri's students and, when Gangiri explained the case, he had shared the information on the condition that it should be used for the cause of dying farmers. Gul's spotless past had a well-hidden court case of criminal negligence from which he was acquitted. But against a serving bureaucrat, this was still live ammunition.

Gangiri had come to know of this case from the newspaper archives in Mityala and the public library. It had taken about a week's stay in Mityala, which punched a small hole in his salary arrears.

※

Since Gangiri's appointment, there had been three meetings of the committee in Mityala. For every meeting, and to investigate every committee member, he had to travel and conduct research. The hole in the salary arrears was growing steadily. Before the fourth meeting, scheduled for that Friday, he had to go to Batoni to deal with the head of the sub-district hospital, a member on the committee whose opinion always created problems. Gangiri felt guilty taking more away from the arrears, it was the only hope of a future for the family.

Of the sixty-eight thousand rupees his brother owed in debts, twenty-three thousand rupees was owed to a bank; part of a crop loan worth forty thousand rupees he had taken two years ago. The rest was for loans of farm inputs from shopkeepers and moneylenders, men who were mostly controlled by Durga Das. For this year's cotton crop, Sudhakar had needed forty thousand rupees but no one was ready to extend him the new loan. He sold his wife's jewellery to raise the amount and planted cotton. But the rains were delayed, destroying the crop. He had no money to re-plant the cotton when the rains finally arrived and no means to support his family without a harvest. That ended Sudhakar's will, and also his life.

From the time Gangiri became a member of the committee, many things had changed. Input dealers and petty moneylenders clamoured for his attention. Seeds, fertilizers, pesticides, power lines, motors, handpumps, cash for labour, everything was his for the asking. He wanted to plant a crop of pulses and the traders fought to loan him inputs for the crop. But the condition was that he should not validate farmer deaths from Gopur and Allur as distress suicides.

Gangiri refused, and the promises were replaced promptly with threats. When those too failed, they all fell silent, waiting to see what he would do next.

But before he did anything, Gangiri had to once again deal with the guilt of imposing his principles on his family. He had to deal with the eager faces of Sashi and Balu waiting for their mother to cook food, waiting for their often-mended clothes to be mended again, waiting for the often-repaired roof to be repaired again. And when the waiting yielded nothing, the children looked away, forgoing desire.

After two meetings of the committee, the villagers realized that Gangiri was turning the verdicts around. They could see that since his appointment, an increasing number of committee members were validating farmer suicides. The names of moneylenders and input dealers were mentioned openly at the meetings. And now, widows had even started receiving compensation. There was an anxiety among the traders and moneylenders about the indifference, and even disdain, they had shown towards Gangiri until now.

That day, after he got to know that two widows of Gopur had received compensation, Gangiri walked to the village kisan kendra. He sat in the shaky wooden chair in the small shop, while the traders watched him with apprehension. The shirt he wore was neat, but needed mending; his skin was the colour of ploughed earth, his eyes patient with knowledge. He did not belong in the desperation of this situation, they could see. He chose it. They had thought he would be a misfit, a teacher trying to be a farmer. But they should have looked more closely.

Then Gangiri spoke, asking if he could borrow the materials necessary to sow pulses in the four acres of his field. He said he would repay after the harvest, with the usual interest on the loan.

The dealers were lost for a minute, taken aback by his politeness, wondering if he had forgotten how they had mistreated him. Then, they quietly took the invitation and advanced him the inputs for the new crop.

5

Wednesday morning, the Jaichand residence, New Delhi

One of the things that had changed with her marriage two years ago was her wardrobe; there were now many sarees in it which Videhi wore in no particular order. She did not notice the ochre yellow saree she wore that day, or that it was paired wrong with a beige short coat.

By the time she walked down to the ground floor, the housekeeper had briefed her about the progress with the changing of the living-room curtains and sourcing options for the upholstery. She was also given the results of the staff-recruitment interviews held in Guwahati and Lucknow for the local residences. She began breakfast by approving the menus of the day and ended it by memorizing the various times at which she could call her husband, who was travelling.

She was thankful for the silence that followed and spent the next half hour reading the newspapers. In the beginning, she often rushed through the headlines, not wanting to keep the staff waiting, unnerved by the watching eyes everywhere. She was now used to the eyes.

Afterwards, she supervised the various chores in the house, the marble floor cheerfully reflecting the sunlight that streamed in through the windows. Videhi walked around, giving instructions in a soft voice. She was a tall woman who looked good in the sarees she wore on weekdays, and the old jeans on Sundays and holidays. She paused to watch the lowering of the chandelier, marking a moment's respect for a surviving witness to the long history of the house. Then she heard with patient attention the housekeeper's explanation of its rare requirements and repairs.

Videhi never betrayed her indifference towards her numerous household duties or her urge to be out of a house that was as warm as a museum. The housekeeper, who struggled to answer Videhi's incisive questions, would never have guessed how eager her mistress was to escape. But Videhi maintained the charade effortlessly, looking forward to her other life that began the moment she crossed the ornate threshold of the front door.

Outside, the gardeners were hovering around the rose beds nervously. In just a fortnight the gardens will be fragrant with roses, she thought as she walked to the car.

For the last year and a half, since she had joined the Centre for Contemporary Societies, Videhi had followed the same schedule in the morning. But the hour at which she returned home in the evening kept extending as she assumed more responsibilities at work. She often wondered about the distance she had travelled in the last few years, mostly alone.

After acquiring a doctorate in Development Studies, Videhi had just begun teaching at a university in Gujarat when she was offered a research position at the Centre. But she had been reluctant to leave the place of her birth for a strange, rambling megapolis like Delhi.

That was till she met Sampat. He had come to the university to deliver a memorial lecture on ethics and business management. The fact that he was Sampat Jaichand had been enough to pack the room to capacity; students were even standing in the lobby that day. Videhi was there as well, curious to hear the seventh richest man in the country, the sole heir to an empire that spread over many countries.

Sampat turned out to be a simple man who spoke directly, and answered questions afterwards for almost an hour. When the dean introduced them at lunch, she noticed that Sampat had the same smile as he did in the lecture hall, polite and stale. So she told him he did not have to smile if he'd rather not. Taken aback, he had stared at her, intrigued but guarded.

'I mean, Mr Jaichand, your face must be hurting with that effort. You can rest it for a while, you know,' she had said a little defensively, wondering if he would take exception to her off-hand comment.

Instead, his smile had widened. 'Thanks for noticing, Dr Dave,' he had said. 'But I am quite willing to endure even more hurt, if you would allow me.'

She fell for his words, for his simplicity that seemed so out of place in his grey-and-gold world. She never quite understood why he fell for her, the daughter of a working man. He always said it was her honesty and kindness. She always hoped it was something more tangible.

Her father asked Sampat personal questions. Finally, Sampat said, 'If I had a daughter, sir, who said she wanted to marry a rich man who does nothing but attend meetings and sit indolently in different offices across the world, I would have forbidden it.

'But if I had a father who could tell you how desperately I need your daughter to be my beacon of hope in this world, you would give us your blessings.' She had never seen eyes so sad, as he added, 'Consider me, sir, for what I do not have. Not for what I do.'

He was thirty-two, she was twenty-nine. They were married four months after they met at the dean's lunch. That was two years ago.

Sampat's family was large, unlike hers. It became a little easier to get acquainted only after Sampat arranged for photographs and special briefings. He held her hand as she gingerly entered his opulent life and submerged without making waves.

A few months after settling down in Delhi, Videhi took up the job at the Centre on Sampat's advice. Initially, she wondered why Sampat insisted on her doing work that kept her so busy that she was barely ever at home. Eventually, she discovered it was because he himself had no time; he paid for his wealth, for his inheritance, with every minute of his life. Every moment of the future was scheduled, every minute of the past was audited. She kept her despair to herself at first, then complained to him when she could not take it any longer.

His evident helplessness, his guilt, his bare explanations, forced her to compromise. But she could also see that Sampat thought wealth should compensate for loneliness for a middle-class girl. It made her resent the wealth around her, and contain herself in an island amidst it. She stayed for one reason alone. Despite the distances, the different time zones and the polite, unhelpful secretaries that separated them, she could still feel the common essence she shared with Sampat, the essence that had made them recognize each other the first time they met.

It was easy to fill up her time with work. The Centre was on the threshold of major expansion and needed to conduct landmark research to grab headlines. At first, Daya had thought the wealthy and influential Jaichands could be roped into donating funds for the Centre. That was, of course, only till he got to know Videhi better. The expectations among her colleagues that her position justified any undue advantage she may get over others, made her work hard. Increasingly, she took her own talents and achievements for granted, and appreciated them in others. In principle, she wanted to be humble about her achievements so that she would strive for excellence. But in practice, she ended up being so self-critical that, at times, it almost broke her.

When the Centre was commissioned to survey districts facing agricultural distress, Daya included Mityala with full knowledge of Sampat's business worries there. Jaichand Industries had a cement plant in Chira village that had run into problems with environmentalists. Daya assigned the project to Videhi, saying that it would help in understanding the ground situation so that the problems could be addressed properly. As Daya expected, Sampat offered assistance with the logistics of the survey in the district, saving the Centre money and effort.

While conducting the survey, Videhi discovered that Jaichand Industries had diversified into other businesses in Mityala that would cause as much damage to the environment as the cement plant had. Every tactic, including coercion, had been used to manage the local people so that the new ventures would not be hampered.

The truth was so disturbing that it took some effort for her to admit that it was Sampat himself who had helped her with the project so that she could suggest ways of making his business strategy more people-friendly. She was surprised it was not just rhetoric; he had meant what he said.

❂

The Centre was housed in a compact building in southwest Delhi. The guard posted at the gate recognized the silver BMW from afar and opened the gates. She was now over her embarrassment of having the longest car in the lot. But then, she hadn't yet brought to office the Mercedes her sister-in-law had gifted her on her wedding.

As Videhi walked into the building, she found a few colleagues gathered at the notice board reading the announcement that Daya had bagged a prestigious award for social welfare. Surprised, she walked towards his office to congratulate him, knowing that he would soon get busy with journalists and interviews.

She found his office crowded with people gathered to wish him. They chatted for a while about how he had deserved to win and why the other candidates had lost. Then he invited everyone to a celebration later and, as they stood up to leave, asked Videhi to stay back.

When they were alone, he said, 'Remember the journalist we met last evening at Kashinath's house? I called him to the Centre at 3 p.m. today to meet the two of us. I hope that is all right with you?'

That was not all right with her, Videhi could still vividly recall the rude words from last evening. 'Why do we need to talk to him at all?'

Daya smiled. 'Because we need all the good press we can get for our work. Remember to always keep the journalists in good humour.'

'And see how long they last?' she asked wearily. 'I will give it a try.'

Videhi walked to her office, irritated that she had to deal with that insufferable journalist again. Each room in the building had access to either the common garden or the common balcony, depending on the floor on which it was located. She walked through her ground-floor office, opened the door to the garden and stood there for a minute, collecting herself. A breeze pushed the fallen leaves around, rolling them down from the stone skirting on to the grass. It was an uncertain morning, sunny, but wanting rain.

The day began with a meeting of the research team, things were hectic in the final stages of the survey. After lunch, Daya prepared for an interview with an international television channel, checked his reflection in the mirror and combed his sparse grey hair once more. The journalist was waiting in his office. The crew arranged lights, pulling heavy wires across the floor. Daya hated journalists who chatted before a show, it left his mind in disarray. But this one was quiet, and sat making notes in her book.

As Daya sat at his desk, organizing his mind, his long bony fingers played with a pencil. *This award signifies a need for tolerance*...no, sounds too much like a political view. *The growing need to redefine the social borders of our minds*...minds? The pencil steadied in his hands and he started writing. *Societies, globally are slowly assuming homogeneity in their aspirations, disappointments, causes and results. In other words*...he hated that phrase!

He thoughtfully felt his forehead and started once more: *The need for tolerance in the future will not just be restricted to conflicts of religion and ideology, but also resources. The ability to share has always been held as a virtue*...no, too pontificating...*The ability to share will not be just a virtue but also*...

The door opened and he glanced up impatiently. His secretary brought in a visiting card. Reading it, he checked the time and was surprised to find that it was 3 p.m. He thoughtfully glanced at the waiting journalist. One television interview was worth ten newspaper articles. But one newspaper article could lead to ten more television interviews.

Outside in the corridor, Nazar turned as Daya emerged from his office and greeted him.

'You know, Mr Prabhakar,' Daya said softly, 'I have been an admirer of Haridas Tulsi for a long time. As I have told him many times in the past, he is one of the few editors in the country still in touch with reality.'

Nazar politely smiled, duly noting as intended, that Daya personally knew the editor-in-chief.

'The thing is,' Daya continued, confidingly, 'I have a television interview scheduled in a few minutes in my office... which is the reason why we are talking here in the corridor.'

'No problem.'

'Thanks. Would you like to talk to Dr Jaichand while I finish the interview?'

'I thought you said last night that the recommendations were yours and not hers,' Nazar reminded him coolly. 'But whatever you say.'

Daya thanked him again and gestured to his secretary. Nazar followed the man through the open corridors that cut through the manicured greenery. As he walked along, he cursed himself for not escaping from this appointment when Daya phoned in the morning. He had a tight schedule for the second half of the day; he had to meet a news source at a coffee shop, collect a copy of a confidential letter from a ministry and, if possible, pick up a gift for his parents' wedding anniversary before returning to office for the editorial meeting in the evening.

Instead...

The secretary knocked on an open door and led him into an office. Nazar entered and froze for a moment. He realized how thick the mist had been the previous evening in the lawns at the Kashinath residence. Amused by a similar surprise in her eyes, he greeted Videhi cordially.

She returned the greeting and waited, looking at the secretary for an explanation for the intrusion. He told her about the television interview and Daya's request for her to meet the journalist without him. She nodded a little impatiently and asked Nazar to take a seat.

They sat in silence after the secretary left, then she reached for a file on the desk. Nazar glanced around, noticing the access to the garden.

'What would you like to discuss?' she asked.

'Anything,' he said, 'that you feel requires improvement.'

'Nothing requires improvement,' she said, 'except perhaps my levels of patience.'

'I can't help you there,' he said, apologetically.

'I thought as much.'

He chuckled. 'Please, Dr Jaichand. This is a peace mission.'

She glanced at the survey file. 'We have found a trend of increased expenditure on consumer items across Indian villages. We believe that the social and financial stress on farmers arises not just from unpaid debts and crop failure, but also from growing aspirations. The steep increase in the spending on FMCGs in rural areas also shows that people are now making more money, which they want to spend and come at par with urban lifestyles.'

'I hope you have factored in education as a major game-changer,' Nazar said. 'You may recall the man Keyur Kashinath was talking about last night, the educated farmer Gangiri, who will not accept injustice. He knows he can fight the system using the disparities contained in it. And he knows these disparities best because he has been a victim for a long time.'

'You are right. These disparities can be the basis of all conflict, social and financial, even political,' Videhi agreed. 'What is history but a clash of circumstances!'

They could see that they were in agreement and fell silent.

'I believe,' Nazar said, to extend the discussion, 'that better support prices for crops have improved rural incomes which are being tapped by the consumer goods' companies. Also, better connectivity, roads and infrastructure have made rural outreach more effective. These reasons have also contributed to the increase in demand for consumer goods in rural areas.'

'And it is expected to improve further,' she added, 'as the government replaces distribution of subsidized food grains through ration shops with direct cash transfers. The scheme will provide money instead of food grains to the poor.'

'But what if the money is not spent on food and is used instead for buying soaps or bribing babus?' Nazar asked. 'Whose welfare are we talking about? The hungry or the greedy?'

'Either way,' she pointed out, 'the changing priorities in rural areas are exerting pressure on a farmer's intentions and income.'

He nodded, once again realizing that there was no difference of opinion.

This time she prolonged the dialogue. 'The pressure is particularly harsh on the marginal farmer because land fragmentation has made agriculture unsustainable. About sixty-three per cent of farmers own less than one hectare of land.'

'That is why expanding cities are engulfing the farm lands that used to produce our food,' Nazar said. 'The cities are now going to the villages to make money, Dr Jaichand, whatever you may say.'

'I agree.'

'In case you don't,' he smiled, 'I can return tomorrow with my research and prove it to you.'

She studied him for a moment, then smiled back. 'Then I better disagree.'

'Thank you,' he said, and checking his watch, stood up to leave. 'Tomorrow, same time?'

She nodded.

He paused at the door and turned. 'Tell me, Dr Jaichand. Does this survey have any political sponsors?'

'No, why?'

'Just checking.'

'We are not a newspaper, sir,' she clarified.

Nazar looked at her patiently, then walked out smiling.

6

Wednesday evening, the sub-district hospital, Batoni town, Mityala district.

The doctor wrote the prescription and pushed it across the table towards the patient. Without looking up, he returned to examining the inventory of supplies of the sub-district hospital that he headed in Batoni town.

'Will my hand be normal again, doctor saheb?'

'Of course it will,' he answered, his finger moving down the printed list of supplies. 'Now please go and get the medicine from the counter. Next!'

Dr Hemant Rao was a man in his late twenties, with thinning hair and thickening glasses. He marked his initials at the bottom of the page and turned to the next page. When he saw the thin arm of a child being extended across the table, he stopped.

'My daughter has fever...' the man said in a concerned voice, speaking in the local language, 'she cannot eat anything, she feels nauseous...'

Rao checked the child's pulse, quickly checked her eyes, throat and stomach. Anaemic, dehydrated...and yes, she had fever too. He recorded the readings and asked, 'How old are you?'

'She is twelve.'

He gestured to the weighing scale and recorded her weight; just twenty-five kilograms. He filled out the medicine slip.

'Do you feel cold?'

'Yes, she has been shivering,' the father answered again. 'We thought it was because the winter has been a bit harsh the last few days...'

'For how long has she had fever?'

'Four...no, five days. But...'

He stopped speaking when Rao looked up. 'Five days?' Rao's voice was sharp. 'Were you waiting for her to die, Somu?'

Somu quickly lowered his eyes. The little girl held his hand tighter. Every one of the patients waiting there that evening knew, or could guess, why Somu could not get to the hospital earlier.

The patients were seated on long benches along the walls in Rao's room and outside in the corridor. Every time a patient was examined and sent away, the sitting queue moved up one position, the soft noise of shifting bodies like the sound of falling pages.

There was silence, mostly, except for the occasional cough, sneeze or gasp of pain. The women were usually accompanied by someone apprehensive or someone indifferent. They were dressed in cotton sarees that were soft with overuse, wore cheap slippers on feet that were used to being bare and beads around necks that used to wear gold. But the unbreakable plastic bangles would probably outlive the hands that wore them.

The men came alone, unless their health was too fragile, in which case at least two or three people accompanied them.

There were about forty patients that day, and every head was turned towards the doctor's room. They could hear the scolding Somu was getting. They could also hear the anxiety in the doctor's raised voice. But they could not hear the remorse he felt for every word he spoke. He understood their helplessness, the reason why they submitted to fate rather than buy medicine. It was far cheaper to have faith.

Sitting towards the end of the queue, Gangiri frowned as he heard the slight trembling in the doctor's voice as he tried to explain the dangers of the delay.

'...and then you expect me to save lives?' Rao's light eyes were bright with anger and desperation. 'If anything serious were to happen, I couldn't handle it here and you would have to go to Mityala. It would cost you more, don't you understand! You are not going to save money by delaying...diseases don't go away, Somu...they have to be treated...'

Somu, who had been standing with his head lowered, slowly looked up and the doctor had to stop speaking. Rao could see the surrender in his eyes, the chilling indifference of total helplessness. The young doctor's expressive face turned emotional as he read Somu's mind. He lowered his head to the notepad, completed the prescription, and sent Somu with his daughter to the counter for medicine. Gangiri watched them as they passed by the benches, the father holding the child's hand in a possessive grip, as if he was ready to defy even destiny if required.

Rao liked to keep his eyes lowered. After two-and-a-half years in the Batoni sub-district hospital, he understood this was the only way to survive. He suffered every time he looked closely at the faces of his patients. He could see their fear of darkness and death, the fear of being forgotten while alive.

He learnt his lessons quickly in the initial months of being transferred here from the medical college hospital. He had been recruited to be part of the government's scheme to increase the number of primary health centres at the zonal and block levels in the districts. He had supervised the setting up of twenty primary health centres under his hospital. Then he had begged his old mentor, the principal of his medical college, to rescue him.

The principal pulled a few strings and Rao finally got the call he had been waiting for from the medical superintendent of the general hospital in the state capital. Rao had another six months to go and then he would be transferred to the capital. He could have left immediately; he wanted to take a month off with the leave he had accumulated and, later, begin life anew in the capital.

In the process of planning along these lines, Rao made a discovery that unsettled him. He could not bring himself around to sending that leave application. Names and faces came in the way, old and young, some well-known, some unnamed, those for whom he cheated the hospital and treated them free.

He stole medicines. He fabricated invoices. He accepted bribes in the form of free hospital beds from the local police. The last, in return for not reporting the illegal detention of a juvenile thief. He even colluded with a temple trust to set up drinking-water dispensers with their emblem in the hospital. Then there was the private ambulance...

Rao wanted to rescue himself from the hope that he had generated. But he knew that any place he travelled to, any thing he did in his life, he would always carry along these men, women and children with him forever. He would always remember the touch of their rough skin, the smell of sweat and earth, the anxiety and resignation in their eyes. He was just a man, yes, but he would never be just one man again, ever.

The sun was setting and he could sense the queue getting restless. Almost everyone had to start work early the next day. There was much to be done on the farms, the cotton crop had just recovered from the dry spell and the late rains. Nothing must go wrong now, the harvest was around the corner. It was a most nervous time for the farmers. They could hardly sleep at night.

His hands worked in a blur as he examined the patients and sent them out with prescriptions. Everyone had to be examined in the presence of others, there was no privacy. No one objected, each knew how tired the other was, no one had the heart to ask anyone to leave the room. Rao was swift, and his comforting hand reached the problem accurately every time.

When dusk fell, he could hear the children getting noisy with hunger and discomfort. As always, he briefly announced that the women and children should come first and the queue rearranged in silence. By the end of the next hour, even the male patients were almost done.

Rao returned to the inventory as he waited for the next patient. But by the silence, he knew his day had come to an end. He called for his assistant to cross-check and glanced up. It was then that he saw Gangiri sitting on the bench along the wall.

'Namaskar, Gangiriji,' he said, surprised. 'Have you been waiting in the queue? You should have sent word!'

'Namaskar,' Gangiri said, bowing his head. 'I like waiting in queues.'

Rao had met Gangiri three times earlier, at each of the three meetings of the suicide committee. Rao's brief interactions with Gangiri had been eventful. At the last meeting, of the fourteen deaths of farmers being considered, Rao had ratified only two as suicides.

Before the committee could vote, Gangiri had requested Collector Gul to provide details of private loans taken by each of the deceased farmers. Durga Das had objected on the grounds that this was an attempt to cast aspersions on him because he had lent money to almost every farmer at one point or the other. Gul, however, brought out the debt details of the dead. Some had outstanding loans with the banks and the moneylenders, and some only with the moneylenders. Some owed fifty thousand rupees, others over a lakh. Some owned land, others had mortgaged it.

It turned out that only two of the deceased farmers owed Durga Das over 1.5 lakh rupees and had already lost their lands. Gangiri had argued that by denying compensation to the widows of the other twelve farmers, Durga Das wanted to seize their land to recover his dues. But, by approving compensation for the two who had no land, he could force their widows to repay debts in cash. The moneylenders would win both ways.

This allegation had created a furore and forced a temporary adjournment. Collector Gul noted that though there had been instances of misuse of money provided as compensation, there was no evidence that it had been done at the behest of the moneylenders. However, all the cases had to be re-examined that day and the meeting extended into the night. Nine of the fourteen deaths were finally declared patra suicides, with a vote of six to four and the families granted compensation.

There was a meeting scheduled for that Friday and Rao could guess why Gangiri had come to meet him now.

'I know my reports on the suicides bother you,' Rao said directly. 'But I follow Durga Das in the voting. He sends me the names the night before.'

'Why?' asked Gangiri, getting angry.

'I can't tell you.'

'You can't tell me here or you will tell me only at the committee meeting?'

Rao considered that. He then said, 'Before my time, this hospital was almost defunct because the then government doctor seemed to like a private hospital in Mityala more than this one. As there were no facilities here, the patients were all referred to that hospital, which billed them heavily. Even the medicines from this hospital used to be siphoned off.' Rao paused. 'Durga Das supports that private hospital in Mityala.'

He pensively felt the plastic corners of the inventory file on the desk. 'They expected me to do the same, but I refused. They offered me almost double my pay to work for the private hospital, but... I could not take it. Durga Das threatened me that there would be consequences.

'And there were.' Rao lowered his eyes to the file. 'From the milkman to the newspaper vendor to the grocer, no one was ready to sell anything to me in Batoni... I was forced to shop in Mityala. I even had to shift into a spare room upstairs in this hospital because no one would rent me a house. Then, as part of the procedure, I was appointed to the district suicide committee. A day before the meeting, Durga Das sent me a message. It said, simply, "No suicides."'

Rao fell silent for a moment. 'That is how it began.'

Gangiri's eyes were hard. 'You never complained?'

'I thought about it. There was a choice before me. I could either prove that those who were dead had committed suicide, or I could treat the living. I chose the latter.' Rao paused again. 'Any smart investigator can prove charges of fraud against me for requisitioning more medicines than the hospital's capacity for patients. Durga Das does not know all these details, but if he did, he will ensure an inquiry against me and this hospital will once again become useless to the poor.'

Rao leaned back weakly in his chair. 'I cannot win against Durga Das. The government is on his side. That is why it does not build better hospitals in villages, or provide clean drinking water, or sanitation or...' he stopped. Then said, 'But I am getting transferred out soon. I can afford to report the suicides honestly till I leave.'

Gangiri met his eyes as he looked up. 'I thought, perhaps, I would have to use your upcoming transfer as a way of getting you to validate the eligible suicides.'

Rao smiled. 'That would have worked, Gangiriji.'

'I am grateful for your support. I am sure you know what it means to every single family in these villages, those who have lost someone...and those who may.'

Rao shrugged, and turned back to his inventory.

Gangiri was walking out when the doctor said, 'You know, there is another member of the committee here in Batoni who is also getting transferred very soon. Your tactic might work well with him too.'

Gangiri's dark eyes turned mischievous. 'I know.'

As is typical with most villages that aspire to be towns, Batoni was expanding along the main highway that led to Mityala. Gangiri walked from the hospital, sensing rain in the air. There was the smell of milk being stirred in pots in the open at the marketplace, the fragrance of camphor and incense from the temple, the sound of weights being juggled on the grocer's scale, the laughter of a child running around the corner with candy.

Gangiri stood in the middle of the market and soon spotted the bank. An aged ex-army man was leaning on his gun, guarding the door. His eyes were habitually wary after a lifetime of looking out for danger. He let Gangiri into the bank with a sigh and a cough.

The office consisted of a long hall with rows of counters starting with 'Enquiries' and ending with 'Cash'. At the end of the narrow hall was a door marked 'Manager'. Next to it was a curious rectangular window with dark glass. Gangiri walked up the hall, guessing that dark glass must be a secret window that allowed the manager to keep an eye on the office from his room.

He also knew that the manager could see him walk up, and hear his cheap shoes, loud and noisy on the vitrified tiles of the floor. When he was close enough to the dark glass window, a bell rang shrilly and a peon came running. Gangiri told him that he wanted to meet the manager about a matter of his life and someone else's death. The dazed peon hurried into the room with the message and sprang out almost immediately. He held the door open and Gangiri walked in.

Amidst the shelves, cupboards, files, air-conditioner, towel stand, pedestal fan, water bottle, pens, and paperweights sat a bald man facing the rectangular window. As he glanced through it, Gangiri could see the hall outside and the peon hurrying out to finish smoking his bidi which had been interrupted by the ringing of the bell.

The bank manager, Ramesh Vaish, was a plump man with sweaty skin and small, flickering eyes. Ledgers were open before him and, after inviting Gangiri to sit, he gestured towards them, complaining that he had no time to even go home. Gangiri explained that he would take no time at all.

'Loan?' Vaish asked, his furtive eyes sizing up Gangiri. Gangiri wore worn but clean clothes, an old sweater, an old watch and carried a plastic pen. His hair was combed neatly, his skin was clean, his nails were trimmed and his eyes waited for the scrutiny to end. Being a man who respected creditworthiness, Vaish found himself confused about Gangiri. The only evidence of his solvency was circumstantial, that he was member of the prestigious suicide committee.

'No, Vaishji.' Gangiri answered briefly.

Flustered, Vaish asked him general questions about health, weather, crops... Gangiri answered politely, asking no questions of Vaish.

Vaish also remembered, amidst commenting on goat-rearing, why he had been disconcerted about Gangiri before. It was because in one of the meetings of the suicide committee, he had discovered that Gangiri spoke Hindi and English, besides his mother tongue. Vaish's experience dictated that educated farmers were usually difficult to do business with. There were a few examples to support this conclusion among the bank's customers.

It made Vaish shudder to recall how diabolical Gangiri had sounded when he spoke at the meetings. And as he started speaking now, softly and with a knowing look in those dark eyes, Vaish felt nervous again.

'We need more people like you, Vaishji,' Gangiri said politely. 'Rural banks need such high levels of commitment.'

Vaish smiled briefly, his small quick eyes flickering to the door and the secret window, as if checking escape options.

'It is a matter of concern for me that a well-meaning banker like you should be transferred out of here and sent to the coastal district.'

'Transferred?' Vaish held his breath.

'The order must be cancelled. You must spend more time with us here in this district,' Gangiri said earnestly.

'Cancelled!' The manager panicked, all other thoughts vanishing from his mind.

Gangiri looked away, as if he was deeply affected by a sudden notion. 'I know what the problem is, Vaishji. It is a common problem among people like you. And I must say, it is to be blamed on the choices you make. Do you know what it is?'

'Greed?' Vaish said uneasily.

'Modesty!' Gangiri was stern. 'You will never own up to what you have done for these villages, will you? But they know, every one of the villagers, what you have done. You know what I mean?'

'That canal contract?' he asked, troubled.

'Personal attention, Vaishji. You have given personal attention to their problems. It is not easy to forget such dedication to duty.' Gangiri leaned forward. 'You hold a special place in their hearts. And that is what I am going to tell your manager when I meet him. Brilliant work, Vaishji.'

Vaish licked his dry lips. 'Well, Mr Bhadra...you are being too kind.'

'Am I not stating the truth?'

'No. I mean, yes...the truth. But...'

Gangiri studied Vaish, the overhead lights made the banker's forehead shine like a clean kettle.

'If we do not take care of you, who will?' Gangiri asked. 'After all, you have taken care of us all this while.'

Vaish reached for the towel on the stand and mopped his face.

'So,' Gangiri continued, 'I will go to Mityala tomorrow to see your district manager. Hopefully, I can return with the assurance that you will not be transferred.'

'Mr Bhadra...' Vaish said urgently, as if preventing him from speaking could prevent him from carrying out the threat. 'Why leave so soon?' Vaish smiled weakly. 'I mean...take more time...think about it...' Vaish fell silent, staring anxiously at Gangiri.

'Do you know the best policy in the world?' Gangiri asked, waiting for an answer.

'To run when you can?' Vaish guessed.

'To never think twice. It confuses me whenever I do. There is nothing to think about. We need you in our little town here, Vaishji, for as long as possible.'

Vaish swallowed hard, remembering what he had promised his wife that very morning. A house in the state capital, air-conditioned and colour-coordinated, celebrations in hotels and holidays in places picked out from movies. Their children growing up in English and finding jobs in companies named after people who lived on nothing but white bread and champagne. He looked frantically at Gangiri. 'Why...would you do this to me? Why tomorrow?'

'Don't you know?' Gangiri asked affectionately.

'For a commission?' Vaish looked hopeful.

'Because I want this done before the next meeting of the suicide committee.'

'Why?' Vaish asked, suddenly suspicious.

'Well... I am sure you know that everyone wonders how you always veto valid suicide verdicts. I shall explain, personally, that you turned down an offer to work in the coastal district. Everyone knows that one year in that district as bank manager is enough to sort out anyone's finances for a lifetime.'

Vaish worried eyes were suddenly still. There was no more confusion.

Gangiri continued, 'Perhaps I should explain this to the villagers tonight and take them along with me to Mityala tomorrow. That way they too can tell their stories about you to your district manager.'

Vaish was now watching Gangiri steadily.

'Is there anything you think we ought to highlight, Vaishji, while speaking about your tenure here?'

'Stop it!' Vaish snapped. 'How dare you threaten me like this!'

'Threaten you?' Gangiri sounded innocent. 'Whatever gave you the idea?'

'You think I am some small fry? You will now see how far I will take this matter, Mr Bhadra,' he said indignantly. 'You are new to this place.'

'I am, yes. Which is why I find myself wondering if you're threatening me not to meet your manager?'

Vaish's voice lost some of its edge. 'Go meet anyone you want to...it will make no difference to me!'

Gangiri smiled. 'I am sure you don't mean that.'

Vaish looked away, too hassled to answer. He turned as

Gangiri took his leave, but waited, watching. Vaish knew the decision had to be made now. He had made money in the district, and the complaints against him had been hushed up by Lambodar. In return, he lied at the committee meetings about farmer suicides. He always said the bank was not aware of the informal loans the farmers took. But he knew. He kept a record. The ledger was right here in this room. And that was not the only truth he was hiding.

Gangiri thanked him for his time and made to stand.

Vaish hurriedly apologized, asking if they could let bygones be bygones.

Gangiri studied the man for a moment. 'I don't know, Vaishji. Is there still time to look for the record of informal loans of the upcoming cases and who the moneylenders were?'

'Sure there is. I will study them tonight.'

'Then, knowing the records, can you vote honestly this time at the committee meeting?'

Vaish realized he had no choice and wiped his forehead again with the towel. 'I will.'

'What made you lie all this while?'

He shook his head in desperation. 'I cannot survive without the help of the moneylenders. I have to meet my credit targets and I have to show loan recovery. They don't want to know at the HQ "how" I do it. And I don't tell them.'

He reached for the towel again. 'Powerful men like Lambodar and Durga Das help me meet my targets, keep the wheels turning with their own projects that help with paying salaries and rent for this office. Sometimes they lend to farmers so that they can pay back the bank loans,' he said and then added slowly, 'and sometimes, when we refuse loans, the farmers have to borrow from the moneylenders.'

'That must suit everyone,' Gangiri said sarcastically. 'After all, banks lending to farmers is a high-risk proposition.'

Vaish nodded helplessly.

Gangiri stood up. 'Vote for the truth,' he said. 'Or retire here in Batoni.'

'The truth it is,' Vaish promised, and watched from his secret window as Gangiri left the office.

7

Thursday morning, Nazar's home, New Delhi

Nazar finished reading the morning papers, listening to the introspective silence of his house. He loved the house, even though it was too big for a single man. He had bought the place for its monolithic silences which had, in fact, cost him extra money.

In the last eight years, there had been many gatherings in the house, large and small, for celebrations, for farewells, for no reason at all. Laughter, loss, anger, relief had seared through its silences. But after every such flight, the house settled back into itself, folding softly, evenly, like the ruffled feathers of a bird, till it was all seamless once more.

He had breakfast, making his own toast and eggs, the sounds creating gentle ripples in the peace. Much against the advice of the designers, Nazar had all the internal walls pulled down, creating a vast space. Light poured in through the great windows on the eastern and western sides. The grey cement floor absorbed the winter morning like a placid sea, the chrome fixtures marked depth and distance like buoys. There were places in the room for the light to rest, for the morning to linger, and for the noon to get dressed. There were places in the spaces between glass vases and book cases for one day to exchange notes with the next.

But the magic of the house lay only within its walls. He stood at the windows, looking at the brief excuse of a lawn outside, a narrow patch of grass that even insects didn't inhabit.

If his life had taught him one thing, he thought, it was that anything that had to be put into words to be understood could also be misunderstood. The doors were not to be opened by hands, and she knew that he was not ready yet. The wreckage from his last relationship was still strewn around in his life and she knew he was the architect of that destruction. It had been months since he returned her calls or replied to her letters. The blue envelope was in the last drawer of the desk in his office where he left letters that could wait. She was waiting outside the final door.

The spacious morning was to blame for his missing the love of another human being. It was a matter of time, the reconciliation of the busy afternoon was not far. He chose this loneliness, acquired it with effort, just like he bought the silences of the house. But every once in a while, he succumbed to the spacious mornings and let someone through the door briefly. He was yet to let anyone stay until afternoon.

Nazar turned as Balram Shinde, his assistant, arrived. Nazar's father, Ameen Prabhakar, had employed Balram when the family lived in Delhi over fifteen years ago. Though there were other children, Balram had developed a special bond with Nazar who was almost the same age as him. Balram was one of the many staff who took care of the ancestral properties in Delhi for Ameen who was mostly in London then, nurturing a construction company. After a few years, when that venture began to flourish, Ameen moved out of India and sold his estates in Delhi.

Nazar, then in his early twenties, had not wanted to leave Delhi, he had been curious about the world outside the tall gates of prosperity. But he had also been curious about the easy destiny that awaited him, a life of power and wealth that was already charted out for him. All he had to do was conform, and when he left the country with his family, that was exactly what he hoped to do.

It first became clear to him, and later to everyone else, that he was not really the conforming type. By the time he finished journalism school, which he had joined much to his father's displeasure, he could no longer recognize his family. He tried his best to fit into the family business, but failed to cultivate the levels of self-assurance and self-obsession required. The inconsequential existence fatigued him and his lonely voice rose in dissent more frequently.

No one was surprised when he announced that he wanted to return to Delhi to work as a journalist. His parents only complained that he did not appreciate the time they had spent securing his future. He said he was grateful they had other children to count on.

The first thing Nazar did on reaching Delhi was find Balram. And in the eight years since, Balram had never told Nazar that Ameen called him secretly and regularly to find out about his son. Nazar never spoke to his parents, he only responded to New Year greetings and sent best wishes on birthdays and anniversaries.

Nazar sifted through the mail Balram brought, and remembered his parents' upcoming forty-fifth wedding anniversary. His sister, Komal, the only member of the family he still spoke with, had called that morning to check if he remembered. Komal Lal was married to a cardiologist and they lived with their daughter in Hyderabad where he worked at a reputed hospital. She was younger than Nazar by three years. He had another sister and a brother, both elder to him. He had no interaction with them; the termination was mutual and much appreciated by both sides.

There was a strong reason for the connection between Komal and him. She was famous for her detachment, for her indifference and for her charity. Only Nazar understood her guilt. It was the same guilt he felt for the excesses of his family.

'A saree for mother, a book for father,' he said.

She approved. 'Where are you buying the saree from? Don't ask me, though. I wouldn't know the first thing.'

'Well, I haven't thought about...' Nazar stopped. 'No, wait! I do know someone I can ask.'

❉

Later that day at 3 p.m., when he reached the Centre, he didn't find Videhi in office. She had not even left a message, unless her absence was itself one. He doubted that, she did not appear to be a coward. Deciding to give Videhi ten minutes, he waited, looking around the beautiful campus with a cynical eye. What an unlikely place to study deprivation and struggle! It looked like a place where definitions were born from third-person experiences, where ideas grew in the bell jars of seminar rooms, where books enjoyed better air-conditioning than half the country's population.

Nazar placed his notebook on a ledge and leaned on the wall, feeling the stillness of the day seep into the vacant corridors. The dangers of a non-reactive atmosphere have often been underestimated by those in love with their ideas. Daya's recommendations could vapourize if they came in contact with the actual world. And so the Centre had to work on fragmenting the actual world into a number of excuses that could be offered for the success or failure of his theories. The ice-cream melted, it could be explained, because of fluctuations in inflation, consumption, supply, demand, manufacturing, technology. But then, Nazar pondered, as a journalist he could say that there was no political will to stop the ice-cream from melting. He was in the same game, just on a different team.

Forty-five minutes later, a silver-grey car glided in through the gates and came to a stop at the doors. Nazar studied the make, appreciating the lines. The driver held the door open and Videhi stepped out, carrying a bag full of papers. A little shocked, Nazar stared as she gave a few instructions to the driver, refused his help with the bag and walked towards the door.

She stopped, seeing Nazar. The bag was heavy, he noticed, and she shifted it from one hand to the other.

He pointed to the car which was driving away. 'Yours?'

She nodded.

'Well, there are just four, maybe five cars of this make on Indian roads. I've always wondered who loves it so much. Now I know.'

'I am not the one who loves this car.' She walked past him, once again shifting the heavy bag to the other hand. He took the bag from her, surprising her, and gestured towards her office.

She thanked him and walked along, asking if he had been waiting for the meeting.

'Yes. I also had to ask you about shopping for sarees,' he said, gesturing to the sienna-yellow saree she wore. 'Where can I buy a saree like this?'

She told him, adding, 'This is a little sombre, but there are livelier versions.'

'I like sombre,' he said, smiling. She smiled back, but he felt something was amiss.

By the time she sat at the desk in her office and reached for the survey file, he was sure. So, he asked her.

'It is nothing, Mr Prabhakar, just a little problem,' she said. 'I can't really bother you with it.'

'All right,' he said, feeling snubbed. Referring to his notes, he said, 'We were talking about the choice between food and soap, the difference between hunger and greed.'

She nodded, focusing on the survey.

'My research as a journalist,' he said, 'shows that landless farmers retain over fifty to seventy per cent of their savings at home in cash. The health of rural India should not be assessed through expenditure on soaps but by the status of these savings.'

'Soaps won't sell if food is more important,' she answered absently. 'And soaps will be bought if there is money to be spared.'

'Money that could have been saved.'

'Well, a drastic fall in rural savings could...' She stared at him, as if a sudden thought had struck her.

'Please try to focus, Dr Jaichand,' Nazar chided. 'The landless, marginal and small farmers spend a major portion of their income on food whereas...' He stopped, it was no use, she was not listening.

He closed the notebook decisively. 'You'll have to tell me what the problem is.'

She hesitated, and looked away.

'Never do this to a journalist,' he chuckled. 'Just the curiosity will kill me.'

She smiled faintly. 'I was only wondering if you could make a phone call, Mr Prabhakar. It could save a life.'

He raised his eyebrows. 'Whose life?'

'Gangiri Bhadra, the farmer responsible for exposing the real suicide numbers in Mityala.'

Nazar did not speak, puzzled.

'I feel,' she explained, 'that Keyur and Lambodar maha sarpanch, the elderly man you met at Keyur's press meet, may be planning to "fix" the problem so that more suicides are not given a valid verdict at the committee meetings.'

'Fix?' he asked.

'I have just returned from a meeting with Keyur...' she said, her voice subdued. 'That is why I was delayed for our meeting here. He wanted to discuss the augmentation of welfare schemes in Mityala. I had proposed some ideas which he was keen on implementing in his constituency.'

Nazar nodded.

'Lambodar joined the meeting a little later. Keyur discussed with the chief sarpanch the measures that we had decided Keyur should announce ahead of the assembly elections. But as the three of us discussed things further, it became clear that the biggest issue in Mityala was the increasing number of farmer suicides. Keyur insisted that the number of debt-related suicides must be controlled immediately. In fact, they must decrease in the very next meeting of the suicide committee.'

She paused, disbelief in her eyes. 'I thought he was just saying that...you know...hoping that the farmer suicide toll would come down. But, no, I gathered from their conversation. He was saying the number of *valid verdicts* must come down!'

'But how?'

'Lambodar said he tried everything and pointed out that as long as Gangiri was on the committee, the verdicts validating debt-related suicides would keep increasing. But he felt that the numbers would fall drastically if Gangiri was removed from the committee. He recalled that before Gangiri's appointment, such verdicts were almost insignificant in number. He also said that Gangiri was solely driven by revenge and was in need of a lesson in humility towards elders. He was anxious that other young farmers might be "misled" by Gangiri's example.'

Videhi stopped and looked at Nazar, worried. 'Lambodar suggested that Keyur complain to the collector,' she continued. 'But Keyur said the collector could not be trusted, as he had not consulted anyone before appointing Gangiri to the committee. He said they would have to "fix" the problem themselves. Lambodar agreed and promised it would be done before the next meeting of the suicide committee, scheduled for tomorrow afternoon.'

'They both would not say any more in my presence.' She added, 'But Lambodar is hurrying back to Gopur tonight, presumably, to take care of the problem in the morning tomorrow.

'I believe, Mr Prabhakar, that Gangiri's life is in danger. He will be forced to resign from the committee at any cost,' she said, fear choking her voice. 'I have seen the anger and determination in their eyes, they will not stop at anything.'

Nazar remained silent, stunned. Even though he had

expected Keyur to try various ways of managing Gangiri, he was still shocked. More than anything, he was sad that a young politician, a bright man who held all the right cards, had all the options, should choose a path so unscrupulous and so cowardly.

Videhi collected herself. 'I pretended as if I had not understood their cryptic words, and continued with the discussion. The meeting moved to the next issue on the agenda, on how to conduct the social impact assessment for new projects.

'But just before I left, Keyur reminded me to keep the issues discussed at the meeting confidential,' Videhi said, concerned. 'There were political rivals ready to take advantage of his problems, he said. I don't know whether I should even be talking to you, Mr Prabhakar... He meant if word got out...' She stopped, distraught.

'If word got out,' Nazar completed gently, 'then his political rivals might corner Keyur by targeting Gangiri. Is that what he meant?'

'Yes,' she smiled gratefully. 'I am sorry, I have never played this game before.'

'I have,' Nazar said grimly. 'What else did Keyur say?'

'Only that he was committed to solving the problems of the distressed farmers. While Gangiri's need for revenge was selfish, Keyur said he himself was actively working on solutions for the farmers.' She paused. 'Keyur then explained that it was not easy being an elected MP. There were re-elections every five years and he had to quickly establish an image of an effective and tough leader. Instances like this served as opportunities for that, he felt.

'I agreed with him,' she added, 'I said the best message

that a leader could give was that of power and control. I complimented him on his vision and offered my help.'

'Offered,' Nazar repeated sardonically, 'your help?'

'Yes,' she said, 'so that he trusts me.' Then Videhi paused thoughtfully. 'Gangiri's resignation from the committee appears to be the only option left to them. They contemplated and dismissed other alternatives, which they discussed as if sympathizing with Gangiri's circumstances. Gangiri seems to have sown a new crop, for which he borrowed material from the local farm-input providers. But till the harvest, the dealers cannot claim repayment. The second option was to get someone to reason with Gangiri. However, being an outsider, Gangiri never needed a local patron. The last option was to force him to resign from the suicide committee.'

Nazar nodded, his face set.

'I am certain,' she said, troubled, 'that they were waiting for me to leave so that they could fine-tune their plans for retaliation tomorrow morning.'

'There will be no retaliation, Dr Jaichand,' Nazar said angrily. 'I will write the story tonight and put an end to it. Give me one quote and I promise you, the story will protect Gangiri tomorrow...' He stopped, frowning.

This was, of course, a great story, a real glimpse into the politics of the young generation, the politics of ruthlessness and arrogance. But it might come too late for Gangiri. Lambodar's plan would have begun by the time the newspaper reached the homes of Keyur's political masters in Delhi in the morning.

Nazar finally said, 'No, it won't work. We will be too late. We have to warn Gangiri now... You are right.'

Videhi did not speak, though she was secretly relieved.

She was not in favour of Nazar filing this as a news story for other reasons. She could guess what would happen if her name was publicly associated with the issue. Keyur would surely get even by exposing the controversies surrounding Sampat's businesses in Mityala. It would be said that she was siding with the farmers to soften their adamant stand against Jaichand Industries. Or that she was helping the political opposition by exposing Keyur's inefficiency. In fact, her role would not be above suspicion whether she supported Keyur or stood against him.

She had called the Jaichand Industries's Mityala office for help with reaching Gangiri. But she could not tell Nazar that without exposing her own motives and her identity. Videhi looked away, uneasy with her predicament.

Just then Nazar asked how she was tracking down Gangiri, and for a brief minute she was silent, upset that she had to lie to him. She forced a smile. 'It's simple, actually. The Centre had appointed a representative in each of the districts we were surveying. I called the Mityala representative and requested him to reach Gopur and deliver a cell phone to Gangiri. When that is done, he will call me on my phone to give me Gangiri's number. Which should be any time now.'

'Any time now!' Nazar was surprised. 'When did you make the call?'

'On my way back from the Kashinath residence. I asked our representative to tell Gangiri that someone from Delhi wanted to talk to him about the suicide committee...Will you please talk to Gangiri and warn him?' she asked, anxiously. 'They may hurt him and his family. There are also two little children...'

'Why don't you want to talk to Gangiri, Dr Jaichand?' Nazar asked, puzzled.

Videhi faltered for just a second, then said frankly, 'For the same reason why I can't give you a quote for the story, Mr Prabhakar. So that Keyur continues to trust me with information.' She paused, then added, 'So that the widows receive the compensation they deserve. So that a farmer succeeds in his fight for justice against powerful men like Keyur and Lambodar...' She stopped speaking. *So that a farmer succeeds against powerful men like my husband*, she thought.

Nazar nodded.

'You know,' he said after a moment, 'you are good at this.'

She stared at him. 'At what?'

'You think on your feet. I like the way you are tracing Gangiri,' he said appreciatively, 'you should have been a journalist.'

'Is that a compliment?'

'It is...sometimes.'

She looked away.

He felt her tension. 'I will call Gangiri.' He smiled. 'Don't worry.'

She thanked him. 'When you talk to him, please be kind and patient...he has been through a lot.'

'I will,' he assured.

'And, you know, he may not be expecting the call. So don't get angry or anything.'

'I am never angry or anything,' he said, tolerantly.

'But try not to shout at him if he does not agree...'

'This is a little insulting, ma'am,' he said, laughing. 'Am I always so difficult?'

'No,' she said kindly. 'Not always.'

8

Videhi left soon after to finish some work before the Centre shut in the evening. Her office was interestingly devoid of any personal effects. There were no photos of family or friends, no drawings or paintings by children, no fresh or dried flowers, no scribbles on the notice board, no reminders of chores to be taken care of on the way home. Perhaps she pigeon-holed emotions as leisure activities; Nazar knew because he did the same and his office looked similiar. He could also guess why she did it. She was apprehensive of being fooled like in the past, insecure of her need for companionship, and never forgot her mistakes.

Nazar walked into the garden and felt the sudden silence in the small pocket of nature, like a hidden corner on a bustling stage.

He had always been intrigued by how the most successful, good-looking and inspiring women were also their own worst critics. Not that it made them vulnerable or easy to impress. It still took a great deal of skill and delicately right degrees of charm, patience and gentle flattery. But it was no longer an exciting game, merely a predictable one. He was tired of his experience, the eyes that could see beyond the façade and a mind that engaged with the mind.

He missed his heart. He missed the self-denying of

treachery, the incorrigible faith in destiny, the tenuous structures of dreams. He felt truly alone, standing under the light grey sky, the colour of the inside of an oyster. If he had even a small piece of his heart left, he would have adored Videhi. Especially for the way she was silently working to protect a stranger some 1,500 kilometres away. But his heart was gone, every last piece of it.

Nazar walked back into the room, focusing his mind on the issue. Videhi returned soon after and cleared her desk of the papers and files. He wanted to know who she was, tell her who he was. He wanted to like everything about her, tell her the best things about himself. Instead, he walked over to the bookshelves and read the titles with interest.

Her phone rang, she wrote down a number and hung up. He walked back to her desk and she pushed the paper towards him.

He reached for his cell phone uncertainly. 'What if we scare Gangiri...and he stops exposing the suicides?'

'And what if we don't warn him and he is killed?' she asked.

Nazar was pensive, unable to decide.

'We have no choice,' she said simply.

Nazar nodded and dialled the number.

The call was quickly answered by a man with a soft voice. Nazar introduced himself and identified his newspaper. In simple terms, and leaving Videhi out, Nazar explained how the increased suicide toll was grabbing headlines in Delhi, discomfiting politicians and how Lambodar was planning to make Gangiri resign from the district suicide committee to bring down the suicide verdicts.

There was a thoughtful silence for a few seconds. Then Gangiri asked, 'Why are you telling me this?'

'To warn you, so that you are on your guard,' Nazar said. 'I received the information about an hour ago. They may act tomorrow morning.'

'The suicide toll makes no political difference to Lambodar maha sarpanch, Nazarji,' Gangiri said politely. 'So, once again...why are you telling me this?'

Nazar smiled, he liked the man. 'Keyur Kashinath is making Lambodar do this. And you will agree, the toll makes considerable political difference to Keyur.'

Gangiri remained silent for a while before he answered. 'I know Lambodar does not like me because he cannot control me. But I am surprised to hear Keyur Kashinath's name. I don't believe you.'

'Then wait till tomorrow morning.'

'Do I have an option?' Gangiri asked gently. 'The increasing toll is bound to trouble the people in power because farmers like us are not supposed to be visible to the government; we are supposed to be a silent, pliant vote bank. But now our lives are drawing attention because of our deaths.'

He paused and Nazar waited in silence.

'My brother committed suicide to escape the humiliation of being a loan defaulter. But he did not opt for invisibility. It was thrust on him by the decision of the suicide committee. My effort is to make sure that that does not happen to any other farmer again. I knew I would not be able to stand for long against these powerful people who are troubled by the real numbers of the suicides, but I had to at least try.'

'I agree that you had to try,' Nazar said. 'But what will you achieve if you eventually give in to these forces? You would only prove, once again, what is already known, that no one wins against them.'

'I don't think like that, Nazarji,' Gangiri said. 'I don't want them to lose. I want them to change. If I am forced to quit, I can be replaced by any one of the deceased farmers' kin. None of us can match the powers we challenge. It is an unequal fight, but we have the dead on our side.'

Nazar could not speak for a moment. Then he grimly said, 'I do hope this warning has given you time to prepare.'

'If what you have told me is true, then the only thing I can prepare is the draft of my resignation letter,' Gangiri said in his soft voice. 'I am not letting anyone hurt my brother's family.'

Nazar glanced at Videhi, worried. He could not advise Gangiri not to safeguard his family and his life. At the same time, he hoped Gangiri would fight back, somehow.

'I did not want to frighten you, Gangiriji,' he said with sincerity.

'But that is exactly what you have done, is it not?' Gangiri said dryly. 'With your story, which is nothing but a threat, you have frightened me enough to either resign or to keep my mouth shut tomorrow at the meeting. Don't worry, Nazarji, I am now thinking of compromising.'

Nazar frowned, realizing Gangiri was mocking him.

'Keyur Kashinath chooses his flunkies well,' Gangiri added derisively.

'You have misunderstood me,' Nazar said, his voice cold.

'Have I? If you really are a journalist, then why don't you write about the dangers I face, Nazarji? Will that not preempt an attack against us? Or, are you not even a journalist?'

'By the time the story is published,' Nazar explained patiently, 'the damage will be done. That is why I am calling you, to save time and lives. Besides,' he asked, 'why would I name Keyur if I *were* his flunky?'

'But then if you are not, why would you make yourself such a powerful enemy by naming him?'

'Because I am not afraid!' Nazar snapped. 'And because Keyur is being unscrupulous and wrong.'

This time the silence was one of curiosity. And there was a hint of respect in Gangiri's tone when he said, 'I believe that.'

'Then also believe that you are in danger,' Nazar said angrily. 'Please be on guard and keep your family safe. You can keep this cell phone with you and call me if you need any help, any time. So goodbye for now.'

'Just a minute, Nazarji,' Gangiri said, concern deepening his soft voice. 'What do you recommend I do at the meeting tomorrow? What would you have done?'

Nazar restlessly looked around the room that was lit by the early evening light. What could he say? He hoped something would tilt the balance in Gangiri's favour. But what reinforcements could destiny send him?

'Don't ask me, I still have things to lose.'

'Like what?' Gangiri asked.

'Like the occasional desire for success. A nagging habit for power,' Nazar replied. 'The adoration of a few, the admiration of a few more. A disease that won't take too long, a death that comes in sleep,'

Nazar closed his eyes and was silent for a moment. 'I would have somehow exposed Lambodar's plans. I would have done whatever it took to be able to validate debt-distress suicides at the meeting tomorrow. You must protect your family, but you must also protect the truth,' he said. 'Honesty without strategy is futile.'

'That is exactly what I think,' Gangiri said.

'You have time to figure out your strategy.' Nazar paused, and added, 'And Gangiriji, please call me if Lambodar's men get too...difficult to handle. I will lie that I am Keyur's lackey and try to intimidate them.'

'We can try that.' Gangiri chuckled. 'Namaskar, Nazarji.'

Nazar wished him back and hung up. Then he glanced at Videhi, his eyes questioning.

She nodded, 'That was the best possible advice.'

'But I am the wrong man to give such advice. I have no idea how to be that courageous. I have never fought to kill or die. I have no idea how to inspire sacrifices. I am just an employee of my ambition. Gangiri is the master of his destiny.'

They were both silent for a minute, worried.

Then she asked, 'Do you think he can survive this?'

'I don't know,' Nazar said, standing up to leave. 'But Gangiri is not here by chance or accident...you and I are.'

She nodded, smiling, and wished him a good evening.

Videhi waited for the sound of his footsteps in the corridor to fade. Then she switched off her computer, sorted out the papers on her desk and walked to the door which opened out to the garden to shut it. She stood there, thinking of the insidious tangibility of the moment and the kind-hearted man who liked her. The early dusk stopped just short of her, a tempting, inviting place for resting the vacancies of life, a patient, capricious place for the textures of emotion. There was no need for simplification, no need for justification. It was going to be night. A sublime, unethical place. A creative, destructive place.

She shut the door firmly and walked away.

9

Friday morning, Gopur village, Mityala

Gangiri could not sleep well and woke up early to a cold winter morning. He sat on the porch, his thin, long limbs folded under a blanket, listening to the silence of the pre-dawn darkness. It was much warmer inside the small house where the wood fire of the night still smouldered. But he slept outside on the porch. Padma and the children were sleeping soundly inside; Sashi and Balu exhausted from playing with the cell phone, their young minds dazzled by the gadget. He thoughtfully reached for the phone. In some ways, it symbolized to him the power of those who sought to oust him. Gangiri knew that in just a few hours, he may have to resign from the district suicide committee.

He had no option. There could be many ways of forcing his hand, any one of the tricks the moneylenders commonly used against defaulters would easily work. The traders could boycott the farmers or get the schools to shut out their children. Or farmers' family members, especially women, could be publicly humiliated. There were more drastic measures, too, reserved for those who had to be made an example of. A defaulter could be imprisoned, sometimes even without food. And everyone remembered Birju from

Allur village. He was thrown into a lake and prevented from coming out of the water for many hours. He died soon after due to fever from the exposure.

Those who battled these atrocities did not battle for long. The police helped perpetrators by keeping complaints from turning formal. The chances of a rebel surviving in these villages were bleak.

No, he would not be wrong in submitting to Lambodar's tactics.

Gangiri shivered as he stared into the darkness. He wished the night would extend for a few more hours and postpone the day. The morning would bring warmth, but it would also bring danger. The journalist was right, whether as a warning or threat, the information did give him time to plan. Gangiri closed his eyes, trying to control the shivering, no longer certain if it was caused just by the cold.

It took time for the morning to emerge from the quilts of fog that lay thick on the fields. The birds sounded disappointed at the dull light and cows raised their heads searching for the day. The sun climbed higher to check if the prospects would improve.

As the weak light reached him, Gangiri opened his notebook and checked the equation once more. It was not a difficult calculation and hardly spanned a single page. He was left with just enough money to provide the family one single, frugal meal a day till the harvest. He was still to investigate Jivan Patel, the district's agriculture officer and the member of the suicide committee who consistently vetoed patra suicide verdicts.

The crop of pulses would not be ready until March or April and even then, half the produce would go to the traders from whom he had borrowed the farm inputs. It would be impossible to finance another crop without a loan, and impossible to repay Sudhakar's debt. The vicious wheel would keep turning.

That morning, more than ever, he was tempted to borrow from the village moneylender. This was no way to treat a family, he frowned, staring at the figures which appeared as meagre on paper as they were in hand. Perhaps he should go to Lambodar before his men came looking for him. Perhaps he should trade with him, promise to vote against suicide verdicts for money. How much would his vote be worth? Ten thousand rupees? Less? More? Could it fetch Padma and the children two square meals a day? *Any* vote was worth that.

Or perhaps he should go to Durga Das, take the early bus to Nula and catch him at home. He could offer to sell the land to him for a good price. Someone said it could fetch him two lakh rupees. Or more? *That* was worth his vote.

But all of this would be possible only before he resigned from the committee. After that, he would be nothing, worth nothing. If only someone would lend them money to survive, help them revive their lands and reap a profitable harvest. But who would have that kind of patience to wait for their losing battle with failing crops to turn into a winning bet? A friend, a guardian, a government that cared?

Padma and the children were now awake. Their voices, which came from inside the house, added to his burden of guilt, and he walked away from them, along the path that led to the field. There was not much to do at this stage of the crop, the seeds had been sown, the long wait had begun. He let water into the field and supervised its spread. Then he walked towards the row of tamarind trees that separated the fields to check on Vadrangi's crop. Vadrangi had replanted cotton that season after the first crop was destroyed. But even this crop was slow to develop, and perhaps the yield would be low.

Around 8 a.m., Gangiri walked back and turned to the path that led to the house. He stopped suddenly in his tracks. At a distance, he could see two men waiting near the house. Their motorcycle was leaning against a tree next to the path.

He started walking again, slowly and anxiously. He could see only the children on the front porch and guessed that Padma must have gone into the house.

As Gangiri reached the bamboo gate, one of the men continued to smoke a cigarette and the other watched him with curiosity. The smoker was short but powerfully built. The taller man was older with thinning grey-black hair, a fatigued face and cynical eyes.

'Namaskar,' Gangiri said. 'Are you waiting for me?'

'Yes, if you are Gangiri Bhadra.'

'I am,' he said. 'What can I do for you?'

The smoker chuckled, and took a step towards him. 'You could tell me why you are being a fool?'

'Being a fool?' Gangiri asked the smoker, glancing at the tall man who was leaning on the fence, watching him.

'Yes, Gangiri, a fool,' the smoker said, amused. 'We know no one is supporting you and you are not getting anything out of all this. Your family is barely alive and your career as a teacher is over. And yet, you want to be a farmer. Why?'

Gangiri studied both men in silence, the morning breeze touching his neck like cold steel.

'Don't tell me you do this out of pride, Gangiri,' the smoker said, laughing. 'Poverty should have cured you of it. Where is the pride in being a farmer when you cannot even feed your children without begging for loans? You have options; you don't have to die here like your brother.'

Gangiri looked at the house, hoping Padma did not hear that.

'Go back to your city school, take Sudhakar's family with you and give them a respectable life,' the smoker said reasonably. 'Or is there no respect in living without begging?'

Gangiri lowered his eyes, the words spreading like pain through his veins.

'Don't worry,' the smoker said kindly, 'this is not surrender. You are just thinking of your family. As you should! And we will help you sell this farm and house, and settle down in the city. We will take care of you, if you promise to take care of your family. Could any offer be more generous than this?'

The smoker paused. 'All this in return for one signature on a letter, your resignation from the district suicide committee.'

Gangiri watched as the tall man pulled out an envelope from his jacket pocket. Gangiri glanced up at the cloudless sky and desperately hoped someone was watching over him. He then looked at the men and said, 'I may be poor but I am not for sale.'

The smoker lost his smile and the tall man straightened. The tall man looked at Gangiri for a long moment, then walked to the house. Realizing that he was headed towards the children on the porch, Gangiri quickly followed him. The tall man stopped near Balu who was standing next to his sister, looking up at him with curiosity.

'Poor, unfortunate children!' said the man in a cold, unconcerned voice. 'Don't they have anything better to wear? And look at those bare, dirty feet.'

He turned to Gangiri, reprimanding. 'Do they even get to eat?' he asked, 'Or are you feeding them your principles? Don't torture them with a life like this, Gangiri. Kill them in one stroke; free them from your mistakes.'

The words cut deep, plunging quickly like knives through soft flesh. Gangiri fought hard to stay calm and appear indifferent. He now knew Padma must have heard every word inside the house. He also knew why she did not come out.

'I know it is not fair to run you down like this,' the man said sadly. 'I am sure you would not refuse any help or money, if they came with conditions that suited you. So saying you are not up for sale is untrue. Is it not?'

Gangiri looked away, his face warm with the insults.

'It is also unfair to their late father,' the tall man said seriously. 'After all, Sudhakar may have never imagined that you would treat his family so cruelly.'

Controlling himself with effort, Gangiri finally said, 'I wish I could have spent more time with you but I now need to travel to Mityala to attend the meeting of the suicide committee. It was very nice talking to you, but we will have to do this some other time.'

He turned to the children and ushered them inside. When the children were indoors, Gangiri turned around, prepared.

The tall man's face was hard, his eyes still. 'Please don't let us keep you from your work,' he said coldly. 'We will wait here.'

Gangiri watched as he gestured to the smoker to join him.

'And while we wait, surely you won't mind us being looked after by your sister-in-law?' He walked towards the house. 'I saw her going into the house earlier. Let me check...'

Gangiri blocked his way and pushed him away hard, making him stumble back. But he recovered quickly and rushed towards Gangiri, his hand swinging. The blows caught Gangiri on the face and, in moments, he was on his knees, his lip bleeding into the dust. He battled for breath, surprised by how easily he was overpowered, how weak he had become.

The smoker pulled him up roughly and the tall man looked at him in silence, waiting. Gangiri finally looked away, unable to meet the uncaring eyes. He saw the children staring at him tearfully from the house, the children who had just lost a father.

He had no choice, Gangiri told himself again, silencing the last, feeble voice within that wanted to fight.

Where were the revolts that started with a single man? Those libraries which treasured heroes, those fables that nourished the dreams of generations, had become obsolete. Ancient words like 'truth' and 'dignity' had waylaid him. Mere words, written and spoken in the shelter of a million thoughts for a better world. Was not one of those thoughts his own? Gangiri lowered his eyes, defeated.

He took the paper the tall man handed him and read it. It was a letter of his resignation from the suicide committee, addressed to the collector and his name typed at the end. The man handed him the pen and he took it without looking up. Gangiri signed the paper with a steady hand and returned it to the man.

The tall man examined the signature, then glanced at Gangiri, intrigued. 'What, no more protests?'

Gangiri shook his head, his eyes dull with pain.

'Smart!' he said. 'We will return with the sale deeds for this house and land. Start packing, you are leaving the village forever.'

Gangiri did not respond and watched them drive away on their motorcycle. He stood weakly in the yard for a moment, the blood from his lip trickling down to his chin. He then slumped down in the dust.

10

Friday afternoon, the district collectorate, Mityala town

For Dhunu, the collector's assistant, that Friday threatened to be one of those days which begins without pace and has to be dragged along like a heavy axle rod in search of a set of wheels. With the collector away from Mityala for half a day, the entire collectorate seemed to recline a little, and the staff enjoyed a holiday in office.

Dhunu lounged in every part of the building where he could legitimately lounge. He gossiped with colleagues, chatted about juniors with seniors, seniors with juniors, spoke about men with women, women with men, and men with men.

Some of the staff remembered errands they had to run, and disappeared. By lunch hour, the results of these furloughs could be seen in the form of bags full of clothes, books and groceries parked next to the desks.

Having no such excuse, Dhunu wandered the empty corridors of the collectorate. He sat in one of the vacant chairs and called home but made the mistake of telling his wife that he was calling because he had nothing better to do.

To alleviate the subsequent distress she plunged him into, he decided to compare his plight with that of the kiosk-keeper around the corner. They exchanged notes on the propensity among wives for wickedness and the pleasure they derived from remembering past disasters with fondness. After agreeing on the pointlessness of man's life in general, and the dispensability of a married man's life in particular, Dhunu slouched back into the collectorate.

He watched as the members of the committee started arriving around 2.30 p.m. for the 3 p.m. meeting. He recognized every one of them; they had all been members for the past seven years. And he could also recognize the new farmer-member, Gangiri Bhadra of Gopur.

Most of the members had their official or personal vehicles. Those who had neither were provided transportation by the administration for the meeting. A small flock of assistants in starched white uniforms was busy like seagulls, guiding members towards the conference hall annexe. There the members waited for the meeting to begin while having refreshments. The annexe was also the place where dinner would be served, if required, which Dhunu was sure would be required today.

The suicide committee meetings these days were long and arduous, unlike in the past when they would end in just a couple of hours. All because of farmer Gangiri who fought for every verdict, each vote. Dhunu knew this because he was present at all the meetings in his capacity as the collector's assistant. He also doubled as the unofficial messenger for the villagers, telling them what happened in the meetings, who fought for whom, and who betrayed whom.

Dhunu, being senior to other assistants, supervised the preparations with a cynical eye and hung about the outer corridor awaiting Collector Gul who was expected any time.

Then one of the assistants came up to him and whispered that he had seen people enter the collector's personal chamber. Dhunu hurried away to check.

Gul arrived ten minutes before the meeting and rushed into his office, barely noticing an unusually harried Dhunu who was desperately trying to explain why he couldn't throw people out of his chamber. Gul hurried into his office and stopped, puzzled.

Gul, an efficient man in his early forties, had a pleasant face with an engaging smile that usually got him undeserved leeway in difficult spots. He had the distinct air of the honest and the upright, which some complained was grossly understated while others believed was a special effect.

That afternoon, however, he was annoyed with himself for being at a loss over a problem. His smooth brow was lined in thought as he walked into the conference room, his eyes barely meeting any others. Dhunu, who knew what worried the ruffled collector, nervously placed a glass of water on his left-hand side and a pen on his right. A set of the case files that were on the agenda that day was distributed to each member. The stenographer prepared to take a shorthand record of the minutes and an audio recorder was switched on.

Gul sat at the head of the long table which seated the other nine members of the suicide committee. He opened the meeting with a brief statement. 'We have thirteen claims for compensation to examine today. It is for us to decide if these deaths were indeed of farmers who killed themselves due to debt and farm distress, as claimed.

'As you all know the procedure, I shall not waste time repeating it. I humbly request that, unlike the last time, we conduct this meeting in peace and with dignity,' he said, adding curtly, 'as befits the stature of this committee.'

He checked the first file. 'The late Chakradhar Rawat, resident of Viri village. Medical facts?'

Hemant Rao was seated a few places away at the table and he reached for his report, his young face anxious as he read from it. 'Organo-phosphate poisoning confirmed, sir. Poison administered through mouth, leading to severe and irreversible thoracic and pulmonary damage, and trauma to the victim. Respiratory failure was the principal cause of death. The chief of police has the other details of the case.'

Police Chief Purandar Reddy, looking strict and sharp in his uniform, referred to his file. 'Chakradhar Rawat was a forty-five-year-old male. Discovered dead in his field by his wife on the morning of 12 November. Cause of death was poison. Motive was established primarily through a suicide note, in which Rawat mentioned that he was forced to commit suicide because he could not bear the pressure of repayment of an outstanding debt.

'The same motive was reiterated by his wife,' Reddy said. 'She said he was distressed that recovery agents of a local moneylender had threatened to disgrace him and his family before the entire village if he did not clear the dues by the end of the month.'

He continued, 'We recorded the statements of eyewitnesses who were present when the recovery agents issued the said threat. We have also questioned the agents named by the widow and the witnesses. There is considerable evidence that Rawat was in the moneylenders' bad books because he had defaulted on loan repayment many times. The widow insists that the default happened because the crop failed, but the moneylenders disbelieved them.'

Reddy glanced around the table. 'We have tried our best but, as has happened in such cases earlier, it is impossible to get accurate information on the moneylenders. Rawat's widow is the only one who can tell us more, but she fears retribution.'

Reddy checked his file again. 'Based on the statements and the evidence, such as the fingerprints of the deceased on the container of pesticide, our investigation proves that it was a suicide caused by debt distress.'

Gul thanked him. He then glanced across at Agriculture Officer Jivan Patel at the other end of the table. Patel nodded, stylishly clearing his throat several times, as if finding the right tone in which to read out his notes.

'Take your time, Jivan bhai,' Gangiri said. 'Just make sure you don't repeat what happened last time.'

The AO glared at Gangiri. 'What is it to you?'

Gangiri's expression accentuated the sarcasm in his eyes, his wounded lip making his smile lopsided.

'Answer me, Bhadra!' Patel demanded. 'I was confused the last time because both cases were from Gopur. What happened was not deliberate.'

'It would have robbed the farmers' families of the compensation,' Gangiri observed wryly. 'I'm just curious, how much do your confusions cost?'

'This is a baseless allegation!' Patel shouted and turned to his boss. 'I shall not stand for this, sir. You know very well how diligent I am with facts and figures, and how little cause for complaint I have given...' He stopped speaking, noting the sardonic look in the collector's eyes.

Gul glanced at Gangiri, then turned to the stenographer. 'Mr Bhadra's last statement is to be struck from the records.'

Patel looked at Gangiri with satisfaction and turned to his notes again. 'Rawat owned three acres of land and he had been cultivating cotton for over a decade. The lands in Viri are not canal irrigated and are heavily dependent on rain. Initially, the yield was high but it started falling over the years and became worse with failing rains. He was unable to clear his dues and became a defaulter with the principal banks which refused to furnish him new loans.

'Rawat had also borrowed money from a private moneylender eight years ago to sink a borewell, but there is no record of the amount. The borewell failed and he was forced to borrow again for another one, which also failed,' he paused. 'The private moneylenders claim that, at the time of his death, Rawat owed them forty-five thousand rupees. He also owed the bank fifty-three thousand rupees.'

Patel shrugged. 'This could easily be a natural death made to look like a suicide because this family, clearly, needs the money.'

Next, Gul asked Ramesh Vaish for his opinion. Vaish was sweating more than usual and his face shone in the flat white light of the conference room.

He wiped his hands as he spoke. 'We, at the bank, have never tried recovering loans through harsh measures. But it is true that Rawat was in desperate need of financial assistance. The moneylenders had abandoned him as he had failed to clear their outstanding debts. He had no money for the next crop and he foresaw a dismal future for his family. The only solution was to repay the debts to regain the trust of lenders, but that was impossible.

'I interact daily with such people who feel they are close to the edge. Nothing they have, or may ever have, would be enough to repay the debts. That is when they start thinking of death.' Vaish's small eyes flickered like moths under the bright lights as he said, 'I think this is a suicide due to debt.'

'This is a *what?*' asked Durga Das, leaning forward in shock, and peering at Vaish through his glasses.

Vaish said defensively, 'It is a debt-related suicide, Durgaji. I know this case. I am sorry.'

Gangiri chuckled, but said nothing.

'No need to be sorry,' Gul said. 'Just give us your vote, one way or the other.'

'No, wait, collector saheb,' Durga Das said, still astonished. 'Are you out of your mind, Ramesh? Have you forgotten you are a banker and not an andolan kaari? What has happened to you?'

There was now a deep frown on the banker's sweaty forehead. 'I know, Durgaji, that this sets a wrong precedent. I, too, am against giving compensation to farmers who have committed suicide and escaped repaying their debts. But that still does not change the fact that Rawat *did* commit suicide due to debt distress.'

Durga Das was silent, stunned. Then his brown, watery eyes slowly turned to Gangiri, who was watching him. The challenge in those eyes was unmistakable.

There was a moment's pause as the collector noted Vaish's vote. Then Durga Das sought permission to cast his vote next. He began by addressing the banker.

'If this suicide happened because of financial reasons, my dear Ramesh, then it is the same as theft,' he said. 'After hearing reports of Rawat defaulting on loans, I started monitoring this case personally. To begin with, I know Rawat's crop did not fail as badly as he claimed it did. Take last year, for instance. The cotton plants in his field reached the healthy height of four feet, which means they received adequate fertilizers, pesticide and water in the initial weeks. The plants were not crowded on a per-unit-area basis and the fibre formation was good. He picked the cotton himself, along with his family, so we have no way of knowing what quantity he harvested. He claimed he handed the entire harvest to the shopkeepers who lent him inputs for the crop. I suspect that the crop certainly gave him more than two good pickings and he made much more from the harvest than he declared.'

'I have personally observed,' Durga Das continued, 'that the utensils from the household were cleaned twice at the community well, which meant food was cooked, at least, twice a day in his house.' He paused, looking around. 'You call this *poverty*? I don't.'

All the members present knew of Durga Das's eye for detail when it came to debtors. No one ever questioned him; no one knew how to.

So they were surprised when Gangiri said, 'Durgaji, I compliment you on your observation skills. But can you tell me if, when you were watching the utensils being washed, there were any dogs nearby?'

Durga Das protested and the collector turned to Gangiri. 'Mr Bhadra, that is impertinent and you will have to be warned again not to misbehave with the members.'

'Sir, I was not misbehaving with the esteemed member. I was asking about dogs.'

There were chuckles along the table.

'That's it!' Gul glanced at the stenographer. 'Make a note that Mr Bhadra is officially warned against misconduct during the meeting.'

'May I,' Gangiri asked, 'now have the answer to the question from Durgaji?'

'If you must!' Gul said tersely and glanced at Durga Das. 'Did you notice any dogs near the utensils, Durgaji?'

'No collector saheb, there were no dogs.' Durga Das was polite.

Gangiri shrugged. 'Well, I ask because when utensils are washed in the open, dogs usually gather around for leftovers. I must conclude that the family was surviving on rice water and salt, not the top favourite among dogs. I know because...' He stopped suddenly and looked away. 'I know because that is what my family has when we have no...' He paused again and completed hesitantly, 'when we are forced to skip meals.'

There was silence in the room. Gangiri sat back in his chair and lowered his eyes, unwilling to see the sympathetic expressions. The members looked at each other, trying to think of something to say. Durga Das glanced helplessly at his friend, Lambodar.

The chief sarpanch was smooth as always. 'I thank you, Gangiri, for giving us this insight. My heart goes out to you and your family. As I am sure you are doing everything in your power to help them, I shall pray that you succeed.' He smiled benevolently and Gangiri thanked him.

'Now, can we return to Durga's opinion, which was interrupted?' Lambodar asked.

When the collector nodded, Durga Das continued. 'Rawat's family had bought a goat under a government scheme set up to promote alternative incomes for farm households. I have always seen the goat provided with ample fodder, its stomach full and rounded.' He paused. 'Where did the money for the fodder come from? Where did the money from the goat's milk go? How is it possible that his stated income was so meagre?'

Durga Das looked around, then continued evenly, 'My complaint is that these farmers come to us crying, begging, but lying all the time. They tell us they are dying and that they need the loan for their daughter, or their parent, or their demanding son. They lie so that we give them the money. And they lie so that we do not ask them to repay.'

He stopped to glance at Gangiri. 'They lie when they are alive.' Durga Das smiled thinly. 'And they lie when they die.'

Gul asked, 'Is that your vote, Durgaji?'

'Of course. It is a natural death,' Durga Das said, 'it is not even a suicide. Unlike some who have spoken before me, my vote cannot be coerced. Rawat's death is not a suicide, debt-related or otherwise.'

'Are you suggesting that this committee headed by me is being rigged?' Gul demanded politely.

'Only in a manner of speaking, collector saheb,' Durga Das hurried to explain. 'I meant my vote was unalterable, unlike the votes of Dr Rao or Vaish.'

Both stared at Durga Das, too flustered to respond.

'Well.' Gangiri smiled at them. 'Don't you think we should favour separate voting rights for the conscience of moneylenders?'

Rao chuckled. 'Only way to find out if it exists!'

There was subdued laughter and Durga Das smiled at Rao. 'You should not ridicule me for my vote, Dr Rao. I remember concluding at the last meeting that some symptoms of these suicides are the same as those of death due to other medical causes. At that meeting, you agreed with me. But, of course, you were singing a different tune then!'

Rao remained silent, his kind face now flushed.

'So tell us, Dr Rao,' Durga Das continued with a sly smile swimming in his watery eyes. 'Where have you lost *your* conscience?'

'You are twisting facts,' Rao answered angrily. 'At the last meeting, Durgaji, I had also listed the reasons why death by poison could not be confused with anything else. I shall repeat the evidence seen in this case, like the bluish tinge of the skin, the froth at the mouth, reduced pupils and severe damage to the tissues of the throat and lungs. My preliminary tests in this case confirm the presence of poison in the stomach. This is a case of suicide.'

Durga Das stared at the doctor for a few seconds, then shrugged. 'Well, I have never trusted doctors. I say it is not a suicide.'

Gul nodded, registering the vote. Then he asked Lambodar, sitting to his left, for his vote.

Lambodar shook his head, his white turban catching the light. 'It is not a suicide, Mr Gul. I know Rawat's family. They are the kind of people who cling to money. For as long as I remember, I have never known the family donate to any cause...'

'That could be because they never had the surplus to donate,' Gangiri interrupted. 'He may have wanted to give money, but could not afford it.'

'That could be it, I don't know,' Lambodar nodded, smiling, 'but nor do you, Gangiri.'

'That is not true. I do know.'

Lambodar's smile faded a little, his metallic voice became

sharper. 'To think that you represent the conditions of all those who are in distress is to think too highly of yourself, Gangiri. There is only one man in this room who truly knows the state of the people in this district, the rich and the poor, the industrialist and the labourer, the moneylender and the farmer. That happens to be Collector Amarendra Gul. That is the nature of his job. No one else can claim to know more than him.'

This politically correct view was naturally seconded by everyone in the room.

Gul waited for the voices to settle down, then said, 'The only way to ever know anything new is to listen when people are telling us something. Mr Bhadra may have a point, Lambodarji, though I hate to admit it.'

'Of course he does,' Lambodar said generously. 'He is one of our most vocal representatives of the distressed farmer community. I am glad he is in this committee to inform us of the ground realities.'

He paused, letting the mockery in his words settle among the listeners. 'My contention is that Rawat's case must be examined in the context of his family. For instance, his crops failed due to lack of proper irrigation. But it is not true that the rains have consistently failed in the last ten years. We have had some very good monsoons in between. I am sure someone here will remember that he extended his house, bought a buffalo and never pledged gold ornaments for money.

'I also agree that the actual decline started only in the last three years. So why did he not repay the debt before that? I remember his words once, when I asked him. He said, "I will pay it, sir, even if I have to die for it."'

There were surprised whispers across the table.

The smile returned to Lambodar's aged face as he showed off his formidable memory. 'So I believe that much before he died, it was decided that his death would be used to gain the compensation. No, Mr Gul, this cannot be called a suicide. It would not be legally sound.'

After his vote, an air of doubt hung over the meeting. Everyone knew apatra Lambodar felt it was his duty to discourage suicides by denying compensation. And yet, the objections he raised seemed valid. Rawat's family was well-known for not repaying debts, for haggling, for not helping others in need. It might have been because of poverty but even then, Lambodar was right. The family was not poor till recently. Lambodar's memory never failed.

The first to notice the change in the mood of the members was another politician and Lambodar's senior, Gauri Shanker maha sarpanch, who sat to the right of the collector. He could discern that Lambodar's stature had revamped the opinion of the group. He did not support the motives behind Lambodar's strategy. Gauri Shanker had always favoured financial help as the only thing the government could do, even if in retrospect, to correct policy shortfalls.

'I believe this is a distress suicide,' Gauri Shanker said briefly. Lambodar looked away, exasperated. As a precaution, Lambodar almost never engaged in a contest with the older man who was held in high regard across the district.

In his typical restless way, Gauri Shanker glanced around at the waiting faces. 'I, too, have known Rawat's family for long. He was a hard-working man, creative and industrious. He was good at many things. For instance, he was a fine carpenter and a useful mechanic. He earned extra money through small orders. But he started depending on these more when the crops began failing.

'Those who say he is a thief, or that he plotted his own death, do not really know that he was a very self-respecting man.' He glanced at Lambodar. 'Rawat was an honest man who woke up one morning, found he could no longer struggle to repay his debts and just killed himself. It happens to all of us; hopelessness. Some of us survive it with help. Others don't *want* to survive it.

'This is a debt-distress suicide whether we admit it or not,' he said. 'But if we do, we will be paying the right homage to an honest, sincere man.'

He sat back, habitually reaching for his old walking stick for support. It was now Lambodar's turn to feel the impact that Gauri Shanker's words had made on the members.

The gathering was plunged into intense thought and questioned their earlier decisions. This happened each time Gauri Shanker spoke after Lambodar. With brief, easy words, he managed to drag people out of the comfort of sharing Lambodar's convictions and forced them to reach their own conclusions.

The only person Gul seemed to like in the committee was Sitabai, even though her opinions were usually the most acerbic of all. Gul now gently asked her for the vote.

'You know, collector saheb,' she said thoughtfully, 'the last time, I was deeply hurt when you requested me to keep my opinion short. Why just me? I've never heard you say this to anyone else.'

'No?' Gul was intrigued. 'I wonder why!'

She studied him with suspicion. 'How can I know if my opinion will be short or long until it is expressed?'

'It may be too late by then,' he replied, amused. 'But please do go ahead.'

'Well, to begin with, I do not think Chakradhar killed himself because of the debt. I agree with Durga Das mahajan and Lambodar maha sarpanch.'

Both men blinked in surprise; it was the first time she had ever agreed with their vote.

Gul asked, 'So you, too, don't think this is a suicide, Sitabaiji?'

'I will get to that if you stop interrupting...'

'Only asking,' Gul clarified, interrupting again, 'Please, continue.'

Sitabai, after a long, patient minute, said, 'Chakradhar did not kill himself because of the debt. He killed himself because of the insults.'

Durga Das cleared his throat noisily and smiled at her, mocking.

'Anyone,' she continued, looking at him, 'would kill themselves if they were hounded the way Chakradhar was hounded for money.'

Durga Das nodded, pretending to be serious.

Sitabai continued, 'The moneylenders believe that the poor, starved people can somehow still repay debts. They want more from us, they want to take away everything...'

'How can a woman understand these things?' Durga Das interrupted her derisively. 'Would you rather that we lend money and forget about it, Sitabai?'

'Forget! Have you ever forgotten a paisa in your life, Durga?' Sitabai demanded. 'Everyone knows you have a record of every rupee you've spent on your son so that you can earn it back in dowry when he gets married.' She paused. 'Is it not true that you have even included the money you spent to get his bicycle repaired when he was a child?'

There were chuckles, the chief of police grinned, and even the collector fought a smile. The doctor whispered something, making Vaish laugh and Gangiri chuckled. Durga Das shifted uneasily in his chair.

Gul remarked, 'Please don't make personal comments about other members, Sitabaiji. Just cast your vote.'

'Is it my fault that moneylenders are part of this committee?' Sitabai retorted. 'It is personal, collector saheb. If these are not suicides by farmers, then these are murders of farmers.'

'Your vote please,' he repeated patiently.

'Chakradhar committed suicide because of debt and everyone knows it.'

'Thanks!' Gul said with real gratitude.

He then glanced at Gangiri. 'Your vote, Mr Bhadra,' he said curtly.

Everyone was used to the harsh manner in which Gul treated Gangiri. He had been uniformly contemptuous and critical of Gangiri from the day he was appointed as a member. Everyone was surprised and intrigued. Initially, they thought Gul must have had a good reason to include Gangiri in the committee. Now, they wondered how it was that Gangiri remained a member despite Gul's disapproval. Gangiri, however, never complained and never disobeyed Gul's orders.

Gangiri could see that none of the members, including Gul, were curious about his verdict on the Rawat suicide. Everyone knew his views, his votes. Only Lambodar and

Durga Das looked at him, waiting. Which one of the two had his resignation? Gangiri wondered. Why had it not been used till now?

Were they telling him that they would not use his resignation if he voted according to their preference? Was this a test? But they were forcing him out of his home and land. In a day or two, everyone in the district would know he had left for the city. Perhaps, then, his resignation would reach the collector, proving to the world that he had sold his membership for a better future.

Gangiri lowered his eyes to his hands. But today, he was still a member of the committee.

'The vote, Mr Bhadra,' the collector said impatiently.

Now everyone turned to Gangiri. Rao frowned and glanced at Vaish who, too, was watching Gangiri. Gauri Shanker waited, hope in his old eyes. Sitabai leaned forward, her face worried. Reddy watched him thoughtfully. But Lambodar was smiling, Durga Das was triumphant and Jivan Patel was waiting.

Gul looked around at everyone and studied the various expressions at length. He then glanced at Gangiri. 'Mr Bhadra, we are waiting.'

Gangiri did not speak for a few moments, then said, 'Chakradhar Rawat, forty-five years old, resident of Viri village, and owner of three acres of agricultural land, committed suicide due to an unassailable debt burden.'

There was silence after he spoke. Everyone could see that the vote had cost Gangiri something. They could see it in the sadness in his eyes, the loss on his lean face, the slump of his shoulders.

Gangiri looked up at Durga Das and then at Lambodar.

Durga Das shook his head gravely and Lambodar remained serene. Gangiri pensively looked away, lost.

Gul recorded the votes. 'Well, I think we don't need my vote to decide. Six in favour of the debt-suicide claim, three in favour of death due to other causes. But for the record, my vote is that Chakradhar Rawat committed suicide due to debt. The compensation is to be awarded to his wife at the time and place of her convenience.'

11

Gangiri watched as Rawat's file was set aside. That closed file opened so many opportunities for Rawat's family, which must surely be on the brink of complete collapse. The widow of a farmer, burdened already with debt, does not have time even to mourn. She has to keep the home and the farm running, generate loans, organize farm inputs, and sell the harvest. The widow whom a farmer leaves behind is thrown into a struggle that she has no choice but to win. Gangiri knew the compensation would mean little in the long run, but days after the death of a farmer, it would mean the world to his family.

Even more important was the impact on the children. The children would remember how their father died, how their mother had fought the odds, how their priorities had changed overnight. They would also recall the onlookers, the neighbours, the friends, the close and distant relatives. They would remember the condolences and the regrets.

Gangiri hoped the children would remember that one assurance held true, that of the state. He hoped the compensation would keep the children from feelings of injustice and discontent, that it would keep the youth from anger, the future from darkness.

He knew, because the verdict in his brother's case had left

a deep crater in his heart that still smouldered with pain. But every time a deserving patra suicide verdict was passed by this committee, a brief spell of rain fell, dousing the fires with hope.

Gul opened a new file. 'Raghupati Naik, thirty-three-year-old resident of Senu village. Suicide due to debt.'

The doctor and the chief of police retold Naik's story and explained the inevitability of the conclusion that it was a suicide. Durga Das, still bitter about the earlier verdict, made snide remarks which forced Vaish to hold back his vote till later. Jivan Patel argued that Naik had misused several crop loans by spending the money elsewhere.

Durga Das, determined to steer the voting this time, said, 'Naik was an indulgent man. He once bought a fan that cost a hundred rupees more than the usual fans. He had a radio which even played FM channels. And then, you should have seen the way he dressed; he really took care of himself. It was also said that he frequented a woman in Mityala here, who was expensive.'

Durga Das shrugged. 'I saw him hurrying off a couple of times and asked where he was going. He never gave a straight answer and always said it was personal work.' Durga Das smiled meaningfully. 'Well, it was personal, he was not lying.'

There were grim smiles around the table, eyes hardened as they perused Naik's file, lips were pursed in displeasure.

Rao's outraged voice broke through their thoughts. 'Naik had to come here to Mityala frequently for his father's treatment,' he said, 'I had recommended that his father, who had a recurrent respiratory problem, be shown to the specialist at the district hospital.'

Vaish wiped his forehead and looked hesitantly at Durga Das. 'That is true, Durgaji. Naik told me about the problem and asked for a loan. But as his land was already mortgaged with us, I had to refuse.'

'I do not trust you any longer, Ramesh. You might be making this up.'

'To what purpose, Durgaji?' asked the collector. There was a frown in his eyes that also lurked in his voice.

Lost, Durga Das looked around for an answer. Lambodar rescued him. 'Purandarji ought to tell us why Naik frequently visited Mityala. Was it, as Dr Rao says, for his father?'

The chief of police shook his head decisively. 'I have no record of Naik travelling to this city in the last three months, ever since his crop failed. He was too busy saving money and trying to earn a living by working in others' fields.'

'But that is no proof that Naik was not using the loan money for purposes other than agriculture,' Lambodar gravely noted. 'I do not, therefore, believe that he committed suicide due to agricultural distress.'

He then smiled cordially at Gangiri. 'I am, of course, not you, Gangiri.'

Gangiri met Lambodar's eyes, 'No, not everyone can be.'

Lambodar nodded in agreement, amused.

Gangiri then asked the collector for permission to vote and Gul nodded dismissively. Even that small gesture showed his disgust with Gangiri.

'Raghupati Naik, a thirty-three-year-old resident of Senu village, committed suicide due to his inability to repay the farm debt,' Gangiri said.

'Please!' Durga Das said, laughing a little. 'What do you get out of this, Bhadra? You can see this man was corrupt, he threw his money around. What is it, really?' He leaned forward keenly. 'Do you receive a cut from the widows, a commission for the compensation?'

Gangiri's smiling dark eyes became suddenly still with rage. His composure deserted him, even though he knew Durga Das was playing a game.

Durga Das liked the change in Gangiri. He said provocatively, 'Tell us the percentage, Bhadra. Is it ten per cent, fifteen per cent of the compensation of one lakh rupees? Or is it paid in kind?'

Gangiri was silent, his thin face rigidly set.

Gul said, 'That was uncalled for, Durgaji, and...'

'I am sorry, collector saheb,' Durga Das said firmly, setting his glasses right. 'I deserve an answer and you will agree this is a valid doubt. Perhaps you, too, would be interested in the answer?'

Gul studied Durga Das for a long moment, and then nodded.

Durga Das looked around at everyone. 'Why is Gangiri Bhadra doing this, my friends? I am sure you have asked yourselves the same question and came up with the answer that he thinks his brother was denied justice. So, is this revenge? In that case, are even normal deaths being passed off as debt-distress suicides? And what is he getting out of this "revenge"? You may think it is the satisfaction of seeing more widows receive compensation. But this, when his own family is struggling with poverty? It is unbelievable!'

Patel shrugged defensively. 'Exactly my thoughts, Durgaji. With all due respect, Bhadra fights for the compensation money as if it were his own.'

'My doubt is,' Lambodar said thoughtfully, 'how does

Bhadra know so much about these deaths, these farmers? Is it possible that he gets to know them well before they die? In that case, why doesn't he stop them from committing suicide?

'Perhaps he makes ordinary deaths look like suicides with the help of the widows,' Durga Das said, his voice hard. 'For a price!'

Gangiri stared at him and the others who made the allegations. He was still sitting back in his chair, but every muscle in his face was tense with control. He finally lowered his eyes to the file in his hands, reasoning with himself that this was to be expected. These were the men who hoped he would fall in line, hoped that he could be tamed. His verdicts today must have come as a rude shock.

'How can you talk like this, Durga?' Gauri Shanker asked calmly. 'You force farmers' widows off their land to recover outstanding loans. You then re-sell the land for lakhs of rupees and pocket the profit.'

Patel objected. 'We have no official record that moneylenders sell the defaulters' lands to recover debt amounts from...'

Sitabai cut him short. 'Yes, but then you don't even have records of loans taken from moneylenders, do you? So don't get into this!'

Gangiri stayed silent, staring down at the file.

Rao was offended. 'Is it of no consequence that I can vouch for the fact that Naik was visiting Mityala often because his father was unwell?'

'I told you, Dr Rao,' Durga Das explained, 'I don't believe doctors.'

Vaish countered, 'But you don't believe bankers either.'

'Do you remember, Ramesh?' Durga Das smiled. 'Once

when your wife was travelling and I invited you home for dinner? As we chatted later on, you told me about the little fling your father had and the change you saw in him. I am surprised you did not find the similarity, Ramesh. Naik behaved just like that, never sparing a thought about money, time, distance. Love, you know!'

Vaish looked away, embarrassed.

'That kind of love reflects Naik's mental weakness,' the chief of police pointed out to Lambodar. 'Perhaps you should support an apatra suicide verdict.'

Finally, Gangiri spoke. 'Naik's father was in no physical condition to travel so often to Mityala, so Naik was bringing the medicines to him at home in Senu. I got to know of Naik's case from one of the Gopur panchayat members who also visits the same doctor. I can give you his name and this can be cross-checked. Dr Rao can give you the name of the doctor whom Naik was visiting. It can be part of the evidence, along with our statements. Similarly,' he glanced at Durga Das, 'can Durgaji provide evidence that I, or anyone who votes in favour of suicide compensation here, is doing so because of ulterior motives?'

'What do you mean "evidence"?' demanded Durga Das. 'You cannot fool me with your tricks...'

'And you, Durgaji, cannot make such baseless allegations,' Gul said, turning to the stenographer to dictate a censure against Durga Das.

Gangiri looked at Durga Das, his dark eyes glinting with anger. 'Moneylenders must be under tremendous pressure to have apatra verdicts passed so that there is no compensation and they can recover their outstanding loans by capturing the property of dead farmers. I am sorry I know so little about all this, I will try to learn more by the time we meet again.' He paused and then added with emphasis, 'and meet again, we shall.'

'Is that a threat?' Durga Das frowned.

'It is an apology,' Gul said testily. 'Now let us get on with the meeting.'

Soon, the second case was also declared a debt-distress suicide and the compensation approved.

Other cases came up for decisions and were sorted out. But the acrimony between Durga Das and Gangiri remained through the meeting. They traded charges, cast aspersions, questioned motives. The collector's official censures against both kept mounting. Finally, the collector had to order Gangiri not to address Durga Das directly, failing which he would lose his right to debate with other members and would be allowed to vote only through ballot.

This ensured peace and by 8 p.m. all thirteen claims were decided, out of which nine were declared patra suicides. According to the minutes, the majority of the committee expressed the view that the farmers who had committed suicide had been hard-working, sincere, helpless, poverty-stricken and desperate. Three members, Lambodar, Durga Das and Jivan Patel, felt that the deceased farmers were alcoholics and gamblers, lazy and depressed. A majority felt the causes for suicide had been debt, humiliation and poverty, but the three members felt that the deaths were due to personal reasons, vices, pride and subterfuge about repayment.

Finally, and with a palpable sense of relief, Gul announced the end of the meeting. Then he paused, the shadows waiting in his eyes. 'Before we proceed for dinner, I want to ask you for something that I need,' he said.

Intrigued, the members waited and glanced at each other.

Gul called Dhunu who was sitting in a corner of the room and whispered a brief instruction. Dhunu hurried out of the conference room. When the doors opened again, the perplexed members saw Dhunu escort a lady and two children into the room. Gul asked them to sit in the few empty chairs along the wall and turned back to the members.

'Dear members,' he said, looking at everyone, 'this is the family of late Sudhakar Bhadra, elder brother of Mr Gangiri Bhadra. This lady and her children are present here because Mr Bhadra could not leave them alone at home. He was afraid, he told me earlier, that their lives were in danger.

'He came asking for my protection and frankly,' the collector's eyes were angry, 'I did not believe him.'

Every member at the table was staring at him, shocked and puzzled. Only Durga Das glanced at Lambodar. They both glanced at Gangiri, who was sitting with his eyes lowered.

'Like Durgaji said today, I thought Mr Bhadra was playing a trick. I thought he was trying to get my sympathy or even my complicity, perhaps. His explanation was dubious, that this morning two men threatened, assaulted, and forced him to sign a letter of resignation from this committee. He said they had done so to stop him from exposing the real suicide numbers in the district. He also said that he was being forced to sell his home and land. That he would be thrown out of the village in a day or two. He said he had no choice; his life and his family's security were at stake.' The collector paused. 'I did not believe him. And I told him so.'

He felt his forehead irritably. 'There were reasons for me to disbelieve him. From the outset I resented the manner in which he had got himself appointed to the committee. I found his methods unscrupulous, however noble his purpose may have been. Two members told me informally that he had approached them. There have been a few anonymous letters stating that he is "blackmailing" members. That is how, it was alleged, we are getting patra verdicts validating debt-distress suicides. Some of you have even asked me to revoke my decision to include him in the committee, and as I had explained then, I would need evidence to take such a step.

'It is true that the number of valid suicide verdicts has been increasing since Mr Bhadra was inducted into this committee,' the collector said. 'But can anyone here prove that it was because the members have been blackmailed and forced to change their vote?'

He paused and said, 'I am referring to this today because I am answerable for the proper conduct of this committee to my seniors and political leaders. So, does anyone here have evidence—not rumours or hearsay—which shows that even a single vote has been manipulated?'

Durga Das said, 'But you said two members were approached by Bhadra?'

Gul glanced at the chief of police. 'Tell them what happened, Reddy'. He smiled at the tough-looking cop. 'You, anyway, look like a man who can be easily blackmailed.'

There were chuckles and even Reddy laughed self-consciously.

He turned to the members. 'Mr Bhadra met me regarding a death in police custody that had occurred under my charge a few years ago. It was a well-reported case and many of you might even recall it. I explained to Mr Bhadra that I had acted against the guilty policemen immediately. There was an inquiry to examine human right violations and, somehow, he felt the incident still had potential to damage my prospects. That was debatable, but I played along just to see what he was up to.

'He was ready to let it lie, he said to my surprise, if I voted truthfully in this committee and without succumbing to any pressure.' Reddy shrugged. 'Naturally I agreed, there was nothing to disagree with.'

Impressed, Sitabai told Reddy that she had not expected this of him. He decided to take it as a compliment.

Gangiri did not look up at anyone.

The collector then respectfully asked if Gauri Shanker would like to speak. Gauri Shanker nodded. 'Gangiri met me, too, to tell me that he had information about the loopholes in the last will of my father. I knew who might have told him this. It has been a long-standing complaint of some of my cousins who were left out of the inheritance. The information, if made public, would have led to some embarrassment and, possibly, a law suit. Nothing I could not have handled.'

He looked at Gangiri and continued in his soft voice, 'Then I considered Gangiri, poor, struggling, but spending his last rupee on gathering information about me to *force* me to tell the truth about the suicide figures.' He smiled. 'I was not blackmailed. I was converted.'

'This is unethical!' Durga Das exclaimed. 'Collector saheb, how can a member canvass like this? It is against the rules of conduct.'

Collector Gul nodded. 'You are right, Durgaji. And that has been the basis of my disgust with Mr Bhadra.'

He turned to look at the members. 'Today the matter has taken a serious turn. Mr Bhadra's life and that of his family's are threatened because of these allegations against him. I request everyone to spare some time, think back and tell me now if they have ever voted under pressure exerted by Mr Bhadra.'

As Durga Das made to speak again, Gul interrupted him. 'The members will have to provide evidence to support their allegations.'

Durga Das looked away and stayed silent, as did the rest of the members. Gangiri still did not look up.

When no one spoke, Gul said, 'I am happy to note that this committee was never compromised. I also sincerely apologize to Mr Bhadra for raising such defamatory questions about his conduct.'

'No need for apologies, sir,' Gangiri said, his voice barely audible.

Gul then glanced at Lambodar and Durga Das. 'This committee is witness to the fact that you, two of the most respected and influential people in the district, are set against Mr Bhadra. I differ with you in principle. I believe that those who show us our mistakes are more precious than those who ignore them. I agreed to Mr Bhadra becoming a member because we need people like him to make our system stronger and more effective.

'I request you, Lambodarji and Durgaji, to take up the responsibility of the security of Mr Bhadra and his family,' he concluded.

There was a moment of shock. Then Durga Das vehemently refused to do any such thing, saying Gangiri was lying.

'Then you have nothing to worry about,' Gul said amicably. 'Besides, I was not asking.'

Durga Das begged Lambodar to do something. Gul watched them both, amused, and everyone smiled with him.

Finally, Lambodar said with graceful restraint, 'As a former sarpanch of Gopur, and now the maha sarpanch of Mityala, it is my duty to protect Gangiri. I shall be happy to take care of him.'

Durga Das stared at Lambodar, then at Gangiri who was watching him, waiting. Infuriated, he said, 'No way... I don't... I won't be made a fool of like everyone else...' He stopped as Lambodar restrained him with a sharp word.

Durga Das took off his glasses, distraught. He then nodded in agreement.

'Thank you,' Gul said. 'I will disregard any resignation letter from Mr Bhadra that reaches me without his personal endorsement. His property must not be sold or bought, and he and his family will be protected against any physical harm.'

Then he smiled. 'It is unlikely that either of you will lapse in your pledge. But in the event that you do, and if something does happen to Mr Bhadra or his family, you will be the first people I visit.' He added tersely, 'You can count on it!'

He then invited everyone for dinner, leading the way to the dining room.

Gangiri too stood up and checked on Padma and the children. One of the assistants was helping them to the dining area, their dirty clothes in contrast with the starched white. He could see Padma hesitate as she walked, embarrassed by the noise her plastic slippers made on the polished floor. Sashi and Balu held her hands, the bright lights reflecting in their wide eyes. Realizing that they were going in to eat, Gangiri slowly sat down in the chair again.

They were going for dinner, he smiled, looking away.

'Won't you have something to eat?'

Gangiri started. It was Gul, gesturing to the dining area.

Gangiri came to his feet quickly. 'How can I ever thank you?'

Gul studied him thoughtfully. 'I can ask you the same thing.'

Gangiri shook his head. 'You would have come to know about Keyur Kashinath's role one way or the other, even if I had not told you.'

'I was not referring to that.'

Gangiri smiled. 'That was a just decision, sir, to make our safety the responsibility of Lambodar and Durga Das.'

'I hope so!' Gul said, nodding. 'I got the idea from your skirmishes with Durga Das and Lambodar, Mr Bhadra. You showed me who your enemies were and why. Very smart!'

Gangiri shrugged. 'I knew you needed the reasons.'

Gul assessed him. 'It was a dangerous game. If even one member had evidence to demonstrate that he or she had been blackmailed, a tape, a note, or a witness, I would have had to suspend you from the committee.'

'I knew that, sir,' Gangiri said. 'Which is why there was no evidence with anyone.'

Gul was silent for a moment, amazed. 'What is the source of your confidence, Mr Bhadra? The way you approached the senior members, including the chief of police, or even the way you walked into my office with your family.'

'Desperation,' Gangiri said briefly. 'But may I say it helped that you dislike me so evidently? It made your stand very objective and above board.'

Gul could not help but laugh. 'I hope my liking you won't change that. Is that what you wanted to hear?'

'Almost...' Gangiri grinned, and winced as his injured lip hurt.

Gul gestured to the wound. 'Can you identify the men who hurt you?'

Gangiri felt the bruise and frowned. 'I'll save that for a rainy day, in case Lambodar or Durga Das forget their duties.'

'I get the feeling that you will never let them forget anything,' Gul said. 'What do you plan to do next?'

Gangiri felt the cell phone in his pocket. 'I have to apologize to a journalist for misunderstanding him. And give him a great story.'

'Make sure you don't give away information on the proceedings of the meeting,' Gul warned. 'Now, let us have dinner.'

'No, sir...' Gangiri said, hesitantly.

Gul put a hand on his shoulder. 'Come on, your family is there too.'

'I know,' Gangiri said, pulling away. *How do I tell you, sir?* he thought and quickly turned away from Gul. *How do I even begin to explain what I will go through if I see Padma and the children eat tonight?*

'What's wrong?' Gul asked, puzzled.

Gangiri wanted to escape, to lie...anything. 'I don't... I am fasting today, sir.'

Gul frowned as he understood the lie. He could not see Gangiri's face, it was averted. But he saw him holding the chair tightly, as if to keep himself from running away.

Gul's frown deepened. 'When was the last time you had a good meal, Mr Bhadra?'

Not since Vijaya Dashami a month ago, Gangiri recalled. *The poor were being fed outside the temple in Allur.*

The memory of that moment, sitting among the destitute on the sidewalk, filled his eyes with tears.

We had rice, vegetables and...we carried some food home. We tried to save the food, but the children were hungry. They cried and kept searching the utensils...

The pleading voices of the children, like a thousand sharp knives, still turned deep in his soul.

My sister-in-law gave them rice water and they refused it at first. But when they felt very hungry, they even had that...they never complained...

He fell in the chair, distraught, the words still blocked in his throat, choking him into silence.

They suffer because of my decisions, sir. I could have chosen to give them a brighter life, but I bartered it for justice...

'Forget everything tonight,' Gul was saying, his voice sad, 'and share a meal with your family.'

Gangiri shook his head, closing his eyes, unable to answer. *I can't, sir, I am sorry. I cannot forget what I have stolen from them. I am nurtured by their tears, enriched by their hunger...I fight for my values with stolen arsenal...*

Gul could see him bent low in the chair in silence, his eyes shut, his hands closed in fists on the table.

These are the smiles I stole from them, sir, Gangiri thought. *These are the smiles I shall steal from them again. This is the food I stole from them. This is the food I shall steal from them again.*

Tears fell on the table, shining under the lights.

Of what use is seeing them happy today, Gangiri thought. *I shall never see them happy again.* 'Of what use is seeing them eat today, sir, I shall never see them eat again...' He fell silent, startled by his own voice, realizing he had spoken the words aloud.

12

Three days later, Monday morning, the office of the Democratic Party, New Delhi

Keyur looked up briefly before lowering his eyes again to the cell phone in his hands. There were four people left, and he knew from past experience that his father would see them all before he finally met him.

The waiting room outside Vaishnav Kashinath's office in the party headquarters had about thirty chairs arranged in five close rows. As Vaishnav always reached office punctually at 8 a.m., most of the chairs were usually taken by that time. So when Keyur arrived at 8.30 a.m. that day there was no place to sit, or even stand, in the room. Then the doorman recognized Keyur and kindly gave up his seat for him.

By 11 a.m., most of the chairs were empty but Keyur still sat next to the door. Every time the door opened, Keyur heard fragments of conversation from inside. His father's staff walked in and out, carrying mail, application letters, requests, recommendations, responses. Vaishnav went through the papers while meeting a steady stream of visitors.

'How is the family? I heard your daughter topped the university,' he was asking someone nearly two hours ago.

'Yes, and now she wants to get into politics.'

'Why not, Anwar? We need more young and educated people to enter politics.'

'Come on, Kashi, don't make fun of me. I don't want my daughter anywhere near this party office. But that is only if I can help it. Children these days have set ideas and she doesn't...'

The door closed before Keyur could find out what that intriguing daughter was up to.

Keyur discovered a trend in the door-closing habits of people. The lower-rung staff shut the door tightly. But the more senior a staffer, the more ajar was the door left. And when party leaders walked in, they left the door wide open, counting on their followers to close it. So, when Keyur saw a peon walking up, he leaned away from the door, knowing he would shut the door himself, leaving no room for eavesdropping.

Then, a former minister of labour for a state walked in and his bodyguard stood at the door, blocking it. Keyur glanced at the standard-issue SMG, and the muscle on the arm that held the weapon lightly. Keyur was convinced the burly man in a grey 'safari suit' had no idea that his posting was the result of a hard-fought battle by the ex-minister.

It all began when the DP lost power in the state to which the minister belonged, in elections held earlier that summer. Only the losing chief minister and his second-in-command, the losing home minister, found their way into the party headquarters at Delhi and were given official positions. Others were left to fend for themselves by negotiating with the new state government. Some of them did well by cashing in on favours they had done for the ruling party when it was in the opposition.

For instance, the former minister for excise managed to get a distillery project approved, the first in the state after twenty-five years, and was said to be making money 24x7. The former minister for environment found a spot as head of a panel that gave environmental clearances for projects, and was said to be turning screws for a secret price.

The ex-minister for labour, however, had spent his tenure in office helping organize labour strikes in opposition-owned industrial units and creating worker unrest in constituencies held by rival parties. So they were waiting for him to lose power.

Those labour union leaders, whom he had used to further his political agenda, had betrayed their cause in the hope of glory and perks, but had received neither. They too were, therefore, waiting for him to lose his office.

In many ways, his fear for his life had good reason. But as he had no evidence to back his fear, the state government easily turned down his request for a bodyguard. When he charged the state government of being guilty of the conspiracy to kill him, they simply retorted saying people in public life should be prepared to make sacrifices, and made an example of his case by publicizing that they believed in providing protection for the common people, not VIPs.

It was then that Vaishnav took the matter up and asked the party high command not to leave a loyal man and a senior leader exposed to the evil plans of a vengeful government in power. The ex-minster finally got his bodyguard and demonstrated his gratitude to Vaishnav by gifting him a golden idol of Lord Shiva. Keyur remembered it very well, and also recalled the precious stones that glittered in it.

But the gift proved to be a little premature. The state government, which soon discovered that he had acquired a bodyguard, began sending intelligence reports to the central government about the reduced threat perception for the ex-minister. And followed it up by leaking the reports to the press.

So now, the ex-minister was fighting to keep the bodyguard, who stood looking around, unaware of the fight between two political parties and two governments about who deserved his protection.

The door opened and Vaishnav escorted the ex-minister out. He was saying, 'I suggest you see Panditji...in these matters, I have found him to be very useful and...'

Almost everyone stood up on seeing Vaishnav and, as he returned to his office, he smiled a greeting at the visitors. Keyur waited till his father walked back into the room before sitting down at the door. He wearily checked his cell phone again. In the one-and-a-half hours that he had been waiting there, he had cleared the messages folder, returned the calls he had not missed intentionally and made notes on what could be done about the stories by Nazar Prabhakar.

It killed him to sit there when almost everyone around him knew why Vaishnav would call his son to the party office when he could have easily met him at home.

This was official business, the party's image was being tarnished and Vaishnav was under orders to deliver a strict reprimand personally and confidentially to Keyur. As with most personal and confidential things in politics, everyone knew everything about it.

The stories by Nazar Prabhakar started appearing in the newspaper three days ago, just when Keyur was beginning to credit Lambodar with the silence from Mityala. The first story was about the nine farmer suicides, validated as being related to debt distress at the latest meeting of the district suicide committee. These deaths had taken place within a fortnight, a steep toll for a single constituency, which even the most seasoned politicians might find challenging to deal with.

Keyur received summons from the minister in charge of agriculture, who was directed by the top office to 'look into the matter'. The result was a long, tedious meeting where it was concluded, as the minister wanted, that the remedies for problems of rural indebtedness lay not with the ministry of agriculture but with the ministry of finance.

The minister said this, casually, to the waiting television journalists before getting into his car outside his office. The statement was briefly reported by news channels and even Vaishnav felt that the matter was at rest.

However, the next day Nazar wrote another story. This one was about how one of the members of the district committee was forced to sign his letter of resignation as he was known for voting to validate claims of farmer suicides due to debt. In the story, Nazar even quoted from a statement made by Gangiri Bhadra, the farmer-member who faced the threats.

Keyur had a brief word with Lambodar and learnt that he was livid about being put in charge of Gangiri's security along with Durga Das. Then Keyur called the collector to ask him why Gangiri's security was in the hands of a maha sarpanch and a moneylender. The collector explained that the temporary arrangement would cease once it was ascertained who sent people to threaten Gangiri and the culprits brought to book. Keyur dropped the matter, suspecting that the collector knew more than he should. Unable to do anything else, in the end he called his father and said he needed the party's permission to speak to the press about the Mityala farmer suicides.

His father asked him to wait. And never got back. Then, this morning, Nazar wrote a third story. It comprised an extensive interview with Gangiri Bhadra which stated his suspicions that local politicians and moneylenders were behind the threats he faced. He even hinted at collusion.

Gangiri had a few questions to ask in the interview. 'What is preventing local politicians from standing as guarantors for farmers with unpaid debts so that they may get fresh loans? Won't that stop the farmers from going to private moneylenders?'

'What is preventing the politicians representing Mityala, like Keyur Kashinath, to announce that those who have defaulted on formal loans in his constituency would be given interest-free loans for just one year to help them break out of the cycle?' Gangiri had asked.

Keyur frowned as he remembered the other questions directed at him. Why couldn't he ensure that the farm-input providers, who lent seeds, fertilizers, pesticides and equipment to farmers, certified a particular yield per acre for the inputs they were supplying? And why couldn't he ensure incentives for those who repaid in time, like zero- or low-interest loans? All of these were potentially workable solutions, even Keyur had to admit to himself.

Then, as with every story by Nazar, there was the last, fatal cut. 'During the last fifteen days of inaction and indifference, there were nine suicides by farmers. How many more fortnights, how many more farmer suicides, will it take for the politicians to save the people who have trusted them with their vote?'

The party president also wanted to know the answer to that question. So he called Vaishnav at 7.30 a.m. Keyur was in his father's office an hour later.

Every time he glanced up, someone reassuringly smiled at him. He smiled back briefly, coldly. But that did not prevent a real estate developer from coming over and inviting him to his farmhouse next Sunday for a party. Or the hotelier who sauntered over to ask if he recalled having ice cream as a child at his restaurant in Connaught Place.

Keyur continued to fiddle with his cell phone, the back of his neck now a little stiff from the posture. The door opened again, people walked out, others walked in, the white curtains swung briefly, letting out bits of phrases before the door shut. Cups of tea that smelt of steam, cookies that smelt of cream. The trays were dull steel, the spoons shiny. The sugar came back untouched.

At about 11.30 a.m., he finally entered Vaishnav's room. 'Yes, Keyur, come in,' he said, gesturing to a chair. 'This will just take a minute.' Keyur waited while his father gave instructions about a few letters to his assistant Joshi.

He sat across the clean table, glancing at the familiar surroundings of the room that had been his father's office for the last decade. The most important feature of the room, present only in one other room in the entire four-storeyed building, was a door that directly connected to the party president's office. Both doors remained locked, except when the party president wanted to meet either or both of the general secretaries.

Keyur heard the quick rustle of papers as his father read, wrote remarks and passed on each letter to Joshi. Occasionally, he gave instructions: 'Make a copy of this.' Or, 'Send by hand.' Or, 'Tell him this is the last time.' Or, 'Write back thanking him.'

Vaishnav Kashinath was a man of medium build who glowed with good health and discipline. He was bald, wore glasses set in a gold frame, dressed in white, coarse hand-spun fabrics that made him look severe. But he had an attractive smile and teeth that still gleamed at the age of sixty-seven. He was also a man of long habits, one of the longest was his habit of carrying two fountain pens in his pocket. The first time he did so was almost twenty-five years ago, when he attended Parliament to take oath as a first-time member. He had been confused whether to sign the book in blue or black ink. He never lost an election and was never confused again, but he still carried two pens in memory of that historic morning.

A large clock noisily ticked off the seconds. Vaishnav's favourite way of ending a meeting was to unsettle his visitors by glancing at the clock meaningfully.

Keyur tried that now. It seemed to work.

'All right, Joshi,' Vaishnav finally said, pushing away the rest of the letters. 'Give me ten minutes with Keyur, then send out a message for a meeting in the conference hall. Only the election observers. Make sure the analysts' meeting takes place after that.'

Joshi nodded and walked out.

Keyur asked, 'So that you are already briefed when you meet the analysts?'

'Naturally, I must know all sides to be able to separate the truth from the truth I want.' He smiled. 'I had a word with Lambodar a short while ago. You have something to tell me, Keyur?'

Keyur shrugged. 'Whatever Lambodar told you is the truth, father. The question is, as you put it, is it my truth?'

Vaishnav's grey-black eyes scanned him steadily. 'You think I cannot afford to sacrifice you.'

It was not a question. Keyur calmly met his father's eyes.

Vaishnav's voice was sharp. 'This is a farmer whose brother was dealt with wrongly by the committee. He is angry and determined, and you thought threatening him to resign was the best strategy!'

Keyur fine eyes shone in defence. 'I had no choice.' He shrugged. 'The district collector should not have included him in the committee. Once he was in it, the suicide toll had to mount.'

'Lambodar feels that the farmer, Gangiri Bhadra, has influenced the collector. That he influences the vote of the committee members. You are an MP. Why could you not influence this farmer, Keyur?'

'He is not that kind of a man.'

'*You* are not that kind of a man,' snapped Vaishnav. 'You don't have either the respect or the fear of people of Mityala. You need to be rescued at every turn by your father. You are impatient to prove yourself but keep making these unforced errors that expose your inexperience. You, dear boy, have been outsmarted by a villager who knows what you don't know—how to survive!'

Keyur looked away, letting his father scold him. He had, from the very beginning, understood a fundamental difference between him and his father. Vaishnav had to hack his way through the jungle of politics and fought every day to survive. Whereas Keyur felt he was born to the position of power and did not have to struggle to prove he was worthy of it. It made him think differently from his father. But he never mentioned this out of respect and affection for him, and now, he heard him out with patience.

Vaishnav, on the other hand, knew his son would have a good explanation. Vaishnav also knew that whatever his son's explanation, he would be convinced by it. He could forgive Keyur anything. He only wanted to convey to Keyur the gravity of the situation.

'If Lambodar is not going public, it is because of me. He is so angry with you for mishandling the situation that it took me not less than ten minutes and two personal favours to get him to relent.' Vaishnav paused. 'And you know Durga Das mahajan funded half your election campaign in Mityala. We must pay him back and keep the heat off people like him.'

Keyur did not answer immediately, but when he spoke, his eyes were still averted, as if he did not want to hurt his father. 'Forgive me, sir, but however valuable they might be, I would not have identified myself with these people,' he said gently. 'That is not to say that I do not need their help, because I know I could not have won without the votes these two men got for me, by force and funds.

'But I would have chosen farmers to be my allies.' Keyur glanced at his father now. 'Or the labourers on farms, the tenants or any of the underprivileged. In almost every single election speech I made, I promised to help the poor and marginalized sections of society. I need to stand by that promise.'

It was difficult to decipher Vaishnav's expression as he heard him in silence. Keyur continued, speaking a little more cautiously.

'I must support the poor labourers, farmers, widows and orphans,' Keyur stressed, 'especially because I was funded by sarpanches and moneylenders.'

Vaishnav watched his son and offered no comment. It had been his strategy to align with local politicians and mahajans. And yet, Keyur could get away with blaming him because he was his son. Anyone else speaking those words in that tone would have not only been out of the door by now, but also out of the DP.

'We should have kept our allies hidden, sir,' Keyur said, employing his usual tactic of generating guilt in his father. 'Now everyone knows I won because the sarpanches and moneylenders coerced the voters.' Keyur gestured to the newspapers lying on the table nearby. 'Farmers like Gangiri are using that knowledge to corner me. They want to prove my complicity by forcing me to save the powerful.'

There was a brief silence after Keyur finished speaking.

Vaishnav then asked, 'If you knew how the farmers perceived you, why did you ask Lambodar to force this farmer Gangiri to resign from the committee? It has only given the farmers an excuse to raise their demand for justice.'

Keyur shook his head. 'We discussed several options but Lambodar would not settle for anything less than the farmer's resignation from the committee. Despite all his claims, it is now clear that Lambodar knew very little about how to handle Gangiri who lives in his own village!

'In a way, I am glad that he is being taught a good lesson,' Keyur said. 'Lambodar wants a hundred acres to build an industrial park next to the river. His own lands are nearby and he stands to benefit from the resultant escalation in land prices. Not to mention the fortune he will make in commissions on related transactions.'

Vaishnav frowned, but did not speak.

'You see, father? Lambodar is thinking of nothing but profit for himself. Over five hundred families in the area will be pushed off their lands and left without a livelihood because of this project. Fertile lands will turn fallow. The river will be flooded with effluents and it will affect crops and people. Generations will question the decision that will...'

'Spare me the rhetoric!' Vaishnav interrupted him sternly. 'The industrial park must come up. You made a promise and the company donated generously to the DP. The figure impressed the leadership, and you know that I confided to them that this was your project. You can't mess this up.'

'I won't, father,' Keyur said meekly. 'I remember how the company softened the DP for me and I shall keep my promise. Besides, we may need them in the future again. So, I have found a spot in Mityala where hundred acres are available and I will finalize the deal soon.'

'Oh good!' Vaishnav said with sarcasm. 'So will the land not turn fallow now? And the effluents not poison the river?'

Keyur replied evenly, 'The land will turn fallow and the effluents will poison the river. But as this plot is some distance away from the villages, I will be spared the criticism.'

Vaishnav heard him out thoughtfully.

'Lambodar, however, feels he will incur a loss. I told him he cannot incur loss on a deal that is yet to be made. But you know him!'

Vaishnav nodded. 'I know him, Keyur, which is why you must let him have his way once in a while. If you are taking away the industrial park from him, give him something else. Rescue him and Durga Das from this farmer-suicide issue. Gangiri has apparently made sure that the finger of suspicion points to them. Lambodar tells me that they are both now responsible for this farmer's welfare. Is that so?'

'I am afraid so, sir,' Keyur chuckled. 'The collector is nobody's fool. And as I said before, Gangiri cannot be handled in the conventional way.'

'Well, the mess could have been avoided if the story had not leaked to the press,' Vaishnav said. 'How did a farmer from Mityala get in touch with this journalist here in Delhi?'

'Or, perhaps the journalist, Nazar Prabhakar, got in touch with Gangiri.' Keyur said, sounding worried. 'What should I do, sir?'

'You should learn to play the game a little, Keyur,' he answered. 'Plant the idea that Gangiri did all this to contest the assembly elections in six months' time. Say that he is looking for a candidature either with the DP or the opposition.' Vaishnav smiled. 'Nothing curtails a man's growing image like misplaced ambition.'

'You want him in politics!' Keyur was shocked.

Vaishnav shook his head. 'Just play on people's cynicism with goodness, the fatigue with hope. We are nervous about messiahs because they bring change. And history has taught us to beware selfish saviours.'

Keyur leaned forward in his chair, curious.

'Make sure that he is no longer the messiah,' Vaishnav said. 'Consider this your training; you will be doing this all your life in politics.'

Keyur nodded, understanding. 'This will provide a motive to Gangiri's actions, destroy his credibility.'

'I would not go that far,' Vaishnav said dryly, 'but it will make for a good story in tomorrow's newspapers.'

'Sure, sir,' Keyur said, smiling. 'I will take care of it.'

Vaishnav glanced at the clock. 'There is one more thing, Keyur. The permission you sought from the party president to speak to the press has been denied.'

Keyur's face fell and Vaishnav hurried to explain, unable to see the look of disappointment. 'You know the rules, no first-time MP speaks officially to the press unless the high command specifically directs it. I still forwarded your request to the president but he turned it down.'

Keyur nodded, knowing his silence would hurt his father the most.

'The DP is very democratic,' Vaishnav continued apologetically, 'and the next generation cannot emerge as leaders before the present one gets a chance. You must be patient with hierarchies.'

Keyur replied moodily, 'It is all right, sir. I only wanted to talk about Mityala and the farmer suicides.'

'Try to understand, Keyur,' Vaishnav lowered his voice. 'They know that, given a chance, you will talk your way out of this crisis beautifully. And they want you to be bogged down for a little while.'

Keyur was forced to smile at this. 'As you say, father. But Srinivas Murty must be enjoying the thrashing I am getting.'

'Murty, like almost everyone in the DP, expects that you will be busy making sure that this controversy dies down and is forgotten within six months before the scheduled assembly polls.'

'The same drill for the voters?' Keyur said playfully. 'Divert them, subvert them, convert them? Make promises that I cannot keep? That no one can keep? I think I can manage that.'

'This is not a joke, Keyur. The assembly elections will be seen as a referendum on you,' Vaishnav said, concerned. 'Murty argues that you may have the silver-spoon advantage, but it is no match to hard, ground realities. I tend to agree with him.'

'You always over-estimate that man because he rose up from the ranks, like you,' Keyur said, unable to restrain himself. 'Murty was only an ordinary state secretary till two years ago.'

'And today,' Vaishnav completed, 'he is in line to be the next party treasurer. That man could be sitting in my chair one day.'

'There are two such chairs and two such rooms in this party, sir.'

'*Now* you're thinking like me.' Vaishnav grinned. 'Go and get this sorted out. And, for god's sake, talk to your mother and tell her I didn't shout at you.'

Keyur promised, and left his father's office. He found a small group waiting near his SUV in the parking lot. Some lower-level party functionaries and non-party cronies were looking for a chance to speak to him on his way out. He patiently met them all, and then drove out of the gates. He liked to drive himself whenever he could, his aides and security personnel followed in another car.

Recalling his father's instructions, he reached for his cell phone. It was difficult for Keyur to recall exactly when he understood the power of guilt in his relationship with his parents. He learnt it, it was possible, from his mother's idea of protecting him from his father's criticism.

Exasperated, Vaishnav would sometimes say, 'Kamala, you do not understand... He must get used to the ways of the world outside. Not everything will be as sheltering and forgiving like his home.'

'And no one will ever vilify him the way you do either, Vaishnav,' she would retort. 'The boy feels you do not love him. Won't that knowledge weaken him when he is fighting the world?'

'That idiot should know it is out of love that I prepare him for life,' his father would say irritably. 'Don't meddle, Kamala. I know what I am doing. Let him take the knocks now and harden up for the real fight.'

'Perhaps all this preparation is unnecessary,' she would insist. 'Perhaps his life will be better than ours.'

'In that case, these lessons are part of my legacy to him,' his father would answer. 'He must inherit these along with the rest of it.'

Keyur knew his loving mother never understood that he did not mind inheriting the lessons. It was a small price to pay for the power he could see coming his way.

Stopping at a red light, Keyur glanced at his phone, smiling to himself. He pressed the call button and glanced up.

The road signs, bright in the noon sun, caught his attention. He could take the straight road and reach the MPs' club where he could invite Nazar Prabhakar for a meeting and plant the story about Gangiri.

Keyur wished his mother when she answered the phone and checked the time, deciding when to have the meeting with Nazar.

His large, dark eyes sparkled as he considered the road ahead. The story would take care of both Nazar and Gangiri.

There were two birds. And he had a stone.

The light turned green.

13

Monday afternoon, the MPs' club, New Delhi

The club was not very crowded that afternoon. Keyur watched through the open doors as Nazar entered and was escorted to the members' sitting room.

His grey-green suit was expensive, so was the narrow, brown tie. The smile at the doorman was polite, the nod to the manager cursory. As he stood up to receive Nazar, Keyur bleakly recalled their three previous meetings. Keyur smiled at him with misgivings and extended his hand, wishing he had an easier journalist to deal with.

'Good afternoon, Mr Prabhakar. I hope I did not inconvenience you by this sudden request for a meeting.'

Nazar smiled, his brown eyes warm with humour. Keyur had always found an irritating recklessness about Nazar, like the way he smiled now, indifferent to the correctness of it.

'It was the least I could do,' Nazar said, 'after the way I must have inconvenienced you in the last few days, Keyurji. Good afternoon.'

'We will get to that shortly.' Keyur smiled stiffly, just to acknowledge the quip.

Nazar found Keyur's charm phony and reacted to it by being unnecessarily direct. 'Could we cut to the chase, please? I have a long day.'

Surprising him, and as if expecting the response, Keyur just said, 'As you wish,' and gestured to the vacant armchair. They were in a corner, some distance away from the rest of the room.

'I would have liked,' Keyur began when they were settled, 'if you had talked to me before publishing your stories.'

'Very kind of you to tell me,' Nazar said, mocking. 'Now I know what you like.'

'Yes, thought you might want to remember that,' Keyur said, amused. 'The reality is a lot different from the stories. I could have issued a press statement explaining just how wrong you were. But I thought it would be much better if you were to present the facts yourself in your next story, revising what you had written in the past.'

Nazar waited as tea was served. Then he said, 'I would have checked the facts with you if I was writing a story about your involvement in the threat to the farmer, Gangiri Bhadra. But the story was not about you, Keyurji. Or was it?'

'It was about my constituency and you presented a wrong picture when I was right here in Delhi, available for comment.'

Nazar studied him sternly. 'Not that I need to explain anything to you, but I had no time. It was not merely a story; a farmer's life was hanging in balance.'

'Did you not think that I could have in some way mitigated the crisis?'

'Frankly, I did not.'

Keyur's eyes glinted in righteous anger. 'Why?'

'I don't have to answer to you.' Nazar sipped the tea.

'You don't?' Keyur was sardonic. 'You asked me widely

publicized questions about the way I work. I am asking similar questions about the way you work. Now, why are you exempt from taking any responsibility? What is the authenticity of your information, your stories? I want to know.'

Nazar could see that Keyur was exploring if he would divulge his source. He found it amusing that Keyur was trying to provoke him, having categorized him as a temperamental man given to outbursts, probably based on his behaviour that evening at his house.

'Do the answers shame you, Mr Prabhakar?' Keyur asked as Nazar remained silent. 'Or, is it because you were being prompted by the opposition parties to malign me? Let's have the truth.'

'You know, Keyurji.' He smiled. 'I have the answers to your questions and I am as answerable as you are. It is just that I am not answerable to you.'

'I am sure you do not believe that, Mr Prabhakar,' Keyur said, in a much lower voice.

'I can see why you called this meeting,' Nazar said thoughtfully. 'You wanted me to know what you like and don't like, and also what I should and shouldn't believe. And now I must leave. As I said, I have a long day.'

'I called this meeting to give you the facts, off the record,' Keyur snapped. 'It is clear from your stories that you do not have them.'

'All right. Tell me the facts off the record, but please make it brief.' Nazar settled back in the chair.

'Thanks, Mr Prabhakar,' Keyur was curt. 'As you know, there are serious reasons why the powerful among Mityala's villagers do not want farmer deaths to be validated as distress suicides eligible for compensation. Gangiri had become a target for moneylenders and those who support them, like Lambodar maha sarpanch, because the number of valid suicides began increasing only after his appointment to the district committee. The suicide toll made life and business difficult for these moneylenders, and they blamed Gangiri for turning the tide against them,' Keyur said.

Nazar heard him in silence, a little taken aback by his truthful explanation.

'If you remember, at the informal press meet at my residence, Lambodar was vehement in his disapproval of Gangiri and his "methods" of manipulating committee members.' Keyur paused. 'I found out that they were planning drastic measures against Gangiri. I called Lambodar for a discussion but he was in no mood to listen. I argued with him that of all the options before him, the most effective was to get Gangiri to resign from the committee. I argued that it would fix the problem without exposing anyone's role.'

Nazar was surprised. 'Are you admitting that it was your idea to force Gangiri to quit?'

'It was the only way to save his life,' Keyur said, acting helpless.

Nazar stared at him, stunned. Then he leaned forward in his chair. 'Keyurji, Gangiri was beaten up, his family was threatened and they almost lost their home and land. Had he not reported the matter to the collector, Gangiri's resignation would have been formalized and he would have been thrown out of Gopur.'

Keyur sounded sincere as he lied. 'I promise you, Mr Prabhakar, I would have never let it go that far. I was planning to warn the collector about the forced resignation.'

'You could have still done that, regardless.'

'I wanted to, but Lambodar said there had been some violence and the police could be involved,' Keyur said. 'I could have been implicated.'

Nazar watched him in silence, getting a little worried. He feared that he may have been wrong, what Keyur was saying was very possible.

Keyur said sadly, 'I realize I don't yet have the stature to control the two powerful men who were behind this. Lambodar wanted to teach Gangiri a lesson. Durga Das wanted his land. Both men wanted Gangiri out of Mityala.'

Keyur met Nazar's eyes frankly. 'I could not have controlled the details, Mr Prabhakar. I just made sure that the lives of Gangiri and his family were not in danger.'

'Would it not have been easier,' Nazar asked, puzzled, 'if you had involved the district administration, the police and your party organization to counter Lambodar and Durga Das?'

'And which of these, do you feel, is independent of people like Lambodar and Durga Das?'

Nazar had no answer to that.

'Perhaps I should have monitored the situation more closely,' Keyur continued after a moment, 'but that would have offended people. I could not risk that. In my short experience, I have learnt that my interventions do no good if local politicians resent them.'

Nazar uneasily admitted to himself that Keyur could be speaking honestly.

Keyur smiled. 'Now they are tamed, thanks to Gangiri. You see, the assembly elections are just six months away. It does not make political sense for Lambodar to antagonize farmers in this way. And even Durga Das will not take the chance of moving against a favourable dispensation like the DP, in which he has already invested heavily. Now, they have a great opportunity to improve their image by protecting Gangiri and his family. I am sure they will use it.'

Nazar smiled back. 'I wish you had spoken like this at the informal media briefing we had at your residence last week. It would have been most impressive.'

'It would have been murder!' Keyur laughed. 'Lambodar would have disowned me and the party would have lost all seven MLA seats in Mityala in the assembly polls.'

'Perhaps.' Nazar nodded. 'But this truth is much better than the excuses that were offered for the rising suicide numbers.'

'I confess, I was worried about Gangiri,' Keyur said reflectively, 'but I also believe that the increasing number of farmer suicides will force the government to act. Eventually I stand to gain, it is my constituency.'

Nazar chuckled, appreciating the candour. 'That is only if you don't implement Dr Daya's recommendations. As I said before, they are nothing but eyewash.'

Keyur nodded, amused. 'The truth is, and I could not mention it then, I absolutely agreed with what you said to his deputy. How can that lady, married to an industrialist exploiting Mityala's resources, talk about farmer suicides?'

Nazar, puzzled, asked, 'You mean Dr Jaichand?'

'Of course. Didn't you know? If she knows everything about Mityala, it is not just because of her research for the Centre's survey. Her information is also derived from Jaichand Industries,' said Keyur, shaking his head in disapproval. 'Sampat has run into environmental problems with the local people of Mityala. His wife is surveying the district so that he can fine-tune his strategy for the villages. Dr Daya told me so when informing me of his decision to include Mityala in this survey.'

Nazar looked away as if disinterested, but his brown eyes were cold. The expensive car made sense now. He should have checked up on her, but he had mistaken her concern for Gangiri as her credentials. And his own infatuation as evidence.

'Please do let me know if you need any help in Mityala,' Keyur was saying. 'Have you been able to talk to everyone? Is there anyone you need to get in touch with?'

'I am in touch with everyone,' Nazar answered, thanking him. 'Will you be visiting the district?'

'Not immediately. I have to be here for party work and Parliament sessions. I think the DP prefers me in Delhi and may let me go only once or twice before the elections.'

'Are all the incumbent MLAs in Mityala from the DP?'

'Six out of seven. It is a DP bastion now after we retained seats in two consecutive assembly elections,' Keyur said. 'The opposition is trying hard to oust us. I heard they have begun selecting candidates, and shortlisted some names. According to my party workers, one of them is Gangiri Bhadra. We have also shortlisted his name here at the DP. He has a good chance of—'

'You mean,' Nazar interrupted him, 'Gangiri Bhadra can contest elections as a candidate for the DP?'

'Why not?' Keyur looked suitably offended. 'Farmers can, you know.'

'Of course,' Nazar said, sheepishly.

Keyur continued, 'Naturally, Lambodar and the other

sarpanches sympathetic to the DP would have to be consulted before finalizing candidates for the polls. With the increasing number of farmer suicides, it has become a big issue in Mityala and every party wants to have one or two candidates who can represent the distressed families.

'The widows are usually not interested because they fear for the well-being of their children. And, usually, none of the relatives of the deceased farmers are popular enough to stand for elections.' Keyur shrugged. 'The exception this time is Gangiri Bhadra.'

Nazar was thoughtful. 'It is a good move.'

Keyur smiled. 'Just survival, Mr Prabhakar. He has managed to keep the limelight on himself and we need that in politics. Besides, I would rather have Gangiri with me than against me, don't you agree?'

They talked for a while, then someone came up to wish Keyur and he stood up. Nazar studied the man, liking his sense of style. The blue-grey tweed was neatly cut, the subdued blue shirt was open at the collar and the grey trousers settled nicely on black shoes. His glowing skin was the result of balanced moisturising and the speaking eyes, the result of a good night's sleep.

There were no traces of anxious fatigue. No rethink. No remorse. He played the game without any effort, Nazar thought as he assessed Keyur. It was his nature, it came easy.

The two parted with a much warmer handshake than when they had met. The twilight loitered between the trees on the lawns of Raj Path, looking for an excuse to stay longer. The night came over Delhi, calling it a day.

14

Tuesday morning, a farmhouse on the outskirts of Delhi

Haridas Tulsi had a rule. He never answered the phone before 8 a.m. He had broken this rule three times in his life because the calls came from the top office of the country. That morning, he had to break the rule for the fourth time for the same reason.

After a brief, polite conversation, he hung up and waited, looking out from the veranda of his farmhouse on the outskirts of Delhi. Birds were flying low over the vast, dew-covered lawns. The slant sunlight fought its valiant way through the white wool of the fog.

He smiled, happy that his newspaper's lead story had caught the attention of the nation's top leader. However many times it might have happened in the past, he loved it every time it happened again.

The phone rang once more within moments. After the initial greetings and mutual inquires of well-being, Vaishnav Kashinath briefly complained about the story.

Tulsi replied, 'The story is based on quotes, Vaishnavji. It is not an analysis. What can I do about it?'

'I leave that to you, Haridasji,' Vaishnav said politely. 'I only wanted to express my grief that your newspaper's correspondent has become a pawn in the rivalry between politicians. My son has stayed away and is above such tactics, but that has not improved the methods of his rivals.'

'If that turns out to be the case, you know very well that I shall not spare these rivals,' Tulsi said. 'We are known for our fairness, Vaishnavji, but we are also known for our fearlessness.'

'I compliment you on maintaining such high standards,' Vaishnav said, 'even during these turbulent times of check on illegal foreign investments in the media. As you know, not everyone could withstand such scrutiny.'

After a slight pause, Tulsi said, 'I heard it is a long list.'

'It is.'

'I believe,' Tulsi cleared his throat, 'that strong and uncompromising foundations are necessary to maintain strong and uncompromising standards of journalism.'

'You are an example for the country, even perhaps the world, on how that is done,' Vaishnav said, his voice respectful.

'You flatter me, Vaishnavji. There are many such examples. Just the other day, I was talking to someone from the Kiteman Trust. They support many businesses that have such uncompromising values. They too have a list.'

Vaishnav did not speak for a second. Then he said, 'I am sure there are others, but you must be an inspiration to all of them. Thank you for speaking to me, Haridasji.'

'Please call me any time you want,' Tulsi said, 'and you do not need to put in a word through the PMO for this. Besides, this is too trivial a case for madam to get involved.'

'As a matter of consideration to the workload of her office, I usually do not share details of every case,' Vaishnav said, 'nor do you, I know.'

'Of course. Besides, with your experience and my relationships across parties, there is hardly any crisis we cannot handle.'

'Hardly. May I wish you a great day? As always, I shall look forward to reading your newspaper. Namaskar.'

'Namaskar and thank you.'

Tulsi hung up and glanced once again at the lawns. The birds had now segregated into three groups of doves, sparrows and mynahs. They restlessly paced the paved paths, their tail feathers touching the ground once in a while, waiting for the sun to rise higher and shine on food chains.

A scrutiny of who funded his newspaper and from which country would destroy him, Tulsi knew. But a scrutiny of the Kiteman Trust would reveal Kashinath's extensive investments abroad, which would destroy *him*.

Tulsi sipped his morning cup of tea and, like the birds, glanced at the sun, waiting for it to rise higher and shine on zero-sum games.

❖

Nazar did not receive any calls that morning and he made none. He picked up his newspaper first from the pile next to his bed and, out of habit, read his own story first. Every story read differently in print than on a computer screen. Besides, it was the moment a journalist waited for, the name in print, the byline on a story. To be judged by strangers, to be anxious and eager to be judged by the world.

Mandip was right, the story looked better with Keyur's photograph alongside.

❖

Keyur answered every call he received that morning, but made none. He knew he could not make any of the calls he really wanted to.

First, he wanted to call Lambodar and ask him what was the use of him being a maha sarpanch if he could not control even one villager in his district.

Second, he wanted to know from the collector of Mityala if members of the district suicide committee had nothing better to do than make statements in the press for the benefit of Nazar Prabhakar. Third, he wanted to call Nazar and compliment him on the perfect charade at their last meeting which had thoroughly fooled him.

Ironically, Keyur's demand for permission to speak to the press was granted that day by the party president. He was asked to hold a press conference and own up to the ideas published in the news story, before the opposition forced him to do so.

Keyur was deeply distressed by the way he was being pushed around by the DP leadership that morning. He patiently put up with his father's anxious advice on how to handle the press conference.

Keyur had also briefed him about the meeting with Nazar. Vaishnav, who had talked to Nazar's boss, Haridas Tulsi, said there would be no retraction, apology, or clarification of the story in the next day's paper.

Vaishnav then advised Keyur to be prepared for sharp criticism and action from the DP as Srinivas Murty had begun raising questions about 'a change in leadership' in the district to improve poll prospects, based on Nazar's stories.

The more he thought of Nazar's story, the more Keyur

realized he actually liked Nazar's move, his bold and fearless response to his own strategy to attribute political motives to Gangiri's campaign.

The more he thought of Nazar's story, the more Keyur yearned for an equalizer in the game.

Mityala MP Should Quit if Farmer Suicides Continue: Demand Voters, Seek Relief Measures

by Nazar Prabhakar

New Delhi: Prominent citizens of Mityala constituency have demanded the resignation of their elected representative, Keyur Kashinath, from Parliament if farmer suicides continue in the constituency. They have called for a fresh election to the Parliamentary seat to be held along with the assembly elections scheduled in six months.

Many sections of the people, especially farmers, are criticizing the DP government for neglecting the issues that contribute to agricultural distress and an increasing number of suicides in Mityala.

Aware of these sentiments, Kashinath is offering Democratic Party candidature in the coming assembly elections to local people as a way of repairing the frayed patience of the voters. However, it is learnt that his recent proposal to offer a party ticket to contest polls was turned down by Gopur villager, Gangiri Bhadra, the brother of a farmer who committed suicide due to debt-related distress.

The high-profile MP, who was elected with much hope, may have a tough time disproving charges of deliberate neglect of farmers for the benefit of moneylenders and local politicians.

Two members of the district committee on suicides,

Chief Sarpanch Gauri Shanker and farmer Sitabai, confirmed to this newspaper that coercion has been used by DP sympathizers to keep the distress suicide numbers low by declaring them as suicides due to reasons other than agricultural debt.

Speaking on phone from village Chira in Mityala district, Gauri Shanker said, 'Some of us have been threatened by representatives of Chief Sarpanch Lambodar and a major moneylender, Durga Das. Some of us are being discredited, saying we want assembly election tickets from the DP. Some of us have even faced risk to life.

'In my long experience as sarpanch, and now maha sarpanch, I have never seen politics slide down to this level. We want to know if the MP Keyur Kashinath has the moral strength to vow that he will step down if one more farmer commits suicide. It will send the right message of accountability across the rank and file and clean up the system,' Gauri Shanker added.

Sitabai from village Karn, also a member of the committee, said, 'Moneylenders are set to gain if farmer suicides are not declared distress suicides eligible for compensation, as the debt-burdened widows have no option but to give up their agricultural lands which had been pledged for loans.'

She also decries the absence of any redressal mechanism which was promised during the elections by the first-time MP. 'No one has even seen Keyur Kashinath since the election day. And now, we do not want to see him either. We want a new MP who can raise our voice in Parliament.'

Gangiri Bhadra made a series of suggestions that could help considerably in bringing down farmer suicide figures.

'I speak only for Mityala and only as a farmer,' Bhadra said, clarifying that it was up to Mr Kashinath to find the merit, if any, in his suggestions. 'First, the repayment of both formal and informal loans taken by farmers holding five to ten acres of land in Mityala can be postponed by one year, without affecting their eligibility for getting fresh loans for the new crop. This will break the loan-debt-repayment cycle and, hopefully, help the defaulters clear their dues.

'Secondly, a combined list of defaulters from the bank and private moneylenders should be compiled. Those who have been on the list for more than two years must be supported through welfare schemes. This will also help in ascertaining the real causes for the farmers' financial troubles,' Bhadra said.

He felt that farm input dealers are central to a farmer's plans as they not only provide the seeds, fertilizers, and pesticide but, in most cases, also double up as agriculture extension agents, giving advice on how to use the particular input for the crop.

'A failure-proof guarantee on farm inputs from dealers should be made mandatory so that they do not sell low-quality supplies. For instance, if seeds are sold on the guarantee that they would need only three sprays of pesticides, then the input dealer must pay for any additional sprays that the crop may require. The extra expense would then be subtracted by the farmers while repaying the dealers who loaned the inputs.'

It is well known that banks face a repayment crisis in villages. Bhadra suggested that banks incentivize repayment by restructuring loans in a way that if the first instalment is cleared within the stipulated time, then there can be a rebate in interest on the second, and so on.

Recovery agents and their methods have emerged as a major cause for suicides by farmers who cannot deal with the humiliation. On that issue, Bhadra said, 'It should be made a law that recovery agents visit households only with the permission of the panchayat and in the presence of witnesses.'

Speaking from personal experience, Bhadra sought that every family in suicide-prone districts like Mityala be provided with counselling about poisons like organo-phosphate pesticides and a medical kit to deal with poisoning. He also felt that both the state and private moneylenders must share the burden of education of the children of the deceased farmers.

Keyur Kashinath, it must be noted, is the son of Vaishnav Kashinath who is known for his decision to quit his post as a minister in the central government, taking responsibility for a mishap that had cost lives. It is, perhaps, natural that such values are also expected from his son by his constituents.

❀

That noon, on his father's advice, Keyur tried to keep it simple and short at the press conference.

'I am travelling to Mityala later today,' Keyur said, looking around at the journalists gathered in the media briefing room at the DP headquarters.

'As I may not be available to the Delhi press for some time, I am here to make a brief statement. Then I shall answer your questions,' he smiled, 'to the best of my ability.'

There were condescending smiles in response, but nothing more. The briefing room windows were sealed for effective air-conditioning during summer. As a result, when the room was crowded, like today, ceiling fans had to be switched on for ventilation even in winter.

Keyur shared the dais with the party spokesperson who introduced him to the press. In front of them were ten rows of chairs, with twenty chairs each. Nazar sat in the middle row, resolved not to ask questions unless absolutely required.

Keyur glanced at the television cameras stationed at the back of the room. 'One media report today listed a series of relief measures proposed by the farmers of Mityala to address farm distress,' Keyur said, starting directly, as suggested by Vaishnav. 'Lack of irrigation, seed incompatibility and exposure to volatile markets have added to debt in rural areas. Despite this, farmers have enhanced farm productivity in the country facing high risks and taking loans at exorbitant rates of interest.'

More journalists walked into the room, but had to remain standing as there was no space left to sit.

'The financial inclusion of poor farmers should remain the burden of the state,' Keyur continued, speaking without referring to his notes. 'I agree with the farmers of Mityala that banks have been battling crises in villages. The flaw lies in the expectations of profitability from individual branches of banks. Efforts are on to correct this by merging such branches from one or more districts into a single, composite unit.'

There was complete silence in the hall, except for the unseasonal sound of the fans whirring overhead.

'The farmers are also right in highlighting their dependence on farm-input dealers. They absolutely cannot deal single-handedly with so many factors, like modern inputs, techniques, traders, prices, finance and other such aspects. I will be collaborating with relevant think tanks to finalize a model for providing micro-planners in my constituency so that farmers receive advice that is tailored to their needs, instead of the generalized suggestions they presently get from various agencies.

'Now.' He leaned forward. 'If there are any questions, I shall try and answer them.'

'Why did it take so long for you to wake up to this crisis?' came the first question from a senior journalist in the front row.

'I have been around for only eight months, sir,' Keyur answered cautiously. 'But even then, I agree that there should have been no delay in dealing with this crisis.'

'Is all this posturing aimed at the assembly elections in the state? You are expected to face a drubbing this time,' asked another journalist.

Keyur was forced to, once again, recall his father's warning that this press conference would be different from the chaperoned, informal meets he held in his backyard. 'I believe it is too early to decide who will get a drubbing,' he said, 'but I shall keep it in mind and work doubly hard.'

As the journalists sensed the tutored answers, the questions became harder.

'There were reports that you have never visited Mityala since you won the election,' asked a journalist from the Hindi media. 'Is it because you were too busy with your social life in Delhi and Mumbai?'

Keyur's hurt expression amused Nazar. Everyone could read him like a book.

'I don't know from where these reports originate! I have not visited Mityala only because I was struggling with Parliament schedules and organizational demands. I do not know how other MPs do it, but it is a gruelling task.'

'But you are not a first-generation politician; you are expected to know how to behave. Doesn't your father advise you?'

Keyur navigated the shoals uncertainly. 'He does, when I ask him for advice,' he answered.

Nazar glanced around, wondering who would ask the question of the day.

It came soon. 'There have been news stories that DP men threatened members of the district suicide committee against exposing farmer suicide numbers. Were you involved in this?' asked a presswoman.

'Of course not!' Keyur frowned, pretending to be shocked by the question. 'I am in touch with the Mityala collector who is ascertaining the identity of the people behind the threats. Strict action will be taken against the culprits so that no one ever tries suppressing the voice of truth again.'

'Are you not alarmed by the increasing numbers of farmer suicides in your constituency?' she asked.

Nazar glanced at Keyur, waiting.

Keyur said, carefully, 'I am deeply concerned, but that is no reason for gagging the district suicide committee.'

'There are demands that you should resign, taking responsibility for the toll,' the same journalist pointed out.

'I am ready to resign today, madam,' Keyur said gently, 'if it can prevent the death of a single farmer, a single human being, not just in Mityala, but anywhere in the country.'

That was a good reply, there was silence for a moment.

'Should we take that as an offer of resignation?' someone asked from the back, making mischief. There were chuckles, but there was also silence as everyone waited to see how Keyur handled the double-edged question.

Keyur was at a loss for an answer, rattled by the general irreverence. He was an MP, he thought a little angrily, he'd won an election, polled thousands of votes. How could anyone—and so what if they were from the press—question him as if he were a nobody?

Noticing his unease, the party spokesperson next to him whispered something in Keyur's ear. He thanked the spokesperson and answered the question. 'The procedure for resignation is laid out in the party rules and a press conference is not mentioned as the venue for it.'

There was now laughter.

'Perhaps, you should quit and make way for farmers like Mr Gangiri Bhadra who know what it is like to live amid farm distress and farmer suicides,' remarked a journalist from a magazine.

Keyur's face was drawn. He had lied to Nazar that the DP could offer the candidacy for an assembly seat to Gangiri. He had made it up just to sow the seed of doubt about Gangiri's motives in Nazar's mind. Now, after Nazar's story made it public, he had no choice but to stay with the lie.

'I have already recommended Mr Bhadra's name to the selection panel of the DP that considers candidates for assembly elections. It is for the party leadership to decide if he should contest for assembly or Parliament.' The spokesperson once again whispered something to Keyur. Keyur nodded, smiling at him, then turned towards the gathering. 'Besides, it is my duty to honour the verdict of the people who elected me.'

The rescue led to a pause as journalists searched for more incisive questions.

'I have a question,' Nazar said, waiting as Keyur searched for him among the faces. There was a little buzz as journalists too looked around to locate Nazar. Everyone knew that the press conference had been called due to Nazar's stories.

'Why do you think the farmers of Mityala refused the DP candidacy?'

Keyur stared at Nazar, realizing it was impossible to answer that. He knew that was why Nazar asked it, to expose the lie. He felt cornered and fought back desperately.

'Naturally, I cannot answer that. You would have to ask the farmers of Mityala.'

'Could it be because the farmers of Mityala have no political ambitions?'

'Yes, it is possible, but as I said, you need to...'

'Or perhaps they are only fighting for their survival and justice for their dead.'

Keyur shrugged, his eyes hardening. 'Take my advice, travel to Mityala and—'

'And what if they had accepted the offer to be candidates for the DP in the forthcoming elections?' Nazar asked, his voice flat, toneless. 'Would it have proved that the farmers of Mityala are raising these issues in the hope of personal political gain?'

The silence in the packed briefing room was absolute. The party spokesperson glanced at Keyur, waiting for him to give the stock reply. The matter now concerned the party, not just Keyur.

As Keyur failed to answer, the spokesperson took over. 'The DP was not trying to malign the farmers or assign political motives to their struggle. I am not aware if the DP has formally chosen candidates or even begun the process yet.'

The pens flew and pages turned as the journalists made notes at the speed of light. After duly noting the clarification by the DP, Nazar requested for one last question for Keyur.

'If the DP was not aware of it, and the farmers were not interested, why did you make the proposed offer known to the press?'

Keyur looked at Nazar in silence, knowing the question had already done the damage. The answer was immaterial.

It was now all in the open before the waiting cameras and the open notebooks. He shook his head, losing patience, and said he had no comment.

The spokesperson moved on to another journalist for a question.

'Will you resign, like your father had, and take responsibility for the deaths that took place under your watch?'

'That was him,' Keyur managed with some restraint. 'This is me.'

'Are you saying you are better than him?' one of the backbenchers asked.

Even the spokesperson turned to Keyur, waiting for the answer. One of the many loyalists of Vaishnav, the spokesperson had been handpicked for the press conference. But even he was beginning to doubt Keyur.

'No, I am not *better* than him,' Keyur said, forgivingly. 'But I am better than all those people who sit on the fringes, and criticize politics and the political class.'

His face was stiff with control. 'You criticize me for not solving problems of the farmers. But you don't appreciate the fact that I am, at least, trying.'

'That is your job, Keyurji,' someone said.

'Then let me do my job!' Keyur snapped. 'Remember that I am not an upstart who has to learn on the job. I have inherited this power; I know what to do with it.'

There was a surprised murmur in the gathering. Nazar could sense questions being furiously revised in the minds of the journalists.

A print journalist said, 'My colleague here asked a question before which went unanswered.'

Keyur waited, trying to focus, his throat parched.

'How are you, Keyur, better qualified than the local people to represent Mityala?' she asked.

Better qualified? Keyur thought to himself impatiently. *Who can be better qualified than the man chosen by the people to represent them? And who could the people choose but him? What a stupid question!*

Keyur felt the weight of every eye, every camera, focused on his face. He wanted to flinch, he wanted to ask for help, he wanted to reach for the glass of water on the table.

He felt himself loosening up, giving in to the stress, answering randomly. 'Then they should not have elected me...They had the choice, there were local leaders contesting the same election as I was. Why did they lose? Why did the people elect me?

'Because it is *me*, you see?' Keyur said with emphasis. 'Yes, I may have an unfair advantage because of my birth, but it is to the advantage of the people and they know it.'

The journalists turned instinctively to check if the cameramen at the back of the room were getting every word.

'Why else do sons of politicians win elections most of the time?' Keyur asked, his eyes mocking. 'People believe we will make better leaders because we are born into political families and into power. They know we can handle it better. And we have.'

A few journalists stopped writing just to study the expression on Keyur's face, a rare mix of fear and arrogance.

'I am sorry but I won the election,' Keyur concluded, adding, 'I can't help it if people trust me, even if you do not.'

'It was a winning seat,' a senior journalist calmly pointed out. 'That is how you won, despite having never visited Mityala before.'

'That is complete nonsense!' Keyur snapped, the hot lights that fell in his eyes burned into his mind, driving him slowly, inexorably, out of control. 'I would have won from anywhere in the country, whether the seat was winning or losing. That is what I was trying to explain to you.'

There was a stunned silence, the spokesperson frowned at Keyur.

'Do you believe you are acceptable as a leader across this country?' the journalist asked.

Nazar watched Keyur's flushed, enraged face. He was sure Keyur must have already made it to the headlines across channels.

'I am not saying that...' Keyur struggled to monitor his words, the waiting silence choking him. 'I am here because the voters love to have someone they are familiar with. It is a continuity of collusion, deals of the past...'

There was a loud murmur among the gathered journalists. The spokesperson urgently whispered to Keyur and declared the press conference over. This fuelled Keyur's anger further as he staggered to his feet, finally letting go of his fury at the way he had been treated by the party since that morning.

The journalists too were on their feet, protesting to the spokesperson that they still had questions they wanted to ask.

'Should the doors of the DP be closed to grass-root politicians?'

'Will you pass on your political clout as inheritance to your children, Keyurji?'

Keyur had turned to leave when one of the questions stopped him.

'What position of power are you aiming at, Mr Kashinath?'

'Aiming at?' he repeated, livid. 'How can you ask me that?'

Noticing the sharpness of his tone, the spokesperson urged him to leave the dais but Keyur paid no heed. 'I may want to serve the common people of this country.' Keyur sneered. 'But that does not make *me* common!'

There was now a sudden silence in the room.

'I do not have to chase positions of power,' Keyur said stiffly. 'I was born to the positions of power. Remember that when you ask me questions about—'

The spokesperson cordially interrupted him but unceremoniously escorted him out of the briefing room.

The journalists sprang into action, television crews followed Keyur into the party office, photographers squeezed in between people to get candid pictures, doors were thrown open and a whiff of fresh air entered the room.

Nazar sat for a long moment in his chair in the middle row, Keyur's words ringing back in his ears.

I was born to the positions of power...

Nazar wondered about the divine right to rule.

I am sorry but I won the election...

He worried about the people's right to rule.

15

Tuesday afternoon, the Centre for Contemporary Societies, New Delhi

The misty afternoon was slipping away from in-between the weak rays of the sun. The sky was the colour of indecision and doubt, the ground beneath Nazar's feet soft with sentiment.

Nazar stood for a moment near his car in the parking lot outside the Centre. He leaned on it, frowning up at the reluctant sun, knowing things he wished he was innocent of. Videhi made him feel the way he must make the women in his life feel. No fact, no risk, no one could chase him away. Except her.

He had never been at these crossroads before. He could understand her, misunderstand her, know her, forget her. A sign of which road he should take had to come from her. That was why he was at the Centre, wishing he knew much less than he did. And hoping she knew as much as him.

He found her working with the survey team, poring over books and reports piled on the desk. He apologized for disturbing them, smiling a greeting at everyone. His greetings were returned by a short man with tired eyes and a lady wearing glasses. A bearded man at the computer did not even look up. Videhi smiled in surprise, then, after looking around at the crowded room, gestured towards the open garden door.

Nazar heard her in silence as she said she had been meaning to call him but found herself submerged in work. She appreciated his stories in the newspaper and complimented him, especially on the story of the day.

He thanked her politely, thinking that the saffron yellow saree she wore compensated for the lost sunlight.

'Why did you lie to me?' he then asked, studying the dark eyes that were too proud to escape his.

'I thought you would misunderstand me.'

I would have, he thought. 'So what if I had?'

'I did not want that to happen.' *And you know why*, she thought.

'Why?' *I want to hear you say it.*

'I wanted to keep Sampat's name out of this controversy.' *And keep you from knowing I am married.*

'It is still out.' *And it would have made no difference.*

She did not speak.

Nazar reached for his phone. 'Gangiri wanted to thank you.' He paused, scrolling for the number. 'I told him about you a short while ago.'

'What about me?'

'Nothing about your family.'

'Then what?'

'Just that you tracked him down in Gopur.'

'And?'

'That you helped me warn him.'

She waited in silence.

'That you cannot be trusted,' he said, 'or depended upon.'

'Was that all?'

'That you are not truthful about critical things.'

'Was it critical?'

'You tell me, you are the one who likes the snares.'

She smiled, recalling their first conversation.

He dialled the number and handed her the phone. 'Remember,' he warned, 'just Videhi.'

She nodded and heard a voice introduce himself on the phone in elegant Hindi. 'I am so grateful to you, Videhiji, for taking the trouble...'

'Please,' she interrupted him hurriedly, 'tell us what can we do to help? Do you feel your family is secure now?'

He said it was and explained to her the various measures that Lambodar and Durga Das had taken to keep a close watch on him.

She smiled when he said, 'It is my belief, Videhiji, that I will have to work very hard to do anything without either of them finding out. Their henchmen are everywhere.'

'This sounds like a great time to show them that you are not manipulating the members of the committee, as Lambodar claimed.'

He was silent for a moment. 'I had not thought of that. But I still need to investigate the agriculture officer of the district,' he said in a concerned voice. 'He must know the truth about the suicides, but he always sides with Lambodar and Durga Das on apatra verdicts. I am sure he must be under some pressure to do so and it is worth finding out why. However, I would give away the sources of my information against the AO if I meet them now.'

'Can't someone else in the village help you with the investigation?' she asked.

'It is not that easy to find someone who can afford to

make such powerful enemies,' he said, adding in English, 'You see, education seems to give me a false sense of security that I may know more than others. I cannot expect others to be this foolish.'

'One used to be enough,' she said.

'Hundreds and thousands are not enough, going by the rising number of farmer suicides,' he said grimly. 'But I am driven by the idea of reclaiming the dignity of the farmers who died like my brother. And I cannot fail because I have staked the only thing my brother valued in his brief lifetime, the happiness of his children.'

'Perhaps you can give instructions on what needs to be done and someone can follow up without the henchmen ever finding out.'

'No, no one can meet me without the world getting to know.'

'Surely you can brief the person on the phone?'

'Of course, that is possible,' he said. 'But how do I find someone willing to help me here?'

'I shall find someone for you,' she said.

'Videhiji, you have already done so much for me. I can't let you do more.'

'Please don't embarrass me,' she said. 'I hope you don't have a problem with me helping you.'

'On the contrary, I am grateful that—'

She interrupted. 'My husband owns the cement plant in Chira village, Gangiriji. The one that is in trouble with local villagers.'

There was again a long silence. 'Then I am doubly grateful to you for helping me, Videhiji.'

'It is I who should be grateful to you for accepting my help,' she said in a constrained tone.

'There is no need. Just because one must live by the destiny set by others, it need not become one's identity,' he said. 'I know something about that.'

The words made her smile. She glanced at Nazar who was watching her. 'I will have someone call you and you can instruct him on what needs to be done. The person will be an employee of Jaichand Industries, like the person who tracked you down and gave you this phone.'

He said, 'I hope a record is being kept of the phone bills. I will pay them one day.'

'Naturally,' she lied. 'And where do you want the investigation of the AO to begin?'

'With his barber.'

Later, Nazar spoke to Gangiri, 'Please keep it a secret that Videhiji is helping you.'

Gangiri agreed. 'What is being planned next for Mityala?'

'Keyur's visit,' Nazar said, explaining the story he had written and the developments which followed.

Nazar said hesitantly, 'I am going to say something now which may anger you, Gangiriji, but I don't care.'

'Neither do I,' he said, chuckling. 'What is it?'

'I want to send you some money,' Nazar said. 'I know this sounds wrong, but you and your family must somehow survive till the next harvest.'

'This is very kind of you, Nazarji,' Gangiri said softly. 'But don't you think it sets the wrong precedent? If I take any help from you, I would prove to the people of these desperate villages that this fight cannot be fought by poor, common farmers.'

'Yes, but what about the two little children, your sister-in-law?'

Gangiri's voice was hollow. 'They pay for my ethics, for my decisions, with their tears.'

They were both silent for a moment. Then Gangiri said, 'I wish I could meet you. And Videhiji.'

Nazar smiled. 'I wish the same.'

Nazar hung up and glanced at Videhi standing a few paces away near the flagstones bordering the garden.

'I will ask the Mityala office to arrange for researchers and give them Gangiri's cell number,' she said. 'Can you please check with him tonight if they have made contact and let me know?'

He nodded, then stood looking at her for a moment. She raised her eyebrows, questioningly.

'You are a kind woman, Dr Jaichand.'

'Mr Prabhakar,' she replied. 'It is as you said, just Videhi.'

'And just Nazar?' He smiled.

'No.' She smiled back. 'Not just Nazar.'

Nazar left the Centre promising to call Videhi after talking to Gangiri in the evening. On the way to an appointment in central Delhi, all through that appointment and later in his office, he kept thinking about her. What was her life like, the life of which she left no evidence in her office? What was Sampat Jaichand like, the man she would not betray? A brief research on the Internet gave him general facts which were not enough even to forget her.

Mandip was demure for a change, appearing as if he were in awe of the splash that Nazar's story had made. Nazar knew better than that.

'Great job, Nazar!' he said for the fifteenth time. 'I have always been against the privileged few who land the best opportunities to get more privileges, only to then abuse them.'

Nazar nodded, and reached for a cookie on the table. They were at the daily editorial meeting where the stories for the day were being decided. Also present were men and women in charge of city reporting, the national news, the news desk, the photo section, the edit page, sports and business sections, and advertisements. Besides Nazar, the two other associate editors were also present.

'Keyur Kashinath's press conference has been playing on television since morning,' Mandip said, discussing the page-one layout, 'so the readers will expect something more in tomorrow's newspaper. What special stories do we have up until now?'

Nazar glanced around with interest. He did not know there were others working on the story.

'We have four special stories,' said the grey-haired chief of the national bureau. 'The first story is based on reactions from the children of politicians within the DP and their view on what Keyur said. None of the sons and daughters of politicians, some of whom are also MPs, found anything wrong with his views. Instead, they blamed the press for cornering him and charged the media for being partisan.'

The bureau chief spoke in an unemotional voice that was modulated by years of covering news under all kinds of circumstances.

'Second, we have interviewed a few politicians from the opposition parties whose children are in politics. They, naturally, found Keyur's behaviour most objectionable.' He smiled wryly. 'They insisted that they would have had their children quit politics if they had behaved so badly in public.

'Third, we have the reaction from the streets on what people think of the children of politicians in power. Fourth,' the bureau chief continued, 'we have a story on Keyur's claim of winning elections from any constituency in the country. As it turns out, the DP had a "voters' mood" survey conducted on its prospects ahead of the elections last year. It was found that voters in ten constituencies of the country would have overwhelmingly supported any candidate from the DP. Mityala was one of them.'

The bureau chief then leaned back in his chair. 'As I see it, Mandip, none of these stories should be the lead story of tomorrow's newspaper. Our main story has to be written by Nazar.'

There was general agreement till Mandip briefly said, 'It will depend on what Nazar has to write.'

Nazar reached for another cookie, wanting to prolong the match. 'Any suggestions?'

The bureau chief remained silent. The news editor, a middle-aged lady, said, 'Well, the question on everyone's mind is what should the measure of a politician's acceptability be.'

'I would not write a story to decide a politician's acceptability,' Nazar said. 'I would vote.'

The young photo editor objected. 'Well, as a voter, the only way I get to judge politicians is by their conduct. And I have dozens of photos of each of these scions driving around in the world's most expensive cars, wearing the most expensive watches, using the most expensive pens and living the most expensive lives.

'In a country where thirty-seven per cent of the population lives below poverty line, I expect politicians to show a little more restraint,' he added.

'Do you mean restraint or guilt?' Nazar asked. 'And if the rich give up their expensive lives, will it save the poor?'

Before the photo editor could answer, Mandip intervened. 'We measure our leaders by strict values. Among other things, we expect them not to give in to the temptations of power and wealth like the rest of us. We believe that such conduct makes them worthy of our trust, our respect and, finally, our vote. Keyur Kashinath made news today because he showed that he gives in to all kinds of temptations, like a spoilt son of any powerful and rich man,' Mandip said, adding after a pause, 'Nazar would know what I am talking about.'

'You mean the temptation to comment on things we know nothing about?' Nazar asked. 'No, I don't know anything about that.'

The bureau chief chuckled, the rest smiled discreetly.

Mandip decided to let it pass. 'What is your story for the day?' he asked a little tersely.

'I was thinking of the aftermath.' Nazar put the teacup down. 'The DP is bound to go into fire-fighting mode. It would be interesting to report the manoeuvres by various party factions. After all, the contest is now between Vaishnav Kashinath and the rest.'

'If by the "rest" you mean the likes of Srinivas Murty,' Mandip smiled, mocking, 'you will have to be sure of your facts. He is famously reticent about speaking to the press and never gives away any story.'

Nazar waited for a few seconds, then said, 'He is coming to meet me here at seven.'

Mandip looked away, his smile fading.

❖

At 7 p.m., the receptionist called Nazar to inform him that Srinivas Murty had arrived. He was led up to the seventh floor and walked the length of the newsroom to Nazar's cabin accompanied by two associates. Every eye that was not glued to a computer screen was turned to him. It was impossible not to notice Srinivas Murty in a room, even in one as long, cavernous and crowded as this. Like with most naturally charismatic people, it was difficult to find the reason for his appeal.

Srinivas Murty and Nazar met cordially, briefly pondered how long it had been since they met last and settled for tea instead of coffee. Nazar knew one of the associates to be a district president and they chatted about life in the lower rungs of the DP organization.

Nazar noticed that when Srinivas's associates spoke, the most avid and interested listener was Srinivas himself. He paid full attention to his men as they answered Nazar's questions. It made his men feel good that the MP himself gave such importance to them in the presence of others. They waited till Nazar's questions ended and then politely excused themselves, saying they would be at the reception downstairs. Srinivas thanked them and waited for them to leave.

Then he turned to Nazar and smiled. He was the same age as Keyur, a fact widely known because of the constant contest between the two. Srinivas had the look of a man contemptuous of any distinction that was not earned and justified. His clothes, a cotton shirt and trousers, were undistinguished; the thick brown jacket he wore sagged at the pockets; the shoes were all-weather; the skin uncared for. But his presence was powerful, his posture erect, his movements agile, and his eyes knowing.

'You have hung Keyur out to dry,' he said with characteristic candour. 'I compliment you.'

'Thanks.' Nazar smiled. 'But it was not done for your benefit.'

'Things done without an agenda can benefit everyone,' he said. 'Including me.'

Nazar mulled that for a moment, then nodded. 'I guess you are right.' He paused. 'I don't think I have asked you before, but I should have, Srinivasji. Why do you oppose Keyur?'

Srinivas did not answer immediately, but his eyes became serious. He then said, 'Force of habit.'

Nazar was surprised.

'For a moment, forget about Keyur,' Srinivas requested, 'and just consider my life. I was born into a middle-class family. My father was an accountant and my mother an instructor at a tailoring school. There were enough brothers and sisters, enough arguments against taking off on a tangent into politics instead of finding a paying job. But I was determined. College politics got me into the youth wing of the DP and I worked my way up.

'I encountered the sons and daughters of local politicians at every level of the organization,' Srinivas said matter-of-factly. 'I patiently fought my way through, and each face-off taught me that I must fight doubly hard to get what these children were born with, the right to power.

'But you see, Nazarji.' Srinivas smiled. 'The greatness of democracy is that elections cannot always be won on the basis of pedigree. You need real politicians to win them for you. That is my profile now. I have no choice but to oppose Keyur, to answer your question.'

'However, you don't want your habit to become your identity,' Nazar said.

'Exactly,' Srinivas said appreciatively. 'Though I don't mind it today, of course. Keyur put on a great show.'

After a moment's silence, he continued, 'I am here on instructions from my party. I need some details about your stories.'

'All the details you need, you will find in the stories.'

'We just want to know if someone from the opposition parties has been helping you with the stories.'

'Opposition parties?' Nazar frowned. 'So you think this story is only political? What difference does it make to me which party is in power if it does not care that people in this country prefer death instead of a life of penury?'

'I am sorry, I did not mean to imply that you were politically motivated,' Srinivas said intently. 'The DP's only concern is to check if this campaign has any political backing.'

Nazar was still frowning.

Srinivas measured him for a long moment, then said, 'You know how it works, Nazarji, we don't want to walk into the wrong wedding.'

Nazar knew how it worked, the DP would not support issues raised by opposition parties, however pertinent they may be. The same was true for the opposition.

He said, 'You make me hate Delhi,'

Srinivas asked carefully, 'Because I am right?'

Nazar shook his head, exasperated. 'No, Srinivasji. My stories have no political backers. The tip off for the story was from a personal friend and I followed my own leads.'

'Thanks,' Srinivas said, relieved. 'I hope you understand that I had to know this directly from you.'

'What does the DP plan to do?' Nazar asked, adding curtly, 'I will write about it in the newspaper so please be factual.'

'Off the record, the DP is contemplating issuing a show-cause notice to Keyur, asking for an explanation for the increasing number of suicides in his constituency,' Srinivas said. 'The DP's short-term concern is to save face and contain damage.'

'And the long-term concern?'

'To keep Keyur out of the limelight.'

'That is where you come in?'

Srinivas smiled.

16

Wednesday, the government guest house, Civil Lines, Mityala town, Mityala district

The parking lot outside the government guest house in Mityala was choked with vehicles that morning. Most of the vehicles had plaques on the fenders declaring, in the local language, the designation of the owner. In most situations, this worked better than a visiting card. The plaques gathered there included politicians of the DP who served on the municipal councils, district committees, village panchayats and gram sabhas. There were MLAs, too, but their vehicles were parked inside the gates.

The visitors were distributed into three rings of importance. The outermost ring included official drivers and their associates who hung about their vehicles in the parking lot, exchanging informal intelligence reports about their bosses in the age-old tradition of their profession. The middle ring, contained in the beautiful lawns of the guest house, comprised aides, assistants and admirers. A neighbourhood kiosk sent a few boys with tea kettles, disposable cups and glucose biscuits to sell among the waiting people.

The third and innermost ring was made up of the men and women themselves, the people who occupied important positions in the local government at the district level. Out of the fifty who had arrived in the morning, thirty-seven were still packed into the dining hall of the guest house.

Every available chair in the small guest house was drawn into the long hall and arranged along the walls. Where the chairs were laid against the open windows, chilly draughts touched the waiting leaders on the neck like the edge of a blade, prompting them to wrap their shawls closer. As the dining hall was not designed to hold more than twenty people, they had to sit quite close to each other.

While there was occasional chatter, there was an overall silence in the packed hall which would have been intriguing to an outsider, especially someone who was not a politician. For, even though these thirty-seven people belonged to the Mityala chapter of the DP, none of them wanted to be in the same room or even on the same page. Each carried a secret list of demands, some in their minds, some in their pockets, which were to be addressed immediately. As these demands sometimes included the sacking of the person who was perhaps sitting next to them in that dining hall, conversation was minimal. The jaws were clenched a little more than usual also because people knew, as they waited for their turn, someone was presenting his or her list to Keyur Kashinath.

Keyur had met thirteen people by 9 a.m.; he had started at 7 a.m. His hopes from the first day in Mityala were being fast replaced with the ambitions of the party's district committee chief. The chief wanted a reshuffle of the committee and was establishing the prevalence of discontent in the ranks. Ahead of the assembly elections, he knew this would make the DP nervous enough to give him the team of his choice.

So Keyur stopped complaining between meetings and heard, with an acquired benevolence, to the reports that the number of visitors was a reflection of his popularity. Keyur did not mention that the morning's one-on-one meetings with local politicians had dispelled any such notions from his mind.

Keyur stood up once again, bowing respectfully to an old man who walked into the room leaning on a walking stick. The man grumbled a greeting in response and sat down in the chair Keyur offered. The old man waited till they were alone and plunged into a caustic analysis of the diving poll prospects of the DP in Mityala.

By late afternoon, Keyur had met each of the leaders, and managed to convey the impression to everyone that they had finally opened his eyes to who his real loyalists were.

He waited as a sketchy lunch was laid out on the tea table in his room. One of his assistants carried in messages from a few local journalists gathered outside, asking to meet him. He sent back a reply regretting his inability to speak without the party's permission.

This was not a ploy to avoid the press, he was telling the truth. It was one of the new commandments issued by the DP, and delivered to him by his father after the disaster at the press conference at the Delhi HQ. He was not to speak or write, either in print or online. He was not to speak about any of the DP's programmes or policies. He was not even to represent Mityala in the national media; this task would be performed by the party's spokespersons. The only place he was allowed to speak publicly was in Mityala, and only when addressing his constituents.

After lunch, Keyur washed his hands and glanced casually

at the mirror. He stopped, staring at his reflection. He had the look of a fugitive, tired and guilty. He frowned, searching his dark eyes, looking deep into the darkness. And there, not too deep, he found what he really felt. Anger.

He walked back into the room to meet another wave of visitors, this time, a group of businessmen and moneylenders. The parking lot outside was once again packed, this time with expensive cars, and the lawns were full of men in business suits. This time, the neighbourhood kiosk sent boys with mineral water and digestive biscuits.

At 6 p.m., the district collector arrived on time for a second, informal meeting. Keyur had already met him at the formal welcome in the morning. He recalled that he had been impressed with the collector during the elections. Keyur had found him to be a good bureaucrat; prudent, polite and political.

'I sent a report this morning to the central government, sir, on the status of farmer suicides in Mityala,' Gul said, adding with sincerity, 'thought I should mention it.'

Keyur smiled at the courteous eyes. 'I am sure you did.'

Gul smiled, and sipped the coffee in silence.

Keyur said, 'You seem to be sure that the DP is not going to retain its MLAs in Mityala in the next elections.'

Gul did not look up from his coffee. 'I am sure that it will.'

'With these figures of farmer suicides?'

'I have great faith in the positive impact of your visit, sir.'

'I am here because of the disturbing trend in the district suicide committee meetings chaired by you.' Keyur studied him. 'My reports state that the suicide toll started increasing only after your unprecedented decision to include a new member, a farmer, on the panel.'

'There was a need to balance the membership of the committee. Mr Gangiri Bhadra has the right background and he fit the profile,' Gul said, adding tonelessly, 'I explained all of this in letters to the state government, the central government, and the PMO. I proceeded only after receiving sanction.'

'Do you then also sanction,' Keyur asked harshly, reacting to the curt answer, 'that these members make statements about the committee proceedings to the press in Delhi that become part of salacious stories against me?'

'The members have only talked of the decisions taken at the meetings and not what led to the decisions,' Gul replied thoughtfully. 'Otherwise, the real story would have been why I was constrained to put Lambodar maha sarpanch and Durga Das mahajan in charge of protecting Gangiri Bhadra's life.'

Gul paused, and continued delicately, 'I thought it would be indiscreet to include Lambodar maha sarpanch's complicity in the forced resignation of Gangiri Bhadra in the report I sent this morning.'

As Keyur had always feared that the collector knew the truth behind the bid to force Gangiri's resignation, this did not surprise him.

'I see that the members of the committee dislike each other deeply,' he noted. 'It reflects badly on you, Mr Gul. Why don't you dissolve the committee and appoint a new one?'

'For two reasons, sir,' Gul said, leaving his cup on the saucer for a moment. 'First, I would have to explain to the state and central ministries, and the PMO, why the committee should be revamped. It is not easy finding the right consensus candidates for non-official positions, for which there are usually many contenders.'

'I have had,' Keyur said with much patience, 'enough of the state, the centre and the PMO in my constituency. Are you basically saying you are powerless? Or that I am?'

'Well,' Gul searched his mind, 'not entirely, I suppose. I can always sack a member from the committee.'

'Then do so!'

'But only if there is unbiased proof against the member,' Gul stressed. 'The subject of farmer suicides and debt distress is such that there is information available against every unofficial member on the committee. To sack one based on such motivated evidence would mean, eventually, sacking all of them. I would have started a revolt in the district.'

'And what is your second reason?'

'Well, I fear that if I reconstitute the committee, I may not remain one of the few people to know of Lambodar's involvement in the forced resignation episode,' Gul said in a concerned voice. 'Word will spread and that cannot be very healthy for the DP incumbents in this district.'

Keyur smiled at Gul. 'You are such an asset!' he said kindly. 'Where will you be posted next, Mr Gul?'

'To some neighbouring district, I think.'

'I will put in a word for the capital.'

'I like the districts, sir.'

'Nonsense!' Keyur said. 'When is your transfer due?'

'In two years'.

'I will also see that the time period is shortened.'

'But I like it here,'

'Yes, I can see that,' Keyur said shortly and returned to the coffee.

They discussed a few other issues before reaching the end of the meeting.

Gul said, 'Chief of Police Reddy informs me that you will be visiting about a dozen villages tomorrow. There has been a high incidence of farmer suicides in this belt and there may be some political action. I recommend you take along additional security.'

Keyur thanked him.

'I shall also send along officers from the agriculture and revenue departments to answer any questions you might have, sir,' Gul added. 'Where do you plan to rest tomorrow? Should I arrange accommodation for you in the Pandaru town rest house? It falls on the way.'

'I will end tomorrow's tour in Gopur village,' Keyur said, adding with emphasis, 'and rest at Lambodarji's residence.'

Keyur enjoyed Gul's stunned silence for a moment, then said, 'I have been served a show-cause notice by the DP for the increasing number of farmer suicides in Mityala, Mr Gul. Kindly keep that in mind when corresponding with anyone about my constituency.'

'I too face the rap for the toll in my district, sir,' Gul said cordially.

'Let's not be naïve enough to compare,' Keyur retorted. 'You have a twenty-year tenure ahead of you and you can't be voted out of office for incompetence. I have a tenure of just five years and I will be judged at the end of it.'

'But look on the bright side, sir.' Gul smiled sombrely. 'I can be always transferred to the capital.'

Keyur chuckled and saw him to the door. Just as they reached it, Lambodar walked in. They exchanged greetings, and the collector left, wishing Keyur a good trip.

'As a favour to me, Keyurji,' Lambodar said as they settled down for a drink before dinner, 'please get this man transferred from Mityala.'

'Are you planning to get me into more trouble?' Keyur joked. 'What will it look like if the government transfers the collector heading the committee which is reporting an increase in the death toll?'

'It will look appropriate.' Lambodar took a deep sip, appreciating the Scotch Keyur had brought from Delhi.

'I know,' Keyur said, smiling. 'My father says we have to be patient.'

'He means *I* have to be patient!' Lambodar said angrily. 'But what else can I do? I am guarding Gangiri Bhadra and his family!'

'Being patient,' Keyur pointed out coldly, 'will get you your hundred-acre industrial park. I will make sure of that.'

'You will not be doing me any favours.' Lambodar's shrewd eyes were contemptuous. 'That company paid for your election candidature.'

'That debt can be repaid in some other way.'

Lambodar's eyes turned hard for an instant. 'You cannot buy my support through the project, Keyurji. I will get the industrial park, with or without you.'

Keyur looked at him patiently.

'You see, I need this project for my son,' Lamobodar said in a lowered voice. 'He does not like a farmer's life. It does not fit into his world view. He lives like a commoner in the city instead. I tried seeing it his way but I cannot live amidst people who think I am just an old man from some obscure village.'

Keyur listened in silence as Lambodar spoke about how

his son had slowly drifted away and was charting a life of his own. As Lambodar explained how the district could be a fertile ground for his son's ambitions, it was not difficult to see that Lambodar wanted to lure his son back by offering him opportunities in politics.

'The days when we could be the lords of our lands are over,' Lambodar concluded. 'But no other family can bind this district together like ours does. That is the reason why the district votes overwhelmingly for the DP. Our family's name evokes that kind of loyalty.'

Keyur refrained from pointing out that the DP had been out of power in the district many times. But it was true that Lambodar's family wielded great influence across the district and he had always been faithful to the DP, a point the party might consider seriously.

Keyur began to feel a little uneasy.

'I supported you, Keyurji, because of your father,' Lambodar said, after taking another sip. 'But to be honest, this is not the constituency for you. You must represent a more urban seat.'

He added after a pause, 'I have tarnished my prestige in handling the case of the farmer suicide committee. If people still respect me, it is because they see no reason why I should indulge in such petty persecutions. However, I must not continue to count on their indulgence.'

Keyur watched calmly, hiding the increasing panic he felt within.

'So you see, Keyurji, saddened as I am by the show-cause notice issued to you, it does present a question before me. Should I put the interest of Mityala before yours?'

Keyur asked, 'Do you find the question paradoxical?'

'I do,' Lambodar said, draining his glass and putting it down on the table decisively. 'I want my son to be in your place. I want him to bring to the constituency a project like the industrial park, that provides jobs and infrastructure in a countryside where failing agriculture has led to poverty and suicides.'

Lambodar observed Keyur for a minute. 'There is a momentum in the villages here for a re-election to your seat, to be held along with the upcoming assembly elections. I am going to support that, Keyurji.'

'Yes,' Keyur said simply. 'I think you should.'

Lambodar frowned, taken aback.

'I understand the seriousness of the situation now.' Keyur nodded gravely. 'And as for your son, this is your home, Lambodarji, and your son's home. I shall personally recommend his name for the seat.'

Lambodar waited, suspicion shining in his eyes.

'There may be some questions about your involvement in the forced resignation of Gangiri Bhadra from the suicide committee,' Keyur said, worried. 'But I can always say that it was my idea,' he added dismissively.

Lambodar was enraged but said nothing, his keen eyes assessing Keyur.

'I wish you could have begun campaigning for your son right away,' Keyur said. 'You know how it takes time for people to warm up to change. Or are you waiting to be relieved of the ticklish duty of protecting Gangiri Bhadra's family? It might take just a well-aimed brick to derail your plans, you know.'

'No such brick shall harm them because Gangiri and his family are under my constant protection,' Lambodar said.

'Then there is nothing to worry about!' Keyur said. 'You see,' he continued gently, 'I am saying this because I care, Lambodarji. If you had told me to go to polls in these circumstances, I would have said sorry, but no, thanks.'

'But that is just me,' Keyur added politely. 'And I am not your son.'

Lambodar looked away, considering Keyur's words as he refilled his drink. Then he reached for the glass Keyur offered, and noticed that Keyur himself did not drink. 'You may have a point,' he grudgingly admitted, 'but it will take just one more crisis for me to abandon you. And knowing you, I know you will not keep me waiting for long.'

'Well, then let us not overtake destiny,' Keyur suggested.

Lambodar nodded.

'What do we do tomorrow?'

'Smile and wave!' Lambodar sighed. 'You know the drill. Just like an election campaign, but without the speeches.'

'That is good,' Keyur said slowly, bitterness filling his voice, 'because I am not allowed to make speeches.'

'You don't have to take the DP stipulations so seriously!' Lambodar chided. 'It could have happened to anyone.'

'But not to me,' Keyur said, the smile frozen on his face.

Lambodar was perplexed.

'I worked so hard to get the leaders in Delhi to approve of me,' Keyur said, his face rigid with disappointment. 'I was on my way to becoming the most promising young leader of the DP. It took a lot of hard work to build that image, nurture that perception of success...'

'It's all gone now,' he said in a low voice, his usually sparkling eyes dull with suppressed fury.

He glanced at Lambodar. 'You should be a worried man,

Lambodarji. This could happen to your son too, if he inherits the same problem.' He paused. 'Especially if you fail to solve it now.'

'What problem?' Lambodar frowned.

'The problem of a single man's revolt,' Keyur replied. 'The problem of a billion rebellions.'

17

Thursday, the government guest house, Civil Lines, Mityala

Much before sunrise the next morning, party workers began gathering at the guest house in Mityala. Their voices and sounds filled the stillness of the early hours, stirring the low nesting birds in the acacia trees nearby.

The cavalcade was made up of eight vehicles. The first and second jeeps carried Keyur's core team, men who had joined the DP only because of him. They were young men from respectable families of the district who had aligned themselves with Keyur to help him during the elections with the campaigning, the money management and the dirty tricks crucial to victory. It had been a gamble, then, to side with a first-time candidate. But today, these men were legends in the district for their political acumen in standing by Keyur and for their prowess that made him win.

They formed a coterie around Keyur when it came to conducting any business of the constituency. But as they lived in the district and Keyur did not, each had developed a powerful coterie of his own which, increasingly, fed their personal political ambitions.

That morning they returned, once more, to their fundamental roles as members of Keyur's core team and took charge of the route he was to travel. Every person Keyur would meet that day, each stop he would make, was meticulously decided by the coterie, down to choosing who would garland and felicitate him. This was not just because it was prudent to plan in detail. His loyalists wanted to make the point in the constituency that their advice was given great importance by the MP in all matters.

When it came to explaining to Keyur their road map, they simply said that they had chosen places where there was a great demand among the local people to see him. Everyone knew it was just a polite explanation, often repeated and rarely true.

The third and fourth vehicles in the cavalcade were dedicated to Keyur's use. These were two new SUVs sent by a local textile mill owner for the trip, with the offer for Keyur to 'keep them if you like them'.

Keyur's vehicle was driven by his personal chauffeur who came by train from Delhi, had two bodyguards in the back seat who came by flight with Keyur and a few weapons under the seat which came naturally. The other vehicles of the entourage carried local party functionaries, officers of the district agriculture and revenue departments, a local businessman who wanted to build the first mall in Mityala, and the police.

Two hours later, exactly at 6 a.m., Keyur emerged from the guest house. Those not used to his punctuality were thrown into a tizzy and ran around to quickly finish their chores. Noticing the minor uproar, Keyur said he would wait and sat in the front seat of his vehicle.

His mind was fresh after a good night's sleep, the darkness around and the silence within the vehicle helped him focus on the task ahead. According to his father's orders, he was to spend close to a week in the constituency. He was to meet local politicians, farmers, businessmen, professionals, policemen, army men, bureaucrats and students.

'Be humble and charm them,' his father had said. After all, it has not been that long since they had elected him, for the voters to start hating him, Vaishnav had added. After touring the district, Keyur was to move to the state capital and perform the same drill, only at a much lower key because it was someone else's constituency.

The idea was, as his father outlined, to kill any resentment among the people with precise damage control. 'Take it for granted that everyone would have read the newspapers or seen the evening news, even in Mityala,' he had said. People would have witnessed the headlines his press conference had made, the long studio discussions that had followed, the DP's immediate action and the heavy coverage of farmers' suicides. Besides all this, they would certainly be aware of the demands for a re-election.

Keyur flinched a little, looking around at the men who were busily loading the vehicles and getting them ready. In all probability, they knew he was there to salvage his image, that he needed them more than they needed him. It was embarrassing, especially because he had never mingled freely, mainly in an effort to give himself an enigmatic appeal. Now, he could only hope that the notoriety would add to that appeal.

Also tragic was the fact that no one in the DP, not even his father, could ask for leniency towards Keyur. Being known for his fairness, Vaishnav could not make an exception in Keyur's case. He had to admit that Keyur deserved to be censured for not paying enough attention to the towering problems of his constituency. However, everyone knew that was the politically correct excuse, the real problem was the way Keyur had conducted himself at the press conference.

Trying to retrieve the situation, Vaishnav had used all his personal rapport with the party president to rescue Keyur by saying he was young and inexperienced. The DP president, a man of few words, listened to Vaishnav with great respect and understanding. At the end, he pointed out that there were other young and inexperienced politicians in the party. For the son of a general secretary to get away with such arrogance and irresponsibility would amount to a serious breach of party discipline. Never really sympathizing with Vaishnav, the party president effectively conveyed that it was his job to ensure that such dangerous precedents were not set.

That Tuesday, both Keyur and Vaishnav lingered in the party headquarters for a long time before and after Keyur's press conference fiasco. But while Vaishnav's signature was necessary for disciplinary action, his presence was not required when delivering the notice to Keyur.

And so they only met briefly at home in the evening. Keyur was about to leave for the airport for the state capital and drive from there to Mityala. Vaishnav was about to leave his boiled chicken untouched and go to bed hungry.

Keyur had been taken aback by how downcast and defeated his father looked. He had never seen him this way. He was also surprised by the way it strongly affected him, as if deep down he knew that this was time itself, giving him a glimpse of its eternal turning.

Keyur had sat with him and assured Vaishnav that he

would follow his directions precisely on what he should do in Mityala. Keyur could feel his father's fatigued anger as he talked about how the rivals were ganging up against Keyur. But Keyur could also see that his father's anger was not that of a tired warrior, it was that of a retired one. It would soon be time for him to rest, Keyur felt.

Keyur lowered the window of the vehicle and let in the winter air. His father's principal desire would be to ensure that nothing happened during his lifetime to sully his impeccable political career, his prestige, his name. Vaishnav would die before his time if his son fell from grace, Keyur knew.

He took a deep breath of the morning air, it was pleasant weather compared to the freezing Delhi winter.

In the aftermath of the conference, Keyur realized that for the first time, he could not blame his father for his failure. It was also the first time his father could not do anything for Keyur. He understood the worry in his father's eyes as he bid him farewell. And he would never forget what Vaishnav had said with affection and concern: 'Don't rush back to Delhi, Keyur.'

Keyur felt the familiar anger welling up inside him again. Just one farmer's decision had changed his life. Gangiri Bhadra's decision not to leave Gopur.

His anger slowly travelled like molten rock down a mountainside into that deep place in the human mind where destiny waits to choose its villains and victims. The dark night turned darker, the breeze stood still, waiting, the birds pulled their feathers closer, the insects finished hunting. Dawn was round the corner of the earth.

❖

The cavalcade finally slid out of Mityala town on to the smooth black highway. After travelling for about 30 kilometres, the vehicles turned off the main road to one of the side roads which connected the villages.

Within a few minutes, they were in a village where even the limited light of early dawn showed signboards on shops announcing the availability of computers, air conditioners and water purifiers. As he watched street after well-paved street of houses with attached garages pass by, Keyur understood that his core team was being nice to him. To make the first stop of the tour gentle on him, they had brought him to one of the villages next to the highway.

Being constantly in the vicinity of development, these 'highway villages' always remained on the rural-urban cusp, absorbing the first waves of modernization. However, as the economic and geographical potential of these villages was no match to the intensity of the modernizing waves, there was often over-absorption. The demands on the social fabric to adapt within a few years to changes which should have ideally been generational, robbed the people of the strength that came from assimilation.

However, almost every one of these highway villages had voted overwhelmingly for Keyur, a reason why the core team thought it sensible to begin the tour with one such village.

As the sun rose over a hazy horizon, Keyur was given a warm reception and complimented for doing a great job as member of Parliament. Keyur knew that if there was any village up to speed on news and television, it ought to be this one. Yet, everyone displayed an appropriate ignorance for which he was grateful. In return, he indulged them by asking questions about agriculture, generously overlooking the fact that they were now merely property dealers masquerading as farmers.

The uncertain morning turned into a warm afternoon amid acres of cotton crop. As he visited village after village, he began feeling the latent anger among the people, living and breathing like a sheath of skin, covering everything, everyone, pulsating with blood. He did not object when his team avoided going to the villages worst affected by delayed rains and where the crop damage had been severe. He did not object as they ushered him back into the vehicles whenever the gathering crowds swelled to more than a few dozen.

After touring the first couple of villages, Keyur got the officers of the agriculture and revenue departments to exchange places with his bodyguards and sit in the back seat of his jeep. They briefed Keyur on the status of the villages, the acreages, yields, taxes, savings, expenditure, debts, deaths. They also pointed out that the cotton crop was getting ready for the first picking.

As planned, he met a few widows whose husbands had committed suicide due to debt and crop failure. He then announced their names as the chosen beneficiaries of a central government scheme, which his father had wanted him to offer as assistance. It included, first, a bank account set up in the widow's name with an opening balance of three thousand rupees. Second, there would be a guarantee from the DP's local MLA for bank loans up to fifty thousand rupees. The welfare scheme, specially designed for farm widows, had been gathering dust and Keyur was merely resurrecting it.

And, as planned, he repeated these promises in all the villages of the two out of seven assembly segments of the district he toured that day. By the end of the week, he would have covered all the assembly segments of Mityala. His team had already done the research and the list of beneficiaries was ready for the entire district. His father hoped that these measures would convince voters to re-elect incumbent MLAs. Vaishnav was sure that nothing could improve electoral prospects better than money placed directly in the hands of the voters.

But after touring villages of two assembly segments, Keyur was beginning to wonder if his father had underestimated the anger of the people and the turning of the tide.

The day's itinerary wound up at close to 5 p.m. The cavalcade headed towards Gopur where Lambodar had made arrangements for everyone to rest. There had been many villages, many names that day. But Keyur waited for this last village, one last name.

✤

Half an hour before Keyur's scheduled arrival, the talathi or the village officer, drove his motorcycle into Gopur village and slowed down at the first crossing. At the centre of the crossing was a small temple to Lord Hanuman that was painted vermilion. The talathi bowed before the deity, drove once around the temple and headed into the village.

It used to be a much larger temple, situated at the entrance of the village to ward off the evil and let in the good. However, when the gram sadak, or the village roads, plan reached Gopur a decade earlier, they discovered that the temple was in the way. It was going to keep both the good and the evil out of the village if it stayed where it was. This problem led to brief spells of emotional arguments, one community swearing by the temple, another provokingly pro-development.

These face-offs were followed by lunches and dinners, organized at neutral venues, for both sides to meet and discuss. As most of these warring men and women had been friends till recently, it was not difficult for the warmth to return.

The side arguing that the temple should be relocated and the side which would hear nothing of it, decided that the temple should remain where it was but must be downsized to allow the road to be built. And to compensate for the loss of space for worship and prayer, a new piece of land was allocated to build a new temple.

The new temple was set up in another part of the village along with the original idol some years ago. But for some of those who used to frequent the old temple, the miniature version at the crossing still remained the genuine thing.

The talathi drove slowly over the village roads, checking arrangements. Banners supporting the DP hung from every tree, pole and statue. Posters of local leaders welcoming Keyur were pasted on the walls of every house, school, office and public toilet. The roads were swept clean and vehicles had been diverted away from the main route to allow free movement.

Then, as he approached a large neem tree, he slowed down. At the base of the tree was a huddled figure, wrapped in a chequered, dusty blanket. The talathi stopped his motorcycle, chuckling. 'Don't tell me you have been here since yesterday, Tika?'

Tikaram did not move.

The talathi's smile faded. He looked closely at the figure,

frowning. He killed the engine and stood the motorcycle on its stand. He did not want to be the one to discover Tikaram dead. It was true, Tikaram had been a lazy man of questionable personal hygiene all his life. But he could afford to be, having leased his land and splurged the rent on all available vices.

However, he had his good points. For one, he always attended every cremation and funeral in the village, and helped the bereaved family in any way he could. To leave such a man dead and unattended on the roadside needed a cold heart, which the talathi did not have.

He walked towards Tikaram, calling out his name. There was no movement, no answer. It appeared as if Tikaram had barely moved since the day before. The huddled figure at the base of the tree was lying on one side, the face lost in the folds of the blanket. Next to the figure were peels of an orange and many bidi stubs. The talathi froze in his steps.

Tikaram, it seemed, had followed his advice after all. Only yesterday, he had warned Tikaram that smoking could kill him and one way to postpone this fate was to eat citrus fruits and build immunity. And only yesterday, Tikaram had grinned cheerfully and asked him to go to hell.

Underneath the grime and grunge, there must have been a sensitive heart that nurtured affection for a friend. If only he had known this side of Tika before, the talathi thought as he knelt weakly next to the figure.

'I wish we had more time, Tika,' he said as he reached for the blanket. 'I really wish.'

First there was a cough, then some movement under the blanket. The talathi jumped back, frightened by this instant response to his wish. A hairy, dirty face finally emerged from the folds and Tikaram peered enquiringly at the shocked talathi.

The talathi quickly collected himself. 'Good to see you alive, Tika!' he said, embarassed. 'I mean, awake!'

Tikaram stared, puzzled, as the talathi sprang to his feet and walked away, glancing around to check if anyone saw him.

'I had come to tell you that the MP Kashinath is expected in a few minutes,' the talathi said, getting on his motorcycle. 'It would be better if you do not greet him lying down.'

'Don't teach me how to greet a VIP!' Tikaram said, yawning. 'I was there when the prime minister came on a visit to Mityala.'

'That was thirty-five years ago,' the talathi said wryly, starting his motorcycle.

Tikaram languidly reached for a bidi. 'I am better than most. Most people die without getting to see who they voted for.'

'You are right.' The talathi nodded. 'You almost did.'

18

Thursday evening, Gopur village, Mityala district

The sun set with the limited colours of winter and Gopur prepared for the long night of darkness. Electricity was available only to some streets of the village, selectively lighting up the homes of important people like Lambodar maha sarpanch.

After the formal welcome, Lambodar led Keyur and his team to his sprawling house where they sat in the open and drank tea. The drivers took away the vehicles for cleaning and maintenance as they knew Keyur would leave early next day, giving them little time for upkeep. The other team members scattered, each finding ways to recover from the gruelling day. The core team members and the two officials sat with Keyur and Lambodar, and discussed the day's events.

Once refreshed, Keyur was ready to meet those widows of the village who were to be the beneficiaries of the welfare scheme, as decided by the core team with Lambodar's recommendations. Keyur was accompanied by Lambodar, the two officials and the talathi as he set out on foot.

But the widows of Gopur were no different from the widows he had met through the day, Keyur discovered.

They said nothing to him. They were not silent, however. They always responded, attentively answering questions, thanking him for his assistance. But they did not *speak* to him.

The chilly evening was beginning to feel like a personal insult.

The widows had been chosen on two criteria. First, the farmer should have committed suicide after Keyur's tenure began; in other words, in the last eight months. Second, the district administration should have recognized it as a suicide due to debt distress. This way, the team felt, they would make sure that the relief would have maximum impact without raising any procedural problems later for the beneficiaries.

Only two widows fit these requirements and Keyur met them both within an hour of beginning his tour of Gopur. As they all turned towards Lambodar's residence to rest for the night, Keyur checked his watch. It was getting to be 7 p.m.

There were two reasons why he had decided to spend so much time in Gopur; politics and public opinion. The stay at Lambodar's home was tailored to promote cooperation with him, that was politics. He now had to take care of public opinion by meeting Gangiri Bhadra.

Keyur took Lambodar aside and requested him to go back home as he intended to meet Gangiri. Lambodar, taken aback, protested that this would be most inappropriate, it was Gangiri who should visit Keyur, he said. But when Keyur insisted, Lambodar excused himself stiffly and walked away.

The talathi led the way and the small group walked along the narrow road in silence. There was the occasional streetlight, but they walked mostly in darkness. The sweet fragrances of the night worked with the ballads of early insects to create the ambience for a sad mystery.

As he passed one poor home after another, Keyur wondered how one man living here, in these circumstances, could make life miserable for him so far away in Delhi. The talathi stopped and gestured to the dirt path on his left, pointing into the darkness. At the end of the path was a small house, a light flickering in its heart to prove it was alive.

The talathi asked Keyur to wait on the road under the streetlight and rushed off to fetch Gangiri. After a while the talathi returned, saying Gangiri was not at home. His sister-in-law had informed that Gangiri could either be with his friend Vadrangi or at the grocer's shop in the marketplace. The talathi said Vadrangi did not live too far off and hurried away to check. The officials volunteered to check the market and left.

A beautiful December full moon was rising amid the delicate foliage of the trees. As it rose higher over the fields, it shone on the cotton bolls, making them look like small pieces of moonlight caught in the fingers of a child.

Keyur sauntered along the cotton fields on both sides of the road, pondering how the same crop could be a source of both hope and despair for the farmers. The hands that sowed this crop had voted for him, but the hands that would harvest it may never vote for him again.

He was pacing the road under the streetlight when he saw a tall man walk up briskly and turn on to the path leading to the house. Keyur could also see another man following, who stopped after noticing him and leaned against a nearby tree, looking away.

Keyur continued pacing and then saw the tall man return to the road. He walked up to him, his expression curious. 'I received a message that I had a guest waiting,' he said in Hindi, 'I am Gangiri Bhadra.'

'That would be me, Gangiriji,' Keyur smiled. 'My name is Keyur Kashinath.'

Gangiri stared at him, stunned, mechanically greeting him with a namaskar. Keyur returned the greeting, amused at his surprise.

'So you are the one who has been plotting against me!' Gangiri said softly.

It was now Keyur's turn to be shocked. Then he said, 'And you are the one destroying my political career.'

'Not on purpose!' snapped Gangiri, his eyes sharp. 'But you sent men to hurt me and my family, to get me to stop validating distress suicides.'

Keyur did not speak, noting that Gangiri knew the truth. He realized it had to be Lambodar who had conveyed this piece of information to Gangiri and even, perhaps, to Collector Gul. Getting enough evidence to back the allegation may not be very difficult, Keyur thought, if Lambodar turned against him and got fervently committed to his ouster from the constitutency to force a re-election.

Keyur quickly reorganized his priorities and thoughts. He had encouraged himself to blame Gangiri for every misfortune and had fondly nurtured various schemes of retribution. All that, of course, had to wait.

The streetlight fell on them at an angle, leaving half their faces in darkness, forcing them to read one half and speculate about the other. Keyur smiled uneasily. 'I see you do not mince words. I won't, either. What do you want, Gangiriji?'

'To prevent farmers from committing suicide,' he said simply.

'Now, how can I...' Keyur stopped speaking as Gangiri turned abruptly and walked away.

'There must be something else you want,' Keyur said hurriedly. 'Something useful for you and your family, like a house, perhaps, a job, money...'

Gangiri stopped in his tracks and turned.

Keyur could see he was furious. 'Now don't give me that righteous anger,' he chuckled. 'Don't ask me absurd "how-can-you-bribe-me" questions. Everyone can be bribed, it is a law of nature, at least in this country.'

Gangiri walked slowly towards Keyur, the dark eyes glinting, his fists clenched tight. Keyur studied his angry face, assessing the chances of being struck by Gangiri.

'All right, you want to know what I want?' Gangiri said, his face close. 'Before you leave Gopur, make a public statement that Lambodar and Durga Das have been falsifying suicide figures since they were appointed to the district suicide committee seven years ago.'

'Why should I?' Keyur shrugged. 'You are the one turning regular suicides into debt-distress suicides by manipulating committee members. This is a simple case of fraud!'

'And what if I can prove that cases in the past were falsified by Lambodar and Durga Das?' Gangiri demanded.

Keyur remained silent, thinking fast. If there really was such evidence against Lambodar, it could be used to tame him, to unsettle him. And he could gain Gangiri's favour by re-examining the verdict in his brother's suicide case.

'I want to see the proof first,' Keyur said.

Gangiri gestured towards the village. 'You can see it now

if you have the time. There are cases here in Gopur that were declared ineligible for compensation because of Lambodar's intervention. It is for good reason that he is called apatra Lambodar.'

'Or,' Keyur said, attempting to provoke Gangiri, 'they may truly be ineligible suicides.'

'The widows will tell you why they are not.' Gangiri said, then paused. 'If you have the courage to meet these widows, that is.'

Keyur nodded. 'Are we being watched?' he asked, curious, gesturing to the man in the distance.

Gangiri glanced at Keyur, amused, '*I* am being watched by Lambodar's men to make sure I am safe. On the collector's orders.'

Keyur smiled when he realized that his every move would be reported to Lambodar.

The talathi, who was returning from Vadrangi's house, joined them. And on their way, they met the two officials returning from the marketplace. After walking through the village, the small group reached the residence of Bimala bai, the widow of farmer Ranganath.

'Is everything all right?' she asked the talathi, worried at finding so many people on her doorstep.

He told her that the MP, Kashinath, was interested in understanding the circumstances that led to the death of her husband. She agreed to speak.

They sat on the porch of the hut as the talathi, with the help of the officials, recollected the case. 'Ranganath was forty-five years old. He had six acres of agricultural land and committed suicide five years ago. He had unpaid debts of up to fifty-five thousand rupees and was said to have owed over a lakh rupees to private moneylenders. He spent every last paisa on liquor. The death was decided as a suicide not eligible for compensation.'

Bimala bai did not move, she did not even look up. She had heard this verdict many times in the past five years. But when Gangiri requested her version, she glanced around nervously and began softly, 'My husband was not an alcoholic...he drank only on the day he killed himself, perhaps to gather the courage...and to stand the smell of the pesticide.

'He committed suicide because the cotton crop that year failed repeatedly due to poor rainfall. We had to sow the seeds three times and yet they failed. The moneylenders harassed him for the repayment, they said they did not trust him. He could not take it anymore.' She paused, before continuing weakly, 'He felt humiliated, he used to cry in the dark...'

She stopped speaking and looked away.

The talathi had nothing to say. Gangiri glanced at Keyur, questions in his eyes. Keyur nodded grimly and they took leave of Bimala.

Next, they went to Varada amma's home. They sat in the open and the moonlight made up for the inadequate oil lamp.

After consulting with the officials, the talathi recounted the incident that took place almost three years ago. 'Srinivas, fifty-two, owned four acres of land. He spent extravagantly on the weddings of his son and two daughters. He had an outstanding debt of one lakh forty-three thousand rupees for almost a decade. There was, therefore, no reason why he should have suddenly killed himself three years ago. He committed suicide due to a domestic quarrel.'

Varada amma quietly said, 'Durga Das mahajan wanted to take away our land. With the help of the landlords, he put immense pressure on us to repay. Our harvest was not good enough to repay the debt at once; we were harvesting only five to ten quintals of cotton per acre. But they said we were lying.

'When the committee refused compensation, I knew there was no hope, the land was lost.' She glanced at the talathi. 'The only domestic quarrel we ever had was when you came harassing and humiliating us to repay the debt. We could not decide whether to abuse you or to ignore you.'

The talathi glanced furtively at Keyur and Gangiri, and denounced Varada amma's allegations.

Much against the wishes of the talathi, Gangiri led them next to the house of Sujata, the widow of Agyaram. She stood waiting politely but did not invite them to sit.

'Agyaram, twenty-five, had taken land on lease but never sowed any crop,' the talathi said, insisting that he remembered the case very well. 'He had a debt of seventy-two thousand rupees at the time of his suicide. He died last year because he could not bear the pain of his stomach ulcer.'

'Are you sure?' Sujata asked in a gentle voice.

'I am only repeating,' the talathi said authoritatively, 'what was decided by the committee.'

She looked at Keyur, 'My husband was forced to lease infertile land with no facilities for irrigation. But the landlord was Lambodar maha sarpanch's friend and we had no choice. The talathi has in his record our reservations and the fact that Lambodar mediated the deal.

'The landlord then forced us to take three loans from Durga Das to dig borewells. All three efforts failed.'

She addressed the talathi again, 'That too is in your records. Along with the fact that there was never any crop because there was never any water.'

She turned to Keyur. 'My husband killed himself when Durga Das sent recovery agents, daily, for the money and the landlord threatened to cancel the lease if he did not repay.'

She waited to see if there were any further questions, then walked heavily back into the house and shut the door. They stood in the questioning silence of the yard for a moment, then walked on to the next case.

Seetal amma's trepidation was clear as they mentioned that they had come to discuss the real circumstances of the death of her husband. Keyur, then, asked the talathi and the officials to wait on the road outside.

When they left, Seetal amma began, 'Lambodar sarpanch said it was not a suicide due to debt.' Keyur could hear the disbelief that still echoed in her voice. 'The committee refused compensation, saying my husband threw away the loan money on luxuries he could not afford.'

She glanced at Keyur. 'You are new here so you might not know. We accept anything Lambodar sarpanch decides.'

Keyur nodded, then glanced at Gangiri.

'Ganesh was a very good farmer, Keyurji,' Gangiri said. 'He started with one acre and made enough profit to expand his holdings to five acres. He helped other farmers with planning their crops, with future investment and with debt repayment. Ganesh's family was big, he had to support his brother and sister, and his own three children. And yet, till the time of his death two years ago, the forty-eight-year-old man had never defaulted on a single repayment of loans.'

'Not until the drought,' Seetal amma said sadly. 'We lost the crop. Then we discovered how many people were waiting for us to fail. The landlords resented us for encouraging farmers to hold on to their lands. The moneylenders hated us for not borrowing enough. And the farm-input providers were angry that farmers trusted us more than them.'

She paused. 'Now, we have no land. My brother-in-law has leased a few acres for cultivation on which we barely survive. We are at the mercy of the landlords and moneylenders.'

As they walked to the next house in silence, Keyur realized one thing. It was not out of respect that the villagers voted for the DP when Lambodar told them to. It was out of fear. If he kept Lambodar happy, he may score again in the next election and retain his seat. It was not the first time Lambodar was doing this for a politician, but Keyur knew that if he had the courage, he could make it the last.

Laxmi welcomed all of them warmly, but when the officer from the agriculture department started speaking about her husband's death, her smile faded.

'Panduranga, thirty-eight, owned three acres of land and took loans from everyone he knew,' the officer began speaking after checking his notebook. 'At the time of his death, he had defaulted on a forty-thousand-rupee crop loan from the bank and reportedly owed twenty-five thousand rupees to moneylenders, fifteen thousand to grocers, and six thousand to relatives. He was disinterested in agriculture because of which his crops failed. He died of malaria last year.'

Laxmi did not speak for a moment, then stood up to go back into the house. Keyur quickly got to his feet. 'Stay please, Laxmiji,' he said in his polished Hindi, 'I am here to find out if the committee was right or wrong in deciding that the suicide was ineligible.'

She glanced at him uncertainly. 'The committee is never wrong.'

Keyur smiled. 'But was it right?'

She shook her head. 'Durga Das mahajan wanted our land and withheld all loans to us. It is true that my husband had malaria, but he killed himself because Durga Das mahajan kept harassing him to sell the land.'

She paused, and glanced at the talathi. 'You conveyed most of those threats to us, so I don't really need to explain.'

The talathi bit his lip nervously and hung about at the back of the group that made its way sombrely out of Laxmi's house. As it was already 9 p.m., they headed back and Keyur asked the officers reasons why the crops in Mityala were so vulnerable to weather.

The officers explained the problems of rain-fed agriculture but also added that the genetically modified cotton crop was never meant to be grown in a place like Mityala, which was mostly deficient in rains.

Gangiri heard them in silence, feeling that Keyur should have had these facts *before* he even contested the elections for the seat. He was disconcerted by Keyur's self-assurance and disappointed by his make-believe sincerity. He remained silent as they all walked together.

At the next crossroads, Gangiri took their leave to head home. Keyur asked if he could visit him again in the morning before he left Gopur and Gangiri reluctantly agreed.

19

Friday morning, Gopur village, Mityala district

After many days of haze, the sun rose that morning to a clear sky. It was warm and bright, and the moisture on the dark soil sparkled like diamonds returning home to earth.

Gangiri knew the earth was happy by just the touch of it, like the touch of a contented lover. For that moment, at that time, everything was satiated, everything had reached its destination. Then the earth turned, placing everything, everyone, a little distance away from their goals.

Gangiri was working in his fields when he heard Vadrangi call his name. He came running with the news that his father's and Sudhakar's suicide cases were to be re-examined by the committee. All cases of farmer suicides deemed apatra, and ineligible for compensation, by the suicide committee in the last seven years would be re-examined. This was announced by the MP, Kashinath, Vadrangi explained breathlessly.

Gangiri stared at him incredulously. He was amazed that Keyur should take such a confrontational stand against Lambodar and Durga Das. Vadrangi said that Keyur had made the statement at Lambodar's residence and was now on his way here.

Gangiri rushed home with Vadrangi just in time to see the long procession of people turn from the road on to the path that led to his house. Unlike before, when he was walking with just his team, Keyur was now accompanied by almost half the village; farmers, labourers, teachers, mechanics, shopkeepers, businessmen. Keyur stopped at the gate and politely wished Gangiri. He then turned around and requested the people that he would like to speak with Gangiri in private. They walked away to wait, and Vadrangi joined them.

Gangiri held the gate of the bamboo fence open and Keyur walked into the front yard. The small house stood in the middle of the plot, half-brick, half-thatch, both halves falling apart. Gangiri's hands were covered with earth the same colour as his skin, the farm implements were next to him on the ground.

Keyur could see the signs of deprivation all around him, the lack of everything. And yet this farmer fought for justice for strangers. If only Gangiri had the advantages he himself had been born with, Keyur thought, he would have changed the world. Was this how nature tamed great forces of change, by containing them in mundane destinies?

Having observed the mood of the villagers earlier, Keyur was now wise enough to understand that the crowd which followed him had not come for him. They had come for Gangiri. The villagers were supporting what they believed Keyur to be doing, paying respect to their hero.

Instead, Keyur gravely noted, he would be subjecting Gangiri to the desperate games of an insecure and unpopular politician.

'I have kept my word,' Keyur said, forcing himself to smile. 'It is your turn now.'

Gangiri thoughtfully studied the blue kurta Keyur wore with black trousers and a black jacket. By now he had got over his initial surprise and understood Keyur's game plan. 'I am grateful for your decision,' Gangiri said. 'You have vindicated the questions raised by people like me.'

'You are welcome.'

'This is the second time you have surprised me,' Gangiri said, the sunlight falling in his eyes, making them sparkle. 'The first time was when you sent those hired goons to threaten and attack me to change my verdicts in the suicide committee.'

Keyur's smile faded. 'I thought you disbelieved Lambodar.'

Gangiri did not correct him that it was Nazar, and not Lambodar, who had warned him about Keyur's role in the assault.

'Lambodar wants to have his son elected MP from Mityala,' Keyur explained. 'He will blame me for all wrongs to get the support of the farmers. I am sure you see that.'

'I do see that!' Gangiri chuckled. 'As also your motive behind the statement to reopen the suicide cases.'

Keyur nodded, shrugging.

'What do you want from me?' Gangiri asked, a little severely.

'Your support to fight Lambodar and his men...'

He stopped when Gangiri began laughing.

'I know it sounds ironic!' Keyur said, a little cross. 'But to keep my hold on this district intact, I need to defeat Lambodar. I may be opportunistic, but I cannot be a good politician if I am defeated. This is not cricket, where defeat is part of the game. This is chess; defeat is the end of the game.'

Gangiri heard him, still amused, but impressed by Keyur's performance.

'This morning,' Keyur said, 'when I discussed the idea of re-examining the ineligible verdicts for Gopur, Lambodar was livid. He was convinced it was your idea. The talathi had reported to Lambodar that we had talked to the widows and dug up suicide cases.' Keyur paused. 'I promised that I would not be partisan and get the collector to examine apatra verdicts from all villages. But I don't think that really appeased Lambodar.'

Keyur looked steadily at Gangiri, at the healing wound on his face, the wound he had commissioned. 'I fear for you, Gangiriji,' he said, getting to the real issue. 'I want you to tell me how I can protect you from Lambodar, which city you will feel safe living in. That is what I want in return for my decision.'

'I could write to the collector,' Gangiri suggested courteously, 'asking him to make an exception and not reopen my brother's case.'

Silence followed his words. Keyur could see Gangiri was neither afraid of the threat nor tempted by the offer. He looked away quickly, the failure cutting him deep. Sudden anger lashed his mind, like white lightning, blinding him. When he looked at Gangiri again, he did not see a poor, determined farmer. He saw, instead, the reason for his disgrace in Delhi, the cause for his downfall in Mityala.

'I have been through much in the last few days, Gangiriji,' Keyur said in a tightly controlled voice. 'My party has demanded an explanation for the high farmer-suicide rate in Mityala. I have been taken apart by the national press due to the news stories which, if I may remind you, quoted you extensively.'

Gangiri listened intently.

'And finally,' Keyur continued, his voice filled with desperation, 'when you embarrassed me by turning down my offer to be the DP candidate for the assembly elections, it triggered a demand for my resignation from the Mityala seat.

'I want to know,' Keyur asked, anger creeping into his voice, 'how is your brother's suicide my fault? Why are you so adamant on humiliating me? Why aren't you willing to settle for a solution that allows both you and me to survive?'

'Please do not get personal!' Gangiri was curt. 'My brother's suicide was no one's fault!'

He paused to collect himself. 'My purpose has never been to humiliate you. But I am not interested in your survival either.'

Keyur threw up his hands in exasperation.

Gangiri continued, anger glinting in his voice, 'In your so-called "offer of candidacy", I saw an attempt to politicize my efforts and I thwarted it. Just as I never publicized your role in the assault on me, knowing well that it would have taken the spotlight off the farmer suicides.'

As the words sank in, Keyur became pensive.

'I never blamed you in the press, Keyurji,' Gangiri stressed, 'I never demanded your resignation. You may want to remember that if you want to continue this conversation.' Gangiri turned away abruptly and walked towards the hand pump in the corner of the front yard.

Keyur watched as Gangiri washed his hands and feet, realizing he had misread the man in so many ways. He could not be threatened or tempted, and he would never be unscrupulous or unfair. Keyur thought it was but natural that he should feel out of his depth when dealing with such a man.

Gangiri walked to the porch and unrolled a cotton mat for them to sit on under the shade of the thatch. He then turned to Keyur, waiting. When Keyur walked to the mat and settled down, Gangiri handed him a glass of water.

'The suicide toll makes me look bad,' Keyur argued, taking the steel glass from Gangiri. '*You* make me look bad.'

'What will make you look good?' Gangiri demanded. 'Widows being denied compensation?'

Keyur slammed his glass down, spilling the water. 'How can you say that? Even after the public statement I just made...'

'It is the truth,' Gangiri snapped, 'and the truth always comes out into the open. I am merely the instrument this time.'

'I am not afraid of the truth!' Keyur retorted. 'I may not know how this job is done, but I want to learn! I don't know how to make a difference, but I know I will!'

He glanced away at the sunlight that filled the front yard. 'Delhi made me believe that it is a game I was born to win. I fell for the alluring assurance that comes from proximity to power centres. This setback has taught me that the centre of my power is my voter.' He paused. 'I am sorry for making so many mistakes... But I am glad that I made the mistake of cornering you with that offer to be a DP candidate.'

He glanced sombrely at Gangiri. 'I have learnt this after meeting you, Gangiriji. You can replace me as a politician, but I can never replace you as a farmer.'

Keyur fell silent, waiting to see if it worked.

'Well, let's try this again then,' Gangiri said dryly. 'What do you want from me?'

'To reach an understanding,' Keyur said. 'Don't you miss the city, the speed, the ease of life there? I can take care of your life in any city of your choice. You could still play a role in Gopur, if you wanted.'

'As a non-resident,' Gangiri said patiently, 'I cannot be part of the suicide committee.'

'There will be no need. I will personally monitor the committee. No eligible farmer suicide will be declared apatra again. Perhaps, in time, I will have the committee reorganized and even drop Lambodar, Durga Das, and others like—'

Gangiri interrupted him. 'Did you really expect me to agree to your proposal, Keyurji?'

Keyur stared at him for a minute, then looked away without answering.

Gangiri just said, 'Thank you.'

They were silent for some time. Keyur said, finally, 'I have never talked like this to anyone, so tactlessly...so directly.'

'Then don't' Gangiri suggested. 'You are wasting your time.'

'It was worth it,' Keyur said, giving up.

'I am flattered.'

Keyur frowned. 'I can see the state of your circumstances. From where do you get the strength, the courage?'

Gangiri remained silent, asking himself the question. Then he said, 'Perhaps from being aware that I am only incidental.'

Keyur was struck by the words and thoughtfully lowered his eyes.

Gangiri could read the disappointment on his face. 'So,' he smiled, changing the topic, 'what did you think of the solutions I suggested to Nazarji in his story?'

'I want to put into practice some of your suggestions,' Keyur said, then stopped, recollecting something. 'But before we discuss that, I have been waiting to ask you a question. How did you get in touch with Nazar Prabhakar?'

'Why?'

Keyur shrugged. 'There would not have been so much trouble in Delhi for me if you had not spoken to a national newspaper and a well-known journalist.'

'It brought you here,' Gangiri pointed out, 'and you have changed the fate of hundreds of widows.'

Keyur could not refute that, if he saw life standing in Gangiri's shoes.

For a while afterwards, they talked about the remedies to help farmers and the variation in implementation required in different parts of the district. They then discussed the assembly segments Keyur was visiting next and what he could expect.

Keyur told Gangiri about the relief measures he had been announcing for farm widows and said he planned to extend the scheme to the apatra suicide cases as well if they were found to be eligible. As the interaction extended to an hour, the villagers who had accompanied Keyur searched for places to sit around the narrow path, waiting for him.

Padma had taken the children to the temple steps where prasad was distributed daily among the poor after the morning puja. When she returned, she found Gangiri talking to Keyur and stopped uncertainly. Her saree did not reach her dusty feet, the hair was tied listlessly and the dark eyes looked indifferently at Keyur.

Keyur stood up when Gangiri introduced Padma. She whispered a greeting and walked into the house. The children came and sat next to Gangiri.

Keyur thoughtfully glanced at the doorway after Padma walked into the house. He had met many widows since he came to Mityala, but meeting Padma made him lose his smile.

The children were telling Gangiri about the prasad they had at the temple steps, when he gently interrupted to introduce Keyur.

'Balu, here, is five years old,' Gangiri said about the boy. 'He is a strong boy who never cries except, of course, when he has had a bad fall. He is also famous in the village for his fairness; he never fights with anyone weaker than himself.' Gangiri paused. 'Of course, few are weaker than him these days.'

Balu smiled at Keyur, his eyes serious.

Then Gangiri glanced at the little girl. 'Sashi is four years old. She is famous among the people of Gopur for her patience. She always waits, unlike other spoilt children, for her turn, never demanding what she cannot have. Only very rarely,' Gangiri smiled down at her, 'she cries like the baby that she is.'

Balu chuckled, and Sashi looked up at Gangiri in protest.

'I somehow feel,' Keyur said contemplatively, 'that Sashi looks very courageous. She cannot possibly cry like a baby.'

Sashi, surprised, smiled at him and turned to Balu triumphantly.

'These are my brother's children,' Gangiri said in English to Keyur. 'They live with their mother here.' He paused, looking at the children's curious faces as they tried to decipher the language. 'They know their father is no more. I have no idea how they have accepted it...but they have.'

Keyur did not know what to say, the sadness in the soft voice was too complete to comment upon.

Gangiri then said, 'I did not stay back in Gopur to settle scores, as you suggested earlier. It was the only thing I could have done. I could have supported this family in the city but how would I have taught them about justice, truth, or even pride?' Gangiri paused. 'I know I am punishing them now, but I know they will appreciate the reasons when they grow up.'

Keyur listened to Gangiri, sensing something fragile about him, something other than poverty. Gangiri was not overwhelmed by the difficulty of his position and the challenge, but he was crushed by the burden of guilt. As he heard Gangiri speak, Keyur understood the personal price the farmer was paying to sustain this fight for justice for farmers like his brother. Gangiri had to choose between this fight and the responsibility for the well-being of his brother's family. Keyur was amazed that Gangiri had opted for the tougher choice.

After almost two hours, Keyur took leave and drove out of Gopur towards the next set of villages in the next assembly segment. Lambodar, who was simmering in anger, expertly covered up his emotions and diligently saw Keyur off to the outskirts of Gopur. He had even got some lunch packed for Keyur, hoping to find the old shortcut to the heart.

Watching the bright afternoon roads from behind his sunglasses, Keyur realized he could never forget this trip to the small village of Gopur. He understood now why neither Lambodar nor his own team ever mentioned the distress suicides which had *not* been found eligible for compensation. The DP could never perform badly in any election, and would never need the dirty tricks of his team, if he worked for the welfare of such families.

Secondly, it helped him politically to know the exact extent of Lambodar's foul play when it came to the verdicts. Keyur could assess the benefits of his decision about re-examining the suicides by the mere fact that Lambodar did not mention the industrial park again.

Thirdly, and frankly, he thought, it was far healthier to be aligned with someone like Gangiri. His suggestions for development were sincere and he clearly did not have political ambitions. Besides, Gangiri could keep Lambodar and his son on tenterhooks merely by being himself.

Keyur glanced out of the window. The meeting with Gangiri was what made his trip to Gopur, to Mityala, memorable. He had wanted to meet Gangiri for retribution. He thought Gangiri had retribution in mind when he stayed back in Gopur. His heart burned with insult, his mind seethed with thoughts of revenge. He wanted to prove that he was not a man to be trifled with, not a man to forgive easily. A man too strong and wily to ever be truly defeated. He planned to subjugate Gangiri one way or the other. But he had found Gangiri to be a smart man, too smart to be tied down by his circumstances. So he tempted Gangiri with what he was looking for: justice in the form of his decision to reopen the ineligible verdicts. Justice to buy him off.

He failed, he now realized, because he had been defeated even before he had reached Gopur. He had become a prisoner of the perception of his own invincibility.

He had underestimated the power of awareness that Gangiri had talked about.

I am only incidental, Gangiri had said.

Perhaps, Keyur thought for the first time in his life, *so am I.*

20

A fortnight later, morning in Nula village, Mityala district

There was absolute silence in the room as Durga Das read the document carefully and his son, Gokul, read his father's face nervously. Durga Das turned another page without comment and Gokul breathed a little more freely.

Then Durga Das glanced up, a reprimand in his watery brown eyes. Gokul, harried, moved closer to look at the paragraph his father indicated. It read: 'The sum along with the interest or its equivalent in produce will be returned by the end of a period of three months'. His father's finger pointed to the word 'equivalent'.

'Equivalent *but not less than*,' Durga Das said in a low voice to his son. 'A certain quantity of cotton which you will specify.'

Gokul understood his error, and apologized.

'Never mind the niceties,' his father snapped. 'Calculate the quantity according to government rates.' He paused. 'But do not mention that in the note.'

Gokul nodded sheepishly. He was a twenty-two-year-old man who had just received a degree in commerce and was spending the winter apprenticing with his father. In a few months, he would be on his way to his first formal job in

Surat with a diamond merchant. And by the end of the first year, he was expected to set up an independent business of his own, as well as a secondary business of moneylending, just like his father.

Durga Das was being patient with his only son. According to Durga, his two married daughters had already inherited what was due to them: his genes. But Gokul was reconciled to being a constant source of disappointment to his father because he found moneylending inadequate as a way of life. He knew, whatever he did, he would always fall short of the cold purposes of his father's trade.

Durga Das turned the page. There were about thirty people in the front room of his house in Nula village which also doubled up as his shop. No one made any noise, no one even coughed or sneezed in that room. They sat on mattresses spread on the floor from wall to wall. The white sheets were dirty with the earth the farmers carried from the fields to the doorstep of the moneylender.

Along two walls were arranged low tables on the mattresses behind which sat six assistants who studied the papers, weighed the gold or silver, checked the precious stones, assessed the customer's creditworthiness and finally conveyed the case to Durga Das. He sat at the extreme right of this assembly line, at one of the oldest tables, with one of the most innovatively manipulated weighing scales in the history of weights and measurements.

For the last few months, his son had begun occupying the table next to Durga Das, the position indicative of the eventual succession. This morning, Gokul had good reason for being so anxious about his father checking the draft agreement. Every eye in the room, of the customers and of the staff, was glued on them.

People could not hear much, Durga Das was speaking very softly with his son. But they knew a cotton field was being pledged for a three-month loan at 1.5 per cent interest per month. This implied that the farmer had a good repayment record, or he belonged to one of the higher castes, or owned land or property in excess of what he was pledging. They knew this because Durga Das seldom charged anything less than 2 per cent monthly interest from farmers who had an average to bad record of repayment or who were from the lower castes or owned less than five acres. He charged 2.5 to 3 per cent from farmers who had been defaulters in the past; the caste did not matter then.

Three musclemen stood just outside the doorway. They swung into action whenever they had to throw out a customer, usually a pleading defaulter whose property was about to be seized. They also helped in fast-tracking repayments from reluctant debtors by giving them shakedowns in Nula's backstreets.

The six assistants took care of various aspects of the business based on their expertise. Two of them were legal experts who studied all documents submitted for pledging. Another one possessed wide technical knowledge, from handpumps to automobiles. One of the assistants acted as a human calculator with special skills and a good memory; he counted and recorded all the money that was transacted during the day. The other two dealt with loans and claims, respectively, for pledged objects.

Moneylenders usually reserved the last job for either someone highly respected and senior or a newcomer to the area who would be presumed neutral. Having no patience with the wisdom that came with the experience of the former type, Durga Das had employed the latter.

Most of the customers these days, in fact, came to deal with the claims assistant. The cotton harvest had begun.

The claims assistant delegated relevant work to his colleagues, but it was primarily his job to return pledged items to the farmers. Nowadays, he was dealing with a lot of women too, because most of the pledged items were their ornaments.

The process of recovery, though bewitchingly simple to the observer, took years of training to master. When an object was pledged, Durga Das gave the borrower a small rectangular slip of paper to be produced when redeeming the object. The paper carried an exclusive cipher that was usually unintelligible to others, a special signature to prove it was written by Durga Das, along with the value and nature of the ornament pledged.

That morning, a middle-aged husband and wife presented such a piece of paper to the claims assistant. He carried it to Durga Das who validated it and sent him to recover the object from the safe inside the house. The farmer held back the repayment and waited to check the object first, indicating his mistrust of the moneylender. The object, a gold chain, was brought out in a small plastic packet and handed to him. The farmer passed it on to his wife to check and she confirmed that it was the pledged ornament. It was only then that the farmer paid the money due and cleared the debt. The woman waited, holding the small packet, for the procedure to be completed and the necessary documents signed. Then she opened the packet, felt the chain on her fingers for a second and wore it around her neck. Her husband watched her and when she glanced at him, smiled.

Not all transactions took place so smoothly. One farmer in a white dhoti and shirt insisted that there were gold beads missing from his wife's mangala sutra, the traditional neck ornament worn by married women, which he had reclaimed just then. The allegation shocked everyone except Durga Das who calmly continued weighing a heavy necklace that belonged to the family of a bankrupt landlord.

The claims assistant passed on the matter to the technical expert who studied the mangala sutra, and declared it had not been tampered with. But the farmer protested furiously, saying they could not be trusted and charged Durga Das with cheating. One of the assistants beckoned the musclemen waiting at the door and the farmer was quickly ushered out for 'further discussions'.

A young girl sat next to her father, who was physically disabled, as he reclaimed an ornament for three thousand rupees. She checked it briefly and placed it deep in her bag, her eyes sparkling with happiness. Others stared as a man paid twenty thousand rupees for a gold necklace and the claims assistant's face betrayed the pain he felt in returning the ornament.

A farmer wanted to buy a gold bead, worth fifteen hundred rupees, to add to his wife's mangala sutra. He held the tiny bead in his palm, staring at it wistfully for a long time. The assistants kept a close eye on him, already knowing he could not afford the bead. Finally, the man returned the bead and stormed out of the shop.

Gangiri watched as the farmer emerged from the shop, looking distraught, and walked away towards the marketplace. Someone should follow that man, thought Gangiri, to keep him from going to the nearest shop that sold pesticide.

He looked at Durga Das's shop again. It was set into the front of the large mansion which was his home. Situated in the heart of Nula's main street, the mansion was a landmark.

In front of it was a tea stall that catered to the visitors to the shop, mainly people gathering courage to mortgage their lands, homes, lives, dreams. The owner of the tea stall, now an expert at dealing with desperation, offered advice along with tea and cookies.

Gangiri had been waiting, sitting on one of the benches since even before the stall opened at 7 a.m. He had offered to leave but the owner had asked him to stay, feeling sad for how troubled he looked. Gangiri helped him put up the yellow tarpaulin canopy above the benches, answering his questions generally but without giving any specific information. He then sat down again on a bench and turned back to studying Durga Das's shop across the road.

It was now 10 a.m. and Gangiri could still not gather the strength to cross the narrow road. He felt a quiet panic, like the silent rise of river water during floods. He had won against the odds he was born with, the odds he had inherited, and the odds he had encountered in life. But that shop across the road symbolized his final, irrevocable defeat.

From the time he entered Gopur, he had been fighting forces which were determined to bring him to that shop, to enslave his spirit. He had been winning until now, and would keep winning till he entered that shop.

However, it was not a question of victory anymore. It was just a matter of the degree of defeat.

He would not be here but for what had happened in the last fortnight, events that took place with the clarity and intent of the quick, deadly movements of an endgame. The threat was so cold that instinctively, though futilely, Gangiri still felt like retaliating.

❖

A few days after Keyur left Gopur, Collector Gul announced that the past verdicts of the suicide committee would be revisited and decided on merit, and given the benefit of doubt. The collector also announced that officials, beginning with village talathis, would face action if it was found that they had misrepresented facts to disprove distress suicides, eventually leading to apatra verdicts.

There was a wave of euphoria in Gopur and people thronged Gangiri's small house, full of gratitude for making Keyur take these decisions. Gangiri explained that he had merely pointed Keyur in the right direction and the decisions were his alone. No one believed him. Including Lambodar, Durga Das, the talathi and the local moneylenders.

Gangiri could feel their anger. The grocers refused to sell him food on credit anymore. As they insisted on payment every time, he could not afford to buy enough food and even for the little he did, he had to pay from what remained of the salary arrears.

Taking the announcement of the review of verdicts as the last straw, an angry Lambodar held a much publicized meeting with the village sarpanch, demanding Keyur's resignation and a re-election in Mityala constituency. There was much sloganeering in open jeeps along village roads against Keyur and also threatening the DP with dire consequences. Finally, posters came up saying there was a need for a 'local' man to represent Mityala. As everyone knew Lambodar meant his son to be that 'local' man, people lost interest.

At about the same time, the cotton harvest commenced. Farmers, who had anticipated very low yields due to the delay in rains, were pleasantly surprised by the first picking.

As the bags became heavy with cotton, the troubles seemed to lift from their shoulders. This added to the sense of independence that the farmers were feeling but increased the despondency among moneylenders.

As a result, at the last suicide committee meeting, Lambodar and Durga Das were more vehement than ever, arguing and voting against every claim for compensation that was on the agenda. But they suffered a setback when AO Jivan Patel quietly voted in favour, deciding that all the suicide cases were due to debt distress and eligible for state compensation.

Both Lambodar and Durga Das knew that their men had shadowed Gangiri constantly for the last few weeks, they had even submitted daily activity reports. They knew Gangiri had not approached Jivan Patel and were worried that the AO might have suffered a genuine change of heart. Only Gangiri knew that the reason behind that change was an uncomfortable photograph, the existence of which was recently impressed upon Jivan Patel anonymously by means of the Mityala postal service. For that bit of research and implementation, Gangiri was grateful to Videhi and had already thanked her on phone.

Gangiri's own crop was doing well, with the first leaves shining with optimism. Other farmers like him, who had opted for pulses, said the prices were riding high due to market demand and that the harvest was expected to fetch a good price.

It was a time for laughing at the fears of the past, for disbelieving the fears of the future. The perfect reflection in the pond had looked real. And even Padma smiled for an instant. Gangiri remembered those moments from just a few days ago as from a different time, a different fate.

Then the stone fell in the water and the spell was broken.

21

About a week ago, Balu had woken up with a headache and a severe cough. Worried that the boy's health might worsen, Gangiri took him to Rao at the hospital in Batoni. Rao prescribed some medicines and asked Gangiri to bring Balu back for a check-up in two days.

But two days were enough for Gangiri to understand that this was no ordinary illness. Balu was barely able to stand when he took him back to Batoni.

Rao diagnosed tuberculosis and sounded worried as he assessed Balu's health. He concluded that as the child was malnourished and weak, the impact of the infection would be intense. Tests also showed that Balu was anaemic, which had affected his strength to fight the disease. Gangiri heard the deadly verdict, distraught, sitting in Rao's small white room in the hospital.

The doctor mentioned the government's free treatment plan for tuberculosis and other schemes for child health care. Rao filled out the few forms that were needed to formalize the treatment under the scheme.

He then closed the files, put away the papers and glanced at Gangiri, asking him not to take it amiss. He apologized for not being able to offer more as he opened his wallet, saying it was almost the middle of the month. He had a few hundred rupees and he offered all of them to Gangiri.

Gangiri, stunned, had refused the money. But Rao pleaded that no treatment of any kind would work if Balu was not given proper food. He insisted that Gangiri take the money and get both the children full meals twice a day for at least a few days.

Even the bright sunlight that morning in Nula could not dispel the darkness he had felt at that moment two days ago in Batoni. In that small room, with the doctor begging him not to starve the children, Gangiri had been scared of himself.

He had wanted to prove that the fight was not about money but about morality. The gods must be on the side of the money. They were surely not on the side of morality. He had finally taken the money from Rao and promised to pay it back after the harvest. The currency notes had felt alien in his hands, unclean to touch.

He had taken Balu home to Gopur in a public transport bus, feeling his weakness and fever as he held him close. What if Padma, who never asked him anything, asked him just one question: 'Why?'

Gangiri had stared out of the bus window, frightened for the first time since he came to Gopur. He knew the next step was surrender. And he knew it was not too far away.

Back in Gopur, he went to the marketplace, meeting one grocer after the other as they turned him down. They refused to sell him anything, even if he paid in cash. They insisted that he first clear his past dues or get a guarantee from Durga Das or Lambodar. The traders resented him for making the farmers aware of their options, of showing them how to fight the system. No one had to organize them, they were united by their hatred for Gangiri.

When he went to the local moneylenders asking for a loan, they said they could not trust a man who defamed them by undermining Lambodar's and Durga Das's verdicts in the suicide committee.

For two days Gangiri returned home empty-handed, realizing that he had to build bridges with either Lambodar or Durga Das to survive in Gopur. When he sought to meet Lambodar, he refused to see him, sending the message that Gangiri was never to call on him again.

The night before, Gangiri had returned home defeated again, and once more put Balu to bed with some rice and free medicines.

❀

The owner of the tea stall watched as Gangiri stood up and walked across the road to the shop. One of the musclemen at the door stopped him and asked for his name, which was then conveyed to Durga Das. In a few seconds, he was invited into the shop.

Gangiri took off his worn shoes before entering and left them among the flock of at least thirty pairs at the threshold. The mattress felt soft under his feet as he followed the man, making his way amidst the waiting people. No one looked up from the low desks, except Durga Das who was watching him carefully.

Gangiri was distracted by his own reflection in a dozen mirrors set in-between wooden cabinets on the walls. Mirrors were a favourite among moneylenders, especially jewellers, to keep an eye on the customers.

Then Gangiri saw Durga Das sitting in a prominent corner of the shop and greeted him. Durga Das cordially requested him to sit across his desk. Gangiri saw that Durga Das was in the middle of a negotiation, his books of accounts open before him on the desk. It was taking time for both parties to decide what the agreed sum should be.

As he watched them, Gangiri was weighed down by a thought. This shop must be the same place where his brother had come to borrow money, the same place his father had come as well. It could be the same place Balu or Sashi might come one day.

He drank the water that was offered and refused the tea, feeling Durga Das observe him even as he wound up the transaction.

Gangiri looked around the shop. There was tension among the people, a heightened level of alertness which pointed to their apprehensions with Durga Das's way of conducting business. He could see that every time a piece of jewellery was valued, people appeared surprised, wondering how it could cost so less. And every time people paid back the loans to redeem their pledged jewellery, they looked worried about how it could cost so much.

Durga Das finally turned to him. 'What is this about, Bhadra? The next suicide committee meeting is still a week away. Or couldn't you wait?'

'You must know very well what this is about,' Gangiri pointed out. 'Your men have been watching me day and night.'

'Yes, well...' Durga Das said smugly. 'I am sorry to hear about your nephew's illness. Tuberculosis seems to mostly affect those who cannot afford it.'

Gangiri smiled patiently. 'Please help me afford it.'

'But how can I?' Durga Das seemed surprised. 'Your brother's loan is yet to be cleared.'

'I just need five thousand rupees to clear the grocers' dues, Durgaji,' Gangiri said. 'It is only till I harvest the crop of pulses three months from now.'

'Five thousand rupees!' Durga Das said, shocked. 'Impossible.'

Then he frowned. 'But you can ask others, surely? Won't the MP Kashinath put in a word for you? He is, after all, your friend?'

'I have nothing to do with the decisions he made when he was here, Durgaji,' Gangiri said, getting to the point. 'He met the widows and came to his own conclusions. You can ask the talathi, I barely spoke during those interactions. But I cannot help it if the women blamed the talathi, Lambodarji and you, for their financial troubles.'

'I asked the talathi,' Durga Das replied. 'He says you instigated the widows. It is part of your campaign against me and Lambodarji.'

Gangiri frowned. 'That is not true.'

'But I think it is true. And I am not loaning you a rupee.'

Gangiri did not speak. He then lowered his eyes, knowing Durga Das was waiting for him to beg.

'I promise I will pay you back after the harvest,' Gangiri tried again. 'You know pulses are set to do well this year.'

'No one from your family has ever paid me back!' Durga Das said sharply, and everyone in the room turned towards them.

Gangiri did not look up, aware of the probing eyes of the people in the room. His voice shook a little as he said, 'I need the loan, Durgaji...'

Durga Das nodded, as if understanding his plight.

'Please.' Gangiri glanced at Durga Das. 'It is a paltry amount for you...'

Durga Das shook his head, his eyes twinkling at Gangiri's desperation.

'Tell me what will make you trust me.'

Durga Das just looked into Gangiri's dark eyes, the knowing, intelligent eyes now pleading.

'What should I do,' Gangiri begged, 'to make you believe my promise?'

Durga Das smiled faintly.

'There must be something I can do...?'

'You are right,' Durga Das finally said. 'There is.'

Durga Das studied him for a minute.

'You have damaged my image in the district, Bhadra,' Durga Das said, curtly. 'You have run me down systematically at the meetings of the suicide committee. You forced suicides to be declared eligible for compensation by casting aspersions on me.'

People now paid attention to the conversation, realizing it was Gangiri Bhadra that Durga Das was talking to.

'You, Bhadra, questioned my integrity,' Durga Das said tersely. 'You made people who trusted me for generations, begin mistrusting me now.'

Gangiri looked away helplessly.

'Even my son here,' he gestured to Gokul next to him, who was listening to the conversation, 'is facing the consequences of what you have done. He has to travel to another state to set up his business. I can no longer be sure that moneylending will be a safe option for him in Mityala. You have done this to my family, Bhadra. Now tell me,' he smiled mockingly, 'what can I do for your family?'

Gangiri lowered his eyes again, unable to answer.

Durga Das studied the downcast face and the drooping shoulders with satisfaction. He said, 'I know you need the money and I will lend it to you. But I have a condition.'

Gangiri glanced at him hopefully.

'You will have to prove to the people of this district that you were wrong about me,' Durga Das said, smiling. 'It is only fair that you undo the damage you have done to me.'

'I had not meant to do you any damage, Durgaji.'

'Words are of no value, Bhadra. But deeds can be of value of up to five thousand rupees. Prove to the farmers that you were mistaken about me,' Durga Das said. He was no longer smiling. 'Prove to me that you are sorry.'

'I will do anything you want.' Gangiri said earnestly, 'Anything.'

Durga Das leaned forward. 'Anything?'

Gangiri nodded resolutely. Gokul glanced at his father uneasily. The people waited, looking at Durga Das.

'Have you ever been to the temple in Pandaru, Bhadra?' Durga Das asked thoughtfully. 'Do you know how they do penance there?'

Gangiri shook his head.

'When the devotees repent their sins, they do penance by kneeling at the threshold of the temple,' Durga Das explained. 'They seek forgiveness of the god by punishing themselves.'

He paused for a moment, then added softly, 'Just as you will kneel at my threshold seeking my forgiveness.'

Gangiri stared at him, his lean face frozen in disbelief.

Durga Das just looked at Gangiri, his watery brown eyes cold and amused.

'I want to see you every day for three days outside this shop from morning to noon,' Durga Das spoke slowly, loving the sound of each word. 'I want to make sure that anyone who wants to witness this can visit Nula and see you here, waiting for me to forgive you.'

There was a swift murmur among the people who were astonished by the stipulation.

Gangiri stared at Durga Das with neither anger nor resentment but a realization. Durga Das saw it as a matter of triumph to insult him. Gangiri knew he himself could not afford that triumph, it was a matter of feeding the hungry children back home.

'I will do it,' he said simply.

Druga Das was incredulous. 'You will?'

'Yes, I will be here tomorrow morning,' Gangiri said, standing up to leave. 'Can I have some money at the end of the first morning please? My nephew is very ill.'

Gokul, who was looking at his father, frowned. He saw something that the others did not understand. There was a change in Durga Das's expression, he was getting angry that his plan was being thwarted.

'What is it about your family, Bhadra?' Durga Das was sarcastic. 'You people can do anything for money?'

Gangiri looked evenly at Durga Das, then controlling himself, turned to walk towards the exit. He could see Durga Das was trying to find other ways to incite him so that he would have an excuse to refuse the loan.

'But for me, your brother would have got the compensation money for which he died,' Durga Das said, boastfully. 'But you are smarter, always have been. You know you don't have to die to make money. What else will you do if I pay you, Bhadra? Cheat, lie, kill, rape?'

Gangiri looked away, feeling anger fill his veins, pounding in his head, making him want revenge for those words. With effort, he refused to give in to it for the sake of Balu, for the sake of a boy who was suffering because of him.

Tears filled his eyes painfully and Gangiri lowered them. He should just walk away, he told himself. *Walk away. Just walk away.*

Then he heard Durga Das say deliberately, 'Don't worry about your nephew. He won't die if there is no money to be made. He won't—'

Gangiri turned abruptly to Durga Das and in one movement reached across the desk and grabbed the front of his shirt. Durga Das gasped as he was rudely pulled up to his feet and stared at Gangiri's face, frightened.

'You are talking about a five-year-old child, Durgaji,' Gangiri said with restraint. 'Don't be unkind.'

Gangiri was about to let go of him when he noticed the fear on Durga Das's face. For the first time the sly look in the brown eyes was replaced by dread at the expectation of retaliation. Both knew Gangiri would be justified in wanting to choke him to death for so many reasons, for so many people. Gangiri's hand left the collar and reached for Durga Das's neck instead, his long fingers encircled it, the tempting horror on Durga Das's face driving him out of control. Then Gangiri frowned, suddenly conscious of what he was doing and quickly stepped away, disgusted with himself.

Durga Das staggered back, and shouted to his men to save him. There was a frozen second when no one moved, aware that Gangiri was stepping back from Durga Das, not attacking him. But as Durga Das shouted again, the assistants pounced on Gangiri and pinned him down to the mattress. The musclemen overpowered him and punched him, holding him down. At first everyone could hear Gangiri's gasps of pain, then there was just the sound of blows as fists hit flesh and bone.

Durga Das ran to the back door that led into the house, ordering Gokul to follow him. But Gokul was too shocked to move, staring at the nine men assaulting Gangiri even as he lay powerless on the mattress, his arms crushed under their feet. Gokul then rushed to them, shouting at them to stop, pushing them away from Gangiri.

Gangiri lay writhing in pain, bleeding, his shirt torn, his skin bruised and bloody. The stunned people quickly gathered around and helped him up. Gangiri tried to lean against the wall, breathing with difficulty, but bent with the pain in his stomach. He closed his eyes, coughing and tasting blood in his mouth.

Then he felt someone wipe the blood on his face and at his lips, and ask about the nearest medical clinic. He felt the same hands supporting his head and he opened his eyes, curious.

Gokul met his eyes, the cloth in his hands soaked in blood. He apologized for his father's behaviour and tried to say something more, shaking his head gravely, making Gangiri smile.

Long after Gangiri was taken away for treatment and long after the shop was declared closed for the day, the doors had to be kept open. People were still coming to the shop, the room remained crowded even in the evening. They gathered around the place where Gangiri had fallen and bled, and they retold the incident to others. A poor man who refused to be insulted by Durga Das, they said. They had thought that such a thing could never happen. And yet, in their silent prayers, they had wished for just such a thing.

They knew their wishes drove Gangiri that day. The man who helped the widows get their due compensation, who helped dead farmers get their due respect.

They had always wished for someone like Gangiri, they had always wanted to be someone like Gangiri. No one spoke, but as they glanced at each other standing in the shop, they all knew what it really was.

They stared in silence at the blood that still shone bright on the dirty white mattresses.

They all knew who he really was.

22

Three days later, the district collectorate, Mityala town

The news travelled to Mityala, burning a trail through the countryside, and reached Collector Gul. He summoned Durga Das and Gangiri to the collectorate for a hearing. Though it was held three days after the incident, they could see that the wounds on Gangiri's arms and neck were still deep, the bruises still vivid.

'Explain your actions, Durgaji!' Gul snapped, gesturing to Gangiri. 'And remember that the chief of police has about a dozen witnesses.'

Durga Das smiled. 'I would love to meet them, collector saheb.'

Gul was momentarily unsettled. 'You are right, they may not be impartial witnesses.'

'Precisely.'

'This can be remedied,' Gul said, reaching for the phone. 'Let us agree on suspending your moneylenders' licence for a month or two. Then the witnesses will have no reason to lie, will they?'

Durga Das quickly glanced at the phone.

'Will they, Durgaji?'

Durga Das's cunning smile had vanished.

'This is not fair, collector saheb,' he said calmly. 'I cannot be held responsible if Bhadra gets hurt in a street brawl somewhere.'

'He did not get hurt in a street brawl,' Gul replied. 'And his safety *was* your responsibility.'

'Who knows what enemies he has made for himself? Everyone knows how unscrupulous his methods are. How can I, or even you, decide whether or not he deserved the punishment he got?'

'Deciding that, Durgaji,' Gul said, picking up the phone, 'is what I do for a living.'

He asked to be connected to the district revenue officer and hung up.

Durga Das shrugged. 'I hope you remember, collector saheb, that this is your cadre state.'

'I hope everyone remembers that,' Gul chuckled.

Tea was served just as the phone rang, it was the DRO. Gul asked him the conditions under which a moneylending licence could be suspended. He made notes and ended the call, asking the DRO to await instructions regarding a case.

He glanced at the notes and looked at Durga Das. 'Use or abetment to use of violence, harassment and assault. Surely you see we have a case for not just suspension but cancellation of the licence.'

'I am quite sure these conditions apply to the conduct of a moneylender towards a debtor. It would be, of course, prudent to discover if Bhadra is indebted to me in any way.'

Gul was lost for a minute.

Durga Das smiled. 'So, you see, we do not have a case for suspension or cancellation of the licence, or anything else. Let us have tea and enjoy the afternoon.'

'I would not agree with you there, Durgaji,' Gangiri said softly.

Durga Das raised his eyebrows. Gul waited, noticing Gangiri did not touch the tea either.

'First, my brother was your debtor, so the conditions apply. Secondly, you insulted, intimidated and threatened me in a manner I consider dangerous to my safety. Thirdly, there is a medical report from the clinic near your shop in Nula that says I was assaulted.'

Durga Das turned away from him, his expression resentful.

'It is better if we sort this out here in my office, Durgaji,' Gul said. 'Otherwise, the police will get to the truth.'

'You would have seen the truth already, collector saheb, if you were on my side,' Durga Das said severely.

'There are no sides here,' Gul replied. 'It is just that I take strong exception to the fact that, despite my specific instructions, someone under my protection was hurt.'

Durga Das shook his head helplessly, and chuckled.

'I shall recommend appropriate action against you when Mr Bhadra files the complaint,' Gul added. 'The scope of punishment, as you probably know, is one year imprisonment or a fine, or both.'

Durga Das stopped smiling.

'Along with the cancellation of your licence which will be notified in the district gazette.'

Durga Das frowned, worried for the first time.

'This is too harsh a punishment, collector saheb, for someone who is innocent. This man pounced on me, tried to strangle me...that is when I had to scream for help.'

'According to your staff,' Gul said, 'Mr Bhadra posed no threat to your life.'

'But he did!' Durga Das was agitated. 'He was in a great rage because I refused him a loan. It took my entire staff to save me from him.'

'And yet you have no wounds, no cuts, not even a single bruise,' Gul observed.

Durga Das had no argument to counter that. There was silence in the room as both Gul and Gangiri watched the desperation on Durga Das's face.

'Durgaji is wrong,' Gangiri finally said, glancing at Gul. 'He is mistaken...'

'I am wrong? I am mistaken?' Durga Das was on his feet, enraged. 'I will finish you, Bhadra, you have no idea what you have—'

'He is mistaken, sir,' Gangiri said again, addressing Gul. 'I was not in his shop. I was hurt when I fell on the road in Nula, where I had gone for some personal work.'

Gul was astonished. Durga Das stood staring at him, stunned.

Gangiri took a deep breath. 'Keeping in view the loss of face Durgaji may suffer in this case, I request that the matter may not be investigated further.'

Durga Das slumped down in his chair numbly.

Gul frowned. 'Why are you doing this, Mr Bhadra?'

'Because it was not Durgaji's fault. He did not violate your instructions, he was not planning to.'

'This is absurd!' Gul snapped, angry, but also mystified.

'I am sorry, sir,' Gangiri replied, 'but this is the truth.'

Durga Das did not speak a word for the duration of the rest of the meeting. Or even later, when he walked past Gangiri to his car in the parking lot. Gangiri paused as the dust from the car's wake blinded him for a few seconds, then resumed his slow walk to the gate.

Gangiri's refusal to lodge a complaint fanned the fire that smouldered in the hearts of the farmers across the district. Many of them came to protest his decision. They argued that this was the first chance in a long time to teach a lesson to a moneylender of Durga Das's stature. They felt that if Durga Das was punished, every moneylender in the district would behave properly towards farmers.

To all their arguments, Gangiri had a simple answer. He gestured at the cuts and bruises on his body. He asked them if they felt any change of heart towards the moneylenders. The answer, always, was no. The answer, he tried convincing them, was not violence or punishment, but reconciliation.

The porch of the small, fragile house was always crowded in the days that followed. People came from other villages sometimes just to see him, as if to know that there was nothing different between them, anyone of them, and him. Some were as poor as him but many were better off. They could see that what he did, they could have done too. They could still do.

❖

The meeting of the suicide committee a few days later was so smooth, so silent and so harmonious that Gul finally asked what was wrong. Everyone wondered what he meant and continued with their excellent behaviour.

Stunning everyone, especially Gul, Durga Das voted that the listed cases were debt-distress suicides and favoured a grant of compensation to all claims. Only apatra Lambodar stayed true to form, opposing Gangiri's arguments and voting against all the cases as always.

When the meeting ended, Gul took Gangiri aside,

complimenting him on his forbearance. He also offered to stand guarantor for any loan Gangiri might want to take from the banks. Overwhelmed, Gangiri thanked him, saying the harvest was still some months away and that the family was surviving on the last of his salary arrears and the money Rao had lent him. He also mentioned that Durga Das had allowed the grocers to lend to him again.

Gul heard him gravely, 'For changing the mind of every member on this committee, you have paid a personal price.'

Gangiri lowered his eyes, the truth in the words hurting him.

'I could not protect you even from the violence,' Gul said, apologetically. 'Durga Das inflicted many injustices on your family but you forgave him. It made him rethink, reform, I understand that. But what about justice?'

'His son took me to the doctor, sir.' Gangiri glanced at Gul. 'Justice was done.'

Gul met the determined dark eyes and smiled. 'You must be a fool to forgive so easily.'

'Or, a farmer,' Gangiri added, dryly.

❈

The next day Rao came to Gopur to check on Balu. He found the boy too weak to even sit up. Rao sat next to his mattress on the floor, noting his temperature and pulse, and joked with Padma that her son was a fighter. He wondered who would need a doctor if all patients were as strong as Balu.

Padma smiled with pride, and held Balu up by his shoulders as Rao examined him. Rao shook his head and said he was going to throw away his medical equipment and try to learn the secret of survival from Balu. He requested Balu to teach him how to be strong like him, how to be invincible. Balu was thrilled and laughed at his words.

When he was about to leave, Padma asked him how long Balu would take to recover. Rao chuckled, saying, 'He is too good a boy to be ill for too long.'

He came out of the house and stopped, noticing the look on Gangiri's face. Gangiri had seen that young expressive face in too many different moods during the meetings of the suicide committee to be fooled by his performance that day.

As he walked with the doctor towards the road, he asked, 'Is that the truth?' Gangiri's voice was choked with concern. 'Balu won't take too long?'

'Yes,' Rao said, looking away quickly. 'He won't.'

Gangiri could not speak for a moment. Finally, he said, 'I should take him to Mityala then, or even the capital...' He stopped speaking, helplessly.

'It would be useless.' Rao confirmed Gangiri's fears. 'There is no time.'

'He is five years old,' Gangiri said desperately. 'He should have time.'

Rao was worried about the devastation he could see in Gangiri's eyes.

'Balu would never have survived this, you know. He was already too...' Rao did not say the words, but Gangiri heard them. His eyes filled up as he looked back at the house.

'I am really sorry,' Rao said. 'I should have been able to do more.'

Gangiri shook his head and walked along, the tears making it difficult for him to find his way.

He stood on the road a long time after the hospital van

drove away. He then wandered the village restlessly, his eyes still tearful, his world torn apart. The great banyan at the lake, the market at the centre, the temple at the entrance, the hillock at the end. Which feature wanted him to stay back in Gopur?

Or was it the people? The greetings of the farmer, the trader, the priest, the teacher. Who was conspiring to keep him in Gopur forever?

He stood still, feeling the village, not just seeing it. It had always wanted him, he smiled, it was not going to let him go. Gopur had made arrangements to keep him here. And to stay, he had to make some arrangements of his own.

❁

The following day brought good news to many families of the farmers whose suicides had been declared apatra in the past by the suicide committee. The district administration, which had reviewed such cases, announced the first list of the names of farmers whose suicides were re-examined and found to be due to debt distress. The family members of those farmers came and met Gangiri to thank him.

The revised verdicts were not just about the money, they were about vindication. He called Padma to meet the families and take part in discussing their plans. When she asked why, he explained that Sudhakar's case could also be re-examined and she should be prepared to fight for justice. She learnt how the process worked, what role the widow of the farmer played, and in case the compensation was awarded, what investment options she would have.

He checked on Balu frequently and, though he no longer asked questions, Gangiri told him about the farmers who came from distant places. Gangiri also realized that he was getting more and more aware of Balu. He could be sitting outside on the porch, talking to people, working in the fields or visiting in the village, he always felt Balu within him, like a tangible, second self. Like the day he was spraying the pesticide a little ahead of schedule, making Vadrangi wonder at the urgency. But Balu, who was with him in his mind, understood the urgency.

On that day he was sitting with the farmers of Chira village who had come to thank him for reversing the trend of apatra cases. Gangiri asked Vadrangi if he could remind him of similar cases from other villages. His friend, who knew him well, realized Gangiri was helping him learn and eagerly participated. Gangiri helped Vadrangi go through the facts of each suicide, correcting his conclusions, helping him understand.

As he sat among the farmers on the porch, Gangiri also knew that that day Balu had been asleep for a longer time than the day before. Till yesterday, he used to sleep for just two to three hours, unable to sleep any longer due to fever and discomfort. But today, he had been asleep since the afternoon and it was already night. When the farmers left and it was silent, he could hear Padma inside the house trying in vain to wake Balu up.

She had tried many times earlier to wake him to give him food and medicines. Now she tried waking him just to hear him call her one last time. Her voice weakened with every futile attempt as she realized he may never call her again. Gangiri could hear her falling apart, he could feel her tears that fell on Balu's burning cheeks as she cried.

Padma held Balu close as each bond of blood came

undone, each silken thread of affection snapped. The silver of the sparkle of his eyes, the gold of the goodness of his heart awaited her permission to return from where they had come. And, though she had called the dust to be her son, she could not let the earth reclaim him yet. And, as if giving her time, time waited.

Gangiri too waited on the porch outside, as still as the night around him. His eyes were dry, his heart was light. For, he grieved for Balu with Balu, not without him. Next to him were the two objects that had seen him through the last few months in Gopur, his book of accounts and the cell phone. He had not needed them lately, as if they were the wings of the dream he had woken up from.

It would just be a short time before the next dream began. He should know, Gangiri thought, he had been woken up from many dreams. Some were awards that he had won in school and college, now locked in showcases. Some were scars like the ones he carried on his skin. Each one could have changed his destination. None had.

He realized suddenly that he had been looking in the wrong place for those who had brought him here to Gopur and were planning to keep him here. Those who wanted him to walk in the shoes of the dead, those who knew they would fit him. He walked into the yard and glanced up at the night sky, realizing he had been searching the wrong world.

Balu was awake when he walked into the house. He had been waiting for him. Gangiri held Balu close as he lay next to him, feeling the heat of fever on Balu's arms as he put them around his neck.

Padma watched them from the corner of the room. Sashi

was asleep next to her on the floor, curled like a new leaf. Padma supervised the ending of what she began, the immortal answers were unlocked from her soul but they were still unable to stop the mortal tears. Gangiri closed his eyes, feeling Balu's struggle as he battled to breathe, his warm forehead pressed against his chest, trembling with weakness.

The question that Gangiri had been asking himself invaded his mind again. He wondered what would have happened if he had chosen the other path, what if he had left Gopur, settled the children and Padma in the city. He knew he would have had to work two jobs to support the family, but he would have worked even three.

The children would have received the education they deserved. He would have made sure they forgot about poverty and deprivation, and Gopur. No, the widows of Mityala may not have got the respect and financial relief they deserved from the suicide committee. And men like Durga Das would not have changed, forcing moneylenders of the entire district to introspect and reform.

But yes, Balu would have lived a better life. He was a smart child, quick to learn and patient with study. He loved competitions and examinations. With the application of that mind in the right direction, he could have become anyone he wanted. He could have been Collector Gul or Chief of Police Reddy or Dr Rao or Nazar Prabhakar.

No, Gangiri thought, Balu would not have been struggling to breathe and waiting to die if he had left Gopur. And it was now Gangiri's duty to make sure that Padma was not robbed of even Sashi.

Sashi was different. She seemed to know the template of

the world, like an artist. She was born to create new meanings, new horizons. Her eyes saw much more, her smile meant much more. With exposure at the right time to literature and art, the sciences and math, she could change the world.

Gangiri felt Balu's struggle stop abruptly, his breathing slow down. He called him once, whispered his name. Then he pulled the blanket over him, holding him close.

He heard the last sigh of the night and the first bird of the morning. Gangiri lay watching the haphazard ceiling of the house, half-concrete, half-thatch, the day breaking through the gaps in between.

Mornings used to be for bright ideas and new theories, for discussing newspaper reports and winning hostel arguments. Mornings were for achieving the impossible, for mutiny against time, for daily immortality. For emergency half-hours in libraries before examinations and for looking up famous quotations before election debates. That one moment for which one is born, mornings were the eternal chance to find that. And also that one moment for which one dies.

Gangiri touched Balu's peaceful face in farewell and kissed his cold forehead. He gently untangled Balu's thin arms from around his neck and walked out to the porch. He brought in the notebook, all the money that was left, the cell phone, and placed them on the shelf beside his books. He touched the volumes, the few friends that had held his hand through life. He then glanced at Padma who still sat in the corner, her eyes lowered, her hand on Sashi's head, as if seeking reassurance.

There were so many things he wanted to say to Padma, starting with his respect for her strength in the past to advice on whom to trust in the future. But he could only say one thing to her that morning before he left. 'Please forgive me.'

She glanced up at him, perplexed, as he walked out. She could see he did not wear his shoes, they were still at the threshold where he had left them yesterday. He must not be going far, she thought.

She was right.

Gangiri picked up the two bottles from the porch as he walked towards his fields. The grocers at the market had been puzzled when Gangiri had bought a bottle of mineral water the day before. So was the local bootlegger, who had never seen Gangiri drink, when he bought a bottle of liquor.

The sky was unfolding the canopies of dawn by the time Gangiri reached the field. The can of pesticide was where he had left it among the tamarind trees. His long fingers worked quickly and steadily as he emptied the water from the bottle. He could still feel the weight of Balu's head as it had rested on his chest. He could still feel the touch of the child's arms around him. He began making the lethal cocktail, the pungent smell of death mixing with the sweet morning air.

Then the sun cleared the hillock in a hurry, the warmth discovering him, the light dissuading him. But his calm, dark eyes sparkled as he summoned the neutral witness of time to pay attention to his last act as Gangiri Bhadra.

23

January, New Delhi

Nazar sat staring at the white envelope on the desk in his office. It was ten days after Videhi had called him in the evening, frantically asking if it was true. She had come to know the news from the staffer at the Mityala office of Jaichand Industries. She had asked him again if it was true. Nazar recalled his reaction, fear. He knew it could be true.

Nazar had immediately called Gangiri's cell phone number, praying that his soft voice would answer once more. But there was no answer. Then he called Gauri Shanker maha sarpanch who was too distraught to give him details. Finally, Nazar called the district collector.

Collector Gul confirmed the news, Gangiri had committed suicide a few hours after his nephew died. Nazar, for the first time in his career, could not ask the usual questions. Gul, however, told him what he needed to know. A fragile crop, a resilient debt, a delicate life, a tenacious disease.

Gangiri had held himself responsible for the boy's death. It was justice, something he had fought for all his life. When Videhi called again, he told her the news was true. And like him, she too fell silent.

In the following days, Mityala district and Gopur village

became the venue for the ritual of news follow-ups. Old questions were churned up again on why farmers committed suicide and old answers given. Haridas Tulsi asked Nazar to write the obituary. Nazar put together his conversations with Gangiri, highlighting his strength to fight for others, his courage to stand alone...his victory, his memory.

Every word sounded hollow, every homage spurious.

Nazar realized that Gangiri had carried a mirror within himself and he seemed to have left it behind in this world.

Keyur Kashinath handed in his resignation as an MP without any major demand for it. Vaishnav asked his son not be emotional, arguing that a member of Parliament does not quit his seat taking responsibility for a farmer's death. Keyur said he was not that kind of member of, hopefully, not that kind of a Parliament. He decided to leave for Mityala to work on the solutions Gangiri had suggested to improve the state of farmers.

Before leaving Delhi, he had called Nazar. 'I thought I owed it to you to tell you, Mr Prabhakar,' he had said on phone. 'Gangiri Bhadra was the solution. You were right.'

It had meant nothing.

Nazar stared at the white envelope on his table. It contained just two lines addressed to Haridas Tulsi, requesting him to accept his resignation. He mentioned no reason, there were so many of them, it was difficult to choose.

He had believed in Gangiri. There would never be another. The ten days of January in that vacuum were enough for him to realize that he could no longer do the job of searching for a conscience in a city of effigies.

Nazar reached for his bag and stood up to leave. He was walking out of the door when his cell phone rang. Nazar checked it and froze on the threshold, mistrusting his eyes. It flashed the name 'Gangiri Bhadra'.

Nazar hurriedly answered and heard a voice greet him traditionally.

'Namaskar,' the voice said. 'I have some news about the suicide committee in Mityala. Are you the journalist Nazar Prabhakar who writes about these things?'

Nazar quickly said, 'Yes.'

'Gangiriji left this phone for me and asked me to call you on this number to give you information about farmer suicides in Mityala,' the voice said. Nazar stood still for an astonished moment, then rushed back into the room, fishing out a notebook from the bag.

'The committee meeting was held today to decide the farmer suicide cases that took place over the last fortnight,' the voice continued. 'For the first time ever in the history of the suicide committees of the state, the members unanimously decided that debt was the main cause that led the farmers to commit suicide and agreed on granting relief to the families.'

Nazar noticed that the man spoke slowly, like Gangiri used to, making it easier for Nazar to take notes.

'One of the cases was that of Gangiriji and the compensation will be awarded to his sister-in-law.' He paused. 'May I give you the names of the other farmers whose cases were heard today?'

Nazar noted down the list, his hand heavy as he wrote Gangiri's name. But the calm voice continued the methodical briefing.

'The committee also decided to appoint a new member in place of Gangiriji as the farmer-member. Along with that it was decided that the second list of review cases of past verdicts would be announced at the next meeting...'

'Who... I mean, yes, who are you?' Nazar asked, interrupting him.

'My name is Vadrangi,' he answered. 'I am the new farmer-member on the suicide committee.'

Nazar was surprised, realizing Gangiri's plan.

'Just wanted to mention that Lambodar maha sarpanch, the man notorious as apatra Lambodar, today voted for all debt suicide cases as patra or eligible for compensation,' he said.

Nazar smiled. 'I wish Gangiriji had been there.'

'I believe he was,' Vadrangi replied simply.

Later, as Nazar re-read the notes, he thoughtfully paused at Gangiri's name. Then he glanced at the table, reached for the white envelope and dropped it in the last drawer of the desk which held his letters that could wait.